You Better Watch Out:
A Christmas Horror Comedy

This book is a work of fiction. Any reference to historical events, real people, or real places are used fictitiously. Other names, characters, places, and events are products of the author's imagination. Any resemblance to actual events or places or people, living or dead or undead, is entirely coincidental.

ISBN 979-8-9853874-1-4

First published December 2021

Cover design and artwork by Matt Keller at matthewkellerart.com

To Matt—

My better half, favorite person, and biggest supporter

Chapter 1

Emmett Branscombe was packing for his annual trip to the cabin in central Maine he had purchased decades ago. He had never gotten to really enjoy it because he was always working, but now that he was retired, he knew this would be the relaxing and rejuvenating excursion he had looked forward to for so long. His ex-wife was remarried. His children were all grown and living their own lives. He'd be back by Christmas. He had nothing tying him down until then.

In the meantime, it would be him, his cabin, and the great outdoors. He'd loved nature his entire life, from the time he first went camping with his family to when he was a Junior Ranger to when he took his own children hiking. Emmett zipped up his puffer jacket over the layers of flannel shirt, long johns, and white undershirt. He was ready for the cold. Used to it after living in Tinselvania his whole life.

The snow outside fell gingerly, lightly covering the ground with a bright white sheen that sparkled beneath the moonlight. If he left soon, he could make it to the cabin before first light and be able to watch the sun rise.

As he grabbed some snacks and water for the drive, he passed by the large bay front windows in his living room. He stopped, his attention focused on the figure that stood in his yard. The blinking rainbow Christmas lights that surrounded the window frame hindered Emmett's vision, but he saw the unmoving shape facing his house, still as a statue.

A motionless figure, partially obscured by the darkness outside but illuminated by the snow and moonlight. Dressed in a fuzzy, dark brown, one-piece costume with a white belly. A stiff, smooth reindeer mask over his or her face and head that completely covered any identifying features. Atop the reindeer head was a set of dark antlers. A red nose shone on the end of the snout. Only the eyeholes revealed any physical characteristic of the wearer. Whoever it was, they were tall and well-built, their silhouette revealing a sturdy form.

"What in the hell's bells?" he grumbled to himself. It had to be one of the neighborhood kids fooling around. The kids in Tinselvania were more considerate and well-behaved than in other, bigger towns, but there were always the ones who used their boredom to play pranks to fill the void in their misspent time. Tinselvania was a quiet, small town filled with friendly neighbors and classic-looking, long-standing, old-style New England houses. Homes that would be featured in travel and historical architecture magazines.

Emmett threw his wool scarf and hat on, then opened the front door to yell at whoever it was to get lost. When he stepped onto his dark porch, the reindeer-costumed figure was gone.

So were the bulbs for his front porch lights. He inspected the empty glass light fixtures. Someone had unscrewed the bulbs from their sockets and taken them away.

"Hello?" he called out. "Who's out there?"

No response came from the night. Emmett chafed at the disrespect of young people. It didn't matter. He'd be gone in a few hours, all alone in a pristine cabin, where he could read his books and cook what he caught in the woods.

Choo choo!

Emmett spun around when he heard the whistling and chugging of his electric train set. It was in his basement. Someone had turned it on. He knew he hadn't left it running. He would've heard it before.

When he turned to go back inside, he saw that the wreath hanging on his door was covered in pictures. Old, grainy, black-and-white photos, cut almost like a collage and taped onto the wreath's leaves. In one of them, a smiling little boy sat on Santa's lap at the mall. Another had the same little boy standing with what appeared to be his parents, taken in front of a giant building.

Choo choo!

The train's whistle snapped Emmett back to the present. Had someone broken into his house to play with his train set? He intended to find out. He went into the kitchen to grab a large chef's knife from a drawer.

He didn't notice the reindeer-costumed person sitting at the table in his breakfast nook, shadowed in darkness. It sat completely rigid, silent, staring directly at Emmett, who was oblivious to the presence. The figure watched Emmett retrieve the sharp, shiny knife and take off downstairs.

Emmett flipped on the light switch at the top of the basement stairs.

"Whoever's down there, you better go now!" he shouted down, taking each step cautiously. "I'm going to have your folks tan your hide!"

There was no sound except for the train circling the tracks. Emmett saw that his electric train set, a replica of the city of Tinselvania, was indeed lit up and in full motion. Nothing else looked disturbed or meddled with.

The colorful burst of Christmas lights, coming from the corner, took him by surprise. Emmett gasped as he saw the decomposed, decayed corpse propped up in a lounge chair, wrapped in blinking lights.

Emmett spun around to run. It was too late.

The reindeer stood face-to-face with him, its black eyes penetrating Emmett's fearful eyes. Before Emmett could react, the reindeer leaned down and thrust forward with all its might and strength.

Emmett didn't scream out loud as the reindeer impaled him on its razor-sharp, pointed-tipped antlers. When the reindeer pulled the antlers out of Emmett's gored chest, blood splattered and sprayed in every direction, soaking the reindeer's outfit.

The reindeer never broke eye contact with Emmett as he fell to the ground, clutching his torso, trying to cover the multiple wounds and holes in his chest with his hands. The reindeer gave Emmett a half-hearted push with its leg, almost like it was bored and wanted to see what would happen if he did, knocking Emmett on his side.

Emmett watched as his blood flowed out of his body, spilling out onto the floor around him.

Choo choo!

He closed his eyes and cried. The last noise he heard was the sound of his model train rollicking down the miniature tracks.

The reindeer gutted and hollowed Emmett out and rearranged the train set. Emmett's corpse was situated so that the miniature train would ride right through the gigantic hole in Emmett's torso on every lap around the tiny track, round and round, in and out.

Chapter 2

Mary Classen stared at her reflection in the mirror as her positive affirmations self-help podcast played over the speakers on her computer. She started every day like that, surrounded by the comfort of her spacious and modest bedroom. She didn't have a lot of material items, aside from an overstuffed closet filled with clothes and shoes. Pictures of her friends and family decorated the walls. Her bedroom was her safe space.

The orator's firm, bold voice implored her to repeat after him and confirm her worth.

"I am a strong, powerful, capable warrior," the voice said. "I am the wind, the storm, the oncoming asteroid hurtling toward Earth. I am a fire-breathing dragon vanquishing those who oppose my rule. Clear the path and waterproof your house!"

"I am a strong, powerful, capable warrior," repeated Mary.

"Say it again, with feeling!" the voice said.

"I am a strong, powerful, capable warrior!" Mary recited, louder and more forcefully.

"I have the fierce soul of an eagle, soaring through the sky, attacking any and all obstacles with courage, dignity, poise, drive, and determination," the voice said. "You can't put me in a box or hold me in your hand. You can't catch my spirit because it's faster than the speed of light. What was that? You don't know because it was so fast."

Mary repeated it, not really convinced. She spoke the words along with the instructor, searching the recesses of her soul to find her most assertive voice. It came out more like an unsure, wavering pontification.

She looked at herself as she spoke the words. She tried her best to summon all her confidence as she brushed her short strawberry-blonde hair. When she was a teenager, Mary wanted to be just like Heather Locklear on *Melrose Place*. She wanted to be beautiful, fashionable, confident, and strong. She wanted to be lovable like Meg Ryan, wise like Oprah, outspoken and courageous like Carrie Fisher, and formidable like Pat Benatar and Debbie Harry. She wasn't sure she'd ever become like those women, but she didn't think she turned out so badly. It wasn't meant to be. She lived a quieter life. She wasn't "cool," but she was okay with that. She liked books and politics, crafts and board games, and listening to her forty-five records on her portable record player. She still had her *Charles in Charge* Trapper Keeper from grade school and celebrated Rex Manning Day every year. She wasn't a fashionista or a supermodel, but she was smart, caring, and driven.

"I put my armor up to protect me against those who do not have my best interests at heart yet will lower the imaginary shield and open myself up to love and new experiences," the voice said. "I am brave, resilient, and brilliant. I am deserving of love and praise. I am not my negative feelings about myself. I am not my mistakes. I am not the pebble in the sand on the beach, but all of the water in the ocean."

"I will create the best bear I can at Build-A-Bear. I will not MapQuest directions to Dunkin' Donuts though the only phone I own is a flip phone without GPS. I will not cut my own hair with a Flowbee because no one will touch me. My milkshake will bring all the boys to the yard. I will not wear jorts under my jeans because I sold all of my boxer briefs to people on their way to a furry convention," the voice said.

Mary gave a cockeyed glance at her computer. She clicked the program off and headed downstairs.

Mary sat at the kitchen counter and finished her third cup of coffee as she put her snow boots on. It wasn't easy to be a high-powered executive at the number one tinsel company in the world. Her life consisted of work and more work. She didn't sleep well or get the opportunity to enjoy the same things that non-high-power executives did.

Sometimes a lonely feeling nagged her at night, adding on to the stress and anxiety she was already feeling. She loved her job and never regretted choosing a career over having children or being in a relationship. But sometimes, she wondered what it would be like to have someone to take with her to the Christmas parade every year. She often saw couples who did things like mountain climbing, pole vaulting, and scuba diving. She was not that person. She got tired watching people do those things, not to mention she was way too uncoordinated and clumsy for them and would probably end up in a body cast.

She wanted to travel more, since she hadn't been to many places outside of Tinselvania. The most adventure she usually had in her life was choosing whether she was having ranch or barbecue sauce with her chicken fingers. Yet, at the same time, she would have been happy to have someone to sit at home with and watch *French Kiss* for the eighty-seventh time. She liked nature and appreciated a good walk on the beach or in the woods but didn't crave the adrenaline rush that so many people did. Plus, she hated being sweaty.

She had lived in Tinselvania her entire life. She still lived in the house she grew up in, a large and spacious abode built in the 1800s. Her mother and aunt lived with her as well, but there was so much room that Mary had her own space. She liked having them around anyway.

Today was the day that another high-powered executive, this one all the way from New York City, would be meeting with her to discuss business. The tinsel industry was cutthroat. Her family's tinsel company had been around since the early 1900s when her great-grandfather founded Tinsel Inc. Since then, all the members of her family had worked at the tinsel factory, devoting their lives to tinsel and the town of Tinselvania.

Christmas was big business and tinsel was the heart of it. The company flourished and remained successful even through the 1960s when tinsel was banned due the amount of lead used in its creation. They had figured out new ways to make it safely and kept tinsel on all the trees across the world. Back then, there were only a half dozen tinsel companies, but Tinsel Inc. drove them all out of business.

Now word had spread that a tinsel conglomerate made up of merciless, aggressive professionals was creating waves in New York City and threatened the lifeblood of Tinselvania. Its citizens depended on the tinsel factory in town to keep jobs and revenue flowing. Without it, the town would fade away. Mary took over the business after she graduated college and her family was beloved in this town. She would not let some out-of-touch New York suit drive her family's business into the ground.

Mary filled her briefcase full of the new tinsel prototypes. Once she was wrapped up in her puffy coat, scarf, and fluffy hat, she walked down the street to the tinsel factory. The early December snow coated the ground, making that comforting crunching sound beneath her boots. She saw the steam rising from the factory's ventilation towers. The comforting feeling of familiarity washed over her. She smiled, knowing that everything would be all right.

Tinselvania was a Christmas town. All the houses were quaint and rustic. The neighbors knew each other's names. Almost every family had at least one member who worked at the tinsel factory. The air smelled like candy canes and pumpkin spice. Christmas decorations and trees remained in most houses all year round, rather than just for the holiday. Christmas music played in all the charming local shops and Minnie's Diner. The recent snowfall had made everything look even more picturesque, like a postcard come to life. It was like a dream to live there. Most people who did never left. It was an old-fashioned way of life, untouched and unmarred by the violence and brutality of cities. Tinselvania was its own bubble and people liked it that way.

Mary's family's home and the factory– a large, imposing two-story building– were on the outskirts of town. Downtown proper was only a few minutes' drive away, separated by forest and lengthy stretches of road.

"Good morning, Estelle!" said Mary to the factory's security guard as she entered the building and headed toward her office.

Estelle McGarrigle had worked at Tinsel Inc. for over thirty years, rising from nightguard to head of security. She wore her crisply starched and ironed beige uniform with pride. Estelle was tasked with keeping unruly Christmas enthusiasts out of the restricted areas of the building and monitoring any suspicious activities such as probable corporate espionage. She was the guardian of all classified information, as competing tinsel companies had sent spies and undercover detectives as plants in the factory to uncover Tinsel Inc.'s secrets.

Mary passed the rows of assembly lines and workrooms, waving at the employees as she passed. They all regarded her highly, as Mary was a fair and empathetic boss. Her coworkers were like another family to her. Without them, the world did not get the tinsel it so desperately needed.

Christmas music filled every room, siphoned in through speakers in the ceiling. The festive atmosphere and congenial attitudes of the workers mirrored the cheerful, lighthearted sounds of Debbie Gibson's "Sleigh Ride" as it played.

The hallways, offices, boardroom, assembly line, breakroom, various workrooms, and packing and shipping department were all decorated with vivid, happy, unmistakable Christmas themes: inflatable snowmen and Santas, wreaths, garland, ornaments, pine trees, twinkle lights, plush dolls that sang Christmas carols, Nativity scenes, and various knickknacks and doodads that had been accumulated and displayed over the years the company had been in business. It was like working in the North Pole. The workers were the elves. Mary half-expected them to start singing in tandem when she saw them all hard at work.

When Mary reached her office, her assistant, Casper Capwell, was ready and waiting with her itinerary. He was a recent college graduate and a snappy dresser, always decked out in an immaculate outfit that was perfectly pressed and flawlessly form-fitting over his fit frame, capped off with a colorful, matching tie that he'd never wear twice. Mary was lucky if she had one clean outfit to take to work with her and carried static cling spray in her bag because everything she owned wrinkled the second she put it on.

"Good morning, Casper," Mary smiled. He stood up from his desk and followed her into her private office within her office, his iPad in hand.

"You have a 9 a.m, conference call with Scrappy Scrapbooks Inc.," he said. "At 10 a.m., you have a video call with the tinsel people in Russia. At 11:30 a.m., you have to go over the colors of the new archetypes for the funfetti tinsel. And at 1:00 p.m., you have the big investors meeting with the board and need to meet with that consultant from the Yule Love It Christmas Corporation. Also, you have to meet with the new hires at your convenience. And we have to pay for the float and decorations at the Christmas Jamboree. And the actors playing Mr. and Mrs. Claus. There's also the food bank, refreshments, driver, manual labor, as well as Christmas bonuses and donations to charity. Oh, and your mom called. She says you are beautiful and smart and don't forget it and she'd like you to give her a grandbaby while she's still around."

"Thank you, Casper. Hold my calls, please."

Mary took off her snow boots and changed into her high heels. The Christmas Snoopy bobblehead on her desk wobbled and nodded as if to say hello. Stacks of files and paperwork greeted her. More numbers to look at and orders to fill. Her computer was covered in Post-It notes, names and times scribbled down on them so she wouldn't forget. Some were just notes to herself: *You got this! You're doing great! Don't give up! What would Oprah do?*

Her office walls were covered with pictures of her family and the factory, many from before Mary was even born. Generations of proud, hardworking tinsel laborers who took a decrepit, abandoned building and made a successful, thriving tinsel factory out of it. Mary was reminded of the legacy she wanted to uphold when she saw their faces every day.

Her father passed away almost ten years ago, but he was the voice in her head that always told her to do the right thing, to work hard, to be honest, to be a good person and treat others with kindness. That was the kind of man he was. When she got her master's degree in business, his gift to her was training her to take over for his retirement. He didn't live to see retirement, but Mary hoped he was looking down on her with approval. His employees were his extended family. His death left a giant hole in the hearts of many people in Tinselvania, most specifically Mary's and her family's.

"These came for you," Casper said, jolting Mary back to focus. He was carrying a bouquet of candy canes. The envelope was addressed to her.

Casper gave her a "you've-been-seeing-somebody-and-haven't-mentioned-it-to-me?" look as she opened the card.

Looking forward to going on a slay ride with you.

"Who sent these?" Mary asked. "The card isn't signed and they spelled 'sleigh' wrong."

"Maybe you have a secret admirer," said Casper. "If my schedule is correct, you haven't been on a date since 2018, and you won't let me make you an online dating profile, so your guess is as good as mine."

Mary sighed. It was probably her mother. In her retirement, her mother had gotten restless and taken up several hobbies to occupy her time. One of them was online shopping and gifting. It wouldn't be the weirdest thing her mother had ever given her.

Chapter 3

By lunchtime, Mary had knocked out her morning responsibilities. Contracts were signed, orders were filled out for shipping, and deals were made.

Tinsel Inc. had a full-service cafeteria on-site. A deli counter, a snack and dessert bar, a water and fountain soda machine, and a hot lunch menu, usually consisting of Christmas-themed foods like ham, turkey, stuffing, mashed potatoes, cranberry sauce, yams, green bean casserole, corn, dinner rolls, and the like.

Mary chatted with the head chef, Alfred Lockridge, and his son, Balthazar, their version of a lunch lady, who took orders and spooned out everyone's portions when they came to the counter. Like Estelle, Alfred had been with the company for decades, with his son following in his footsteps. He wore his white chef's apron as a badge of honor. Balthazar was Alfred's mini-me; whereas Alfred was tall and broad, his son was thin and demure. Balthazar looked like the inside of an Alfred-shaped Russian doll.

The lunchroom was bustling with people eating their lunches and discussing their lives. Mary took her meatloaf sandwich and Diet Pepsi and sat at a table with her best friends, her girl gang: Kara Halloran, Liza Wells, and Robin Landes. She had been friends with them since they were kids. They had been each other's confidantes, support system, and secret keepers their entire lives, and they all worked at Tinsel Inc. together.

"I heard you got flowers today," Robin said. She was the public relations manager, in charge of all social media, press releases, and keeping the factory's image and good name number one in the tinsel business. She knew all the trends, from social, economic, and political, all the way to which celebrities were posting about Tinsel Inc. tinsel on any of the eight hundred social media sites out there.

Robin always dressed like she was part of the cast of *Dynasty*. Anything shiny, ostentatious, and glamorous, from pantsuits to broaches to dresses. She had always been the "pretty one" of Mary's friends, with long, blonde hair and a healthy figure.

"They were candy canes," said Mary. "And how did you hear about that?"

"Small town, not much news," answered Robin. "I was excited because I thought I'd be able to take you shopping for some date underwear and not those granny drawers you wear."

"They're comfortable and don't ride up my buttcrack," reasoned Mary. "I don't need fancy undies to fill out spreadsheets and meet with vendors."

"You need to stop buying your clothes at gas stations and convenience stores," Robin said. "One day we're going to find you in your attic, surrounded by fidget spinners and sock monkeys, staring out the window and talking to a Pop-Tart."

"Do you guys want to go to Minnie's Diner for the pig roast tonight?" Liza asked. Liza was the company lawyer, in charge of the in-house legal department. She was the "responsible one" of the group, who Mary and her friends turned to for help with taxes, mortgages, and anything else adults were supposed to know how to do. Liza dressed sensibly, usually in slacks and long-sleeve button-down shirts beneath a V-neck sweater. Her brown hair was pulled back in a ponytail.

"I can't," Robin said. "I have a date with Angus and I may let him put his Elf on a Shelf in a very bad place."

Mary, Kara, and Liza groaned.

"I swear I'm going to turn the hose on you, Robin," laughed Kara, who worked in the art department, tasked with the visual aspects, design, build, and overall look and aesthetics of the tinsel. "Don't you ever want it to be something special, something beautiful?"

"I'll answer that if you can say what you really mean by 'it,' Kara," smiled Robin, knowing Kara would never say the word "sex" in public. "I can't even picture you and Nick's dirty talk. *'Do you want bologna on your sandwich? Me too.'* You and Mary would be the stars of *Girls Gone Mild*."

"I'm going to get you one of those ticket dispensers like they have at the deli so the men outside your bedroom know when their number is called," laughed Kara. She was the "den mother" of the gang. She cooked and baked everything from scratch, gave hugs whenever they were needed, was active in the PTA, cried if anyone even mentioned *The Notebook*, and spent far too much time worrying about everyone she loved. She had a wild mane of wavy, reddish-brown hair that resembled Julia Roberts' in *Sleeping with the Enemy*.

Kara was married with two daughters, Liza was married with one son, Robin was single and always on the prowl, and Mary was single and watched *Supermarket Sweep* reruns from 1991 at home alone while she filled out order forms for the factory. Mary loved that even though their lives and opinions varied, it never affected their bond of friendship.

"I have dinner at my sister's tonight," said Mary.

Kara, Liza, and Robin groaned again.

"Why do you keep saying 'yes' to going over to Noelle and Jed's?" Liza asked. "You see her every day at work. She's had a stick up her butt since we were kids. I saw her arrange the rocks on the beach once because she thought the ocean left them too disorganized. She was a hall monitor in school who grew up to be a hall monitor in life."

"The whole family is going, so I have to," shrugged Mary. "I'll text you about all the taste-free vegan food they serve. I'm going to McDonald's beforehand to eat several Big Macs in preparation. I have a date with the Hamburglar."

"Just remember," said Kara. "No matter how bad you feel about yourself, there are women who write love letters to serial killers. You're not there yet."

"That's not helpful at all," laughed Mary. "Should I get a big sandwich sign to wear that says, 'I'm pathetic' and walk up and down Main Street?"

"That's not what I mean, you goober," Kara said. "And don't we have anything else to talk about? We're interesting, smart, accomplished women. Our lives don't revolve around men."

"Mary's definitely doesn't," said Robin.

"I have no complaints about my life," Mary said, giving her friends a serious face. "It's a small life but it's valuable. I have amazing friends and family and I love my job. That is all I could ever ask for. If 1980s Steve Guttenberg wants to come along and marry me, I wouldn't say no. But that would be a bonus, not the goal of my life. I'm forty-five. I think if I were going to have a whirlwind romance, it would've happened by now."

"Oh, '80s Guttenberg," said Robin. "Sometimes *High Spirits* plays on cable late at night and it's him, Peter Gallagher, and Liam Neeson all young, shirtless, and strapping. Those are the days I get carpal tunnel in my hands."

Mary, Kara, and Liza stared at Robin, then burst into laughter.

"What do you think the *Sliding Doors* version of our lives is like?" asked Liza. "Mine is the leader of Earth and everyone has to follow my rules. Everyone takes a siesta at 2 p.m. Work weeks are two days a week, of your own choosing. Wine is free everywhere. The vein in my forehead that pops out when I'm upset does not exist. Everyone gets to have special X-Men superpowers, like being able to magically transport from one place to another. *Shark Week* lasts all year. Everyone sleeps one hour a night and feels rested."

"Oh, bull corn!" interrupted Mary in a hushed, angry whisper. She had accidentally flipped over her empty meatloaf plate onto her lap, the remaining gravy now all over her outfit.

"Best friends team assemble!" said Liza. "Force Field Code Brown! Activate human shield! Number 37 formation diagram in the instruction manual. Just like we practiced."

Liza, Kara, and Robin all stood, surrounding Mary and forming a blockade, guarding her from view as they walked her in tandem back to her office. Mary waved at people as she walked by, her gravy-stained clothes hidden by the human chain her friends had formed around her.

Chapter 4

Bright Harmon was not a fan of quirky small towns. He loved his life in New York City. He needed the noise, the chaotic atmosphere, the hustle and bustle. Tinselvania was the opposite of that. People said hello to him wherever he went, asking him how his day was going, genuinely expecting an answer and follow-up conversation. He longed for the empty "How are you?" when he passed by coworkers, the unspoken understanding and agreement that neither of you really cared to hear the reply so you'd do a drive-by acknowledgment and keep it moving.

He wore fancy suits and shiny shoes whenever he could, worked out regularly to keep in shape, and had the "tall, dark, and handsome" market cornered, as far as he was concerned. He worked hard at his looks, knowing full-well his business associates judged him and others on their outward appearance.

As soon as Bright's Lyft rolled into town, it was like crossing an imaginary border into a different, bygone era. One where they clearly loved Christmas, as every building, edifice, and house was completely covered in holiday décor. Most of the houses were modest suburban dwellings, uniformly lining each street like an old-fashioned Americana painting, featuring twisty, hilly residential streets with large yards.

The town square was a snow-covered park with gazebos, jungle gyms, a playground, and a large ice-skating rink in the center, surrounded by local-owned shops. A gigantic Christmas display of a plastic Santa and his elves was set up in the center of the square, alongside a massive model Christmas village. The streetlights were adorned in sparkly, glittering decoupage snowflakes and homemade stockings. He counted at least five payphones, wondering if Tinselvania had such modern amenities as Wi-Fi and Alexa and Google. People were sledding and tubing down snow-covered hills, Christmas music blared over speakers in the square, and nobody seemed to have a care in the world or be aware of life outside of their tiny bubble. He felt like he was headed into Whoville.

What he would give right now for a real slice of pizza. To witness a fight between two cracked-out junkies. To be in the vicinity of a museum or art gallery or somewhere with culture. To sleep in his own bed with the sheets with the high thread count. To look out of his windows and see the almost-panoramic view of the city from his vantage point on the thirty-sixth floor of the luxury high-rise he called home. Anywhere but here, one of these towns that were attached to their antiquated traditions and habits, their way of life hopelessly mired in conventional, conservative social norms, values, graces, standards, customs, and rules. It bored him as much as it frustrated him.

Bright knew he was in town under false pretenses. The CEO of Tinsel Inc. thought the sole purpose of Bright's visit was to go over ways to be more efficient, to reach more investors and vendors, and to analyze and assess risk, among other business ideology. However, the President of the company Bright worked for, Yule Love It Christmas Corporation, had arranged this visit for a different reason. It was open-ended for as long as it would take to convince the town to allow Yule Love It to buy out Tinsel Inc. and take it over. Tinsel Inc. was fierce competition. Their name was synonymous with Christmas. Yule Love It wanted their stock, their business model and plan, and their workers for cheap.

"Would you like some eggnog?" Bright's Lyft driver asked, holding up a pitcher of the drink.

"No, thank you," Bright said curtly, waving the driver's offer away.

His assistant was already at The Happy Goose, a local inn they would be staying at for their visit. Bright pictured a run-down shack with ancient amenities like an outhouse and Atari players in each room. Being in Tinselvania didn't assuage Bright's predisposition for mild seasonal depression. He felt like he was being sent to a prison island to work on a chain gang.

He did his breathing exercises and visualization techniques to ease his anxiety. His inner sense of disquietude began to disperse as he imagined himself on a sunny beach with a cocktail in hand. No work, no distractions, no frustration, no fears and unease over responsibilities and tasks that needed to be completed. Just him and the ocean waves, far away from the daily grind and this lame podunk town.

"I hate Christmas," he grumbled as he stepped out of the Lyft and felt the cold air, holiday decorations, and picturesque face of The Happy Goose assault him all at once. He steeled himself, remembering he was there on a mission. He had goals and plans to accomplish. Nothing was going to sideline him.

Joseph Lowery, Bright's assistant, greeted him in the lobby. He was a recent college graduate, eager to please and on his way to working up the ranks at Yule Love It. He greeted Bright professionally and quickly, immediately handing over a stack of papers and some files. Joseph was the epitome of "dress for the job you want." His brown hair was perfectly cut and groomed. His wardrobe consisted of suits, pants, and sweater vests that he couldn't afford, but his credit card companies appreciated him buying.

Joseph knew Bright was heterosexual and supported his lifestyle, but he couldn't help having a crush on him. Bright was driven, smart, successful, and handsome. He was also the only constant man in Joseph's life, even if that meant Joseph was just his errand boy.

"I did some cursory research on Tinselvania and its citizens," he said. "The population rarely fluctuates other than births, and over half of the adult workforce is employed by Tinsel Inc. Mary Classen, the CEO, unmarried, no kids, Harvard Business School graduate, no social media other than the company's accounts."

Bright thanked him as Joseph took Bright's suitcases and walked with him to the front desk.

The Happy Goose was a quaint, homey lodge with a log cabin vibe. Stained, exposed wood was bedecked in, what else, Christmas decorations. A massive Christmas tree with gift-wrapped presents stood mightily in the corner. A couple of squishy couches sat next to a fireplace full of blazing, crackling wood.

"Well, hello," the cheery, curly-haired, rosy-cheeked older woman behind the front desk said. "I'm Mrs. Havighurst. You must be Bright Harmon."

Bertha Havighurst had lived in Tinselvania her entire life, as did most of her family, who were in construction. Her family had actually built most of Tinsel Inc. when it was erected. She could have retired years ago but ran The Happy Goose. She wasn't ready to stop working and she liked the interaction with people. Her husband had passed away many years ago and her children were grown. Even though her own kids still lived in Tinselvania, they had lives of their own to lead. Her house was very quiet and lonely at night, so she preferred the warmth and comfort of the inn.

"Yes, thank you, Mrs. Havighurst."

She handed him his room key. Bright chuckled. It wasn't a fob or a card. It was an actual key on a key ring with a picture of a dancing, smiling goose on the tag.

"Would you like me to carry your bags upstairs for you?" she asked.

"No, I've got it," Joseph said, unwilling to let her take his job away from him.

"Everything is all set up for you," she smiled. "If you have any questions or need anything, please just call down to the front desk and I will help you. We just baked a gooseberry pie. Would you like me to bring some up to your room later?"

"No, thank you," Bright said. "I am a high-powered executive and have a meeting to get to."

"Welcome to The Happy Goose!" Mrs. Havighurst said as Joseph led Bright to the elevator.

"It looks like the North Pole exploded in this place," Joseph said. "I feel like we're in *The Twilight Zone*. Everyone in this town looks like the kind of people who won't make a gay wedding cake. Do you want to go over the numbers one more time?"

Bright was pleasantly surprised at how cozy and warm his room was. It was comfortable and welcoming even if it was on the smaller side. The bed had fluffy down comforters and a brightly-patterned quilt with two soft pillows. The room had a faint and unobtrusive cinnamon and nutmeg smell. It reminded him of the Christmases he'd had with his family as a kid, opening gifts and having hot chocolate with his grandparents, watching Rankin/Bass Christmas specials on television and later piling up in a toboggan together, dressed in their warmest winter clothes. Before the horrible accident that had wiped his entire family away.

Holidays were something he got through and survived, not celebrated.

Bright's thoughts turned to Candeeee. His girlfriend had dumped him unceremoniously only a few months ago, out of the blue and with no indication she was unhappy in their relationship. She was a hat model who Bright had hired for the Yule Love It catalog, using her earnings to pay her way through astrophysics school. Once she graduated with her doctorate, she told Bright that they "had to talk" and he learned she'd been sleeping with his best friend for the last six months of their relationship. So he'd not only lost the woman he loved but his best friend too.

Now, several months later, he wished she were with him in his Christmassy little room in this bumfuck town. Candeeee was modeling hats for the new Woolworth's catalogue and her paper on magnetohydrodynamics in galaxy formation and evolution was going to be printed in the newest issue of *Hat Modeling Astrophysicists Monthly* while he was stuck fighting for his professional life in *Twin Peaks*.

"Bright?" Joseph said, snapping him back to reality. "We have to get going for your meeting. Remember that the longer it takes to convince them to let us buy them out, the longer we are stuck here in this shithole, dollar-store, bargain-bin, Christmas nightmare hellscape. Tweeting is not a verb here. It's the sound the factory workers make as they work."

"Google me," answered Bright, waiting on Joseph's facts and figures.

"Tinselvania was founded in the 1600s when Puritans and Pilgrims came over on the *Mayflower*," Joseph read from his copious notes. "Back then, the town was called 'Die-Witches,' but once the tinsel factory opened in the early 1900s and became the town's major and only source of revenue, the name was changed to Tinselvania. The Classen, Branscombe, and Persimmons families all owned and operated it until Mortimer Classen bought out their shares. His family has owned and operated it since, with the other families whose relatives helped open it, as well as the rest of the community, gainfully employed and benefitting from the factory's existence. Tinsel Inc. has vendors, investors, and purveyors all over the world and their tinsel is sold in almost every country. Mary Classen has turned down several offers over the years to sell, so she'll be the biggest obstacle to overcome. Convincing her that it's in her best interest to sell, letting her know Yule Love It will drive her out of business otherwise, is your best play."

"Do we know what the other companies Candeeee turned down originally offered?"

"You mean Mary?" asked Joseph. "Is that where your mind is, Bright? You are much better off without her. You deserve someone who respects you and sees you for the intelligent, successful, driven man that you are. Someone whose name doesn't have four Es at the end. Someone who will make you happy and understand what's inside your heart. Someone who may have been in front of your face the whole time."

"How do I look?" asked Bright.

"Like a cross between Ben Affleck in *Armageddon*, Channing Tatum in *Magic Mike*, and Jude Law in *The Talented Mr. Ripley*," said Joseph, fixing Bright's tie.

Bright was completely oblivious. Joseph sighed and took out his cell phone.

"I'm calling an Uber," he said. "Oh God, do they have ride shares here or does everyone just get around on a horse and buggy?"

Chapter 5

Mary sat in her office while Casper ran back to her house to get her a proper change of business attire. In the meantime, she was in the Meowy Christmas sweater her mother had given her as a gift even though they'd never owned cats. Every time Mary looked down at the bulky gray monstrosity she had on, its drawing of a dancing kitty celebrating with Christmas cheer, she wondered how she did so well in school and at work but still did things like knocking gravy plates all over herself. Kara had lent her some SpongeBob SquarePants exercise leggings to wear as well, cementing her current wardrobe as less of a fashion victim and more of a fashion catastrophe.

She could hear her mother's voice in her head scolding her right now, saying, "I always told you to bring a change of clothes to the office!" Mary was determined that her mother would never find out about her wardrobe malfunction.

"Hello?" a voice called from the hall. "Is anyone here?"

"I'm on the phone," Mary lied. "Just be a few minutes!"

She picked up her phone to pretend she was on a call but she wasn't fast enough. Into the room entered two well-dressed men with expensive haircuts.

"Yes, I will donate that $100,000 to Platypuses Across America," she said into the receiver with steely determination to the imaginary person on the other end, hoping her fake-phone call gambit was convincing but fully aware she had not sold it as well as she hoped. She put the receiver down and folded her hands together as if she'd closed a monumental deal.

"I'm Bright Harmon and this is my assistant, Joseph Lowery," Bright said, hand extended. Mary stood, wanting to crawl into a hole and be swallowed up by the earth to avoid her embarrassment at her hideous outfit, and shook his hand.

"I'm Mary Classen," she said. "Nice to meet you."

"Nice to meet you as well, Mrs. Classen."

"Welcome to Tinsel Inc. We're happy to have you. You can call me Mary. We're not super fancy here."

"I see that. There was no one at the desk, but your security guard let us in. I hope we're not interrupting."

"No, just doing business. Tinsel never sleeps."

"Nice sweater," said Bright, neither mocking her nor really complimenting her.

"It's Casual Friday," Mary chuckled.

"Today is Wednesday," said Bright.

"It's Casual Friday-Wednesday," Mary corrected herself, hoping she could play off her lie. "It's something we do here, a tradition of sorts."

"Should we get down to the numbers?" he asked, uninterested in her explanations.

"I thought maybe you'd like to attend one of the board meetings with me," Mary said. "Meet the members of the board and familiarize yourself with how we do business around here."

"Sure," he answered, though his tone said "no."

"I can show you to your temporary office," said Mary. "We thought you might want somewhere to set yourself up, since your stay is indefinite."

Mary brought Bright and Joseph to their work quarters and left them so they could acclimate. Bright and Joseph inspected the décor. The office was set up with standard desks and filing cabinets but also adorned with cheerful Christmas lights and a plate of homemade Christmas cookies. A gift basket filled with tinsel, ornaments, and a stuffed plush of The Abominable Snowmonster from the North was atop Bright's desk.

Though Bright's initial reaction was one of contempt and disgust at the downhome quaintness of it all, he was loath to admit to himself he found it all slightly charming. As if his values were suddenly swayed by some chintzy, warm-and-fuzzy gifts. He wouldn't let himself get soft. He was on a mission.

"Who am I?" he whispered, almost laughing at himself.

"What?" Joseph asked from his adjacent assistant's office.

"Nothing," Bright said. "Temporary insanity. I'm going to do my 'thing.'"

Joseph knew what that meant. They closed the office blinds and locked the door. Bright queued up Queen's "Flash's Theme" from *Flash Gordon* as Joseph shined his phone's flashlight at him. The song began and Bright posed, stretched, and summoned the warrior within. He collected the strength and power of Freddie Mercury and Flash Gordon, with Joseph as his hype-man.

Flash! Ah-ah!

This was Bright's ritual. Ever since he was a kid and announced he wanted to be a "turnpike man" (the person who takes the tickets on the highway), he used this song as his confidence builder. As the song played and Bright channeled Sam J. Jones as Flash, he felt himself feeling strong, impervious, and capable. He reached his arms to the sky, flexing his muscles as he pretended he was preparing to go into battle against Ming the Merciless. He was going to crush this visit. He would help take over Tinsel Inc. and nothing would stop him.

Chapter 6

Dr. Sylvia Post had spent her life trying to help others. Her decades of work in psychiatry and decoding the puzzles of the human mind, bolstered by the many scientific papers she'd had published in reputable medical journals and awards she'd won for her service, had made her one of the leading experts in the field of human behavior.

She was in her office in Neve, Maine, when she received a phone call from a friend and former coworker to inform her that one of her most violent patients had escaped the maximum-security psych ward he was confined to for the past decade.

She had met Chester Persimmons when he was in his early forties, over two decades ago. He had committed a series of vicious and brutal murders, including some of his family members. He was tall and muscular, with an imposing stature, yet a calm demeanor. By the time Sylvia had met him, any light in his eyes had evaporated.

He was one of her many patients at The Calista Asylum for the Criminally Insane, located on Calista Island seven miles off the coast of Neve. When Calista Asylum closed, he remained in her care. In all the years she counseled and guided him, he never explained his motives or the reasoning behind his killing spree. Sylvia had her theories and hypotheses but could not prove any of them.

Eventually he was moved to his most recent psychiatric care center in upstate New York. Sylvia had not seen him in the years since. She regarded him as one of her major failures, never reaching him or ascertaining any methodology or insight into his crimes or his mind. He was quiet and polite yet drifted off into lengthy periods of comatose-like behavior, staring blankly at the walls and looking right through whoever he was barely speaking to. He never showed remorse or regret, shame or fear, any relatable emotions. He had grown up in Tinselvania until he moved his family moved out West, which is where he began his massacre.

She would never forget the pictures of him, wearing his reindeer onesie and mask, covered in other people's blood.

Why now? Why did he escape now? What was the catalyst that sprung his plan of freedom into action? Sylvia pondered these questions.

She felt as if she should've helped him more, should've reached him so that he could tell her why he'd slaughtered all those people. She could have used that information to identify similar behaviors in others, thereby preventing more killing.

His immediate family had already been notified of his disappearance. Sylvia read through her old notes and files on Chester Persimmons: videotapes, audio recordings, newspaper clippings, her own records, and journal remarks. There had to be something there that could give her a clue as to his next step.

She froze when she realized.

He would go back to Tinselvania.

Chapter 7

Bright and Joseph took seats at the back of the conference room. This was the official board room meeting place. Mary, still in her Meowy Christmas sweater and SpongeBob leggings, stood before the long, shiny table where the board members waited in their plush chairs.

Behind her was a white screen next to a whiteboard stacked with dry-erase markers. Her computer was set up with all the important graphs, charts, and spreadsheets for her PowerPoint presentation.

Her Uncle Cobden, her father's brother, had retired years back and was spending his newfound freedom by going on various cruises, vacations, and travels with his wife, Mary's Aunt Hepzibah. In his place, his son Ethan served as chief financial officer and his son Josh as chief operations officer. They were both around Mary's age, with families of their own, and were at the meeting for support and friendly faces. They both offered silent nods as she entered.

The board consisted of Classen family members, all of whom had retired by now but maintained stakes and interest in the company. Silent partners and legacies whose family members, the next generation, worked at Tinsel Inc.

Uncle Oscar, Aunt Aurelie, Uncle Armand, Aunt Jeanette, Uncle Lionel, and Aunt Leona turned their attention to Mary. She felt the unspoken judgment directed toward her ludicrous get-up. Seated next to them were several stone-faced, serious-looking investors from all over the United States who had been brought here by the board for Mary to pitch Tinsel Inc., to get them on board with giving her company their business and securing even more orders of tinsel throughout the country.

She greeted them, trying to maintain professionalism, and made no acknowledgment of her outfit. She passed out yearly projection reports to her waiting audience, then introduced Bright and Joseph, who gave cursory waves.

The first slide went up. A multi-colored graph with percentages, numbers, and figures. She felt the eyes of judgment and expectation focused solely on her. She'd never gotten used to that.

"What's the first thing you think of when you think of tinsel?" she asked. "Happiness. Family. Christmas. Playfulness. Holiday cheer. What do we need to survive this crazy world? Love. Food. Water. Shelter. And tinsel. In the past year alone, our tinsel sales have gone up by 367 percent. Our initiatives and social media influence have pushed consumers to add tinsel to their everyday lives, their home décor, their holidays other than Christmas. Having a Sweet Sixteen? You need tinsel. Your cousin bought a wombat farm? Decorate it with tinsel. Making cards for announcements or invites to your cool party bash? Cover it in tinsel. Tinsel is the go-to, easy-to-find, accessible spangle that turns a bronze project into a gold one. Why do you need confetti or balloons or piñatas when you can have tinsel? Answer: you don't. Tinsel makes a party, just like it makes your life. Tinsel is not the opening act. It's the main event."

She clicked on the next slide, with a list of company names and dates.

"In the past half-century, these are all of the tinsel companies that we have put out of business because their product was inferior or a generic rip-off of the quality we provide with our tinsel. What makes our tinsel so special? One word. Love. Every strand, every piece, every shiny bauble that comes from this warehouse not only is made with passion and care but the love of those creating it. The people of Tinselvania."

She clicked on the next slide, a picture of happy, excited people frolicking in a field with tinsel sprinkling and falling from the sky on to them.

"We don't just sell tinsel here. We sell a way of life. We ask people, 'Do you want a boring, dull existence or do you want it to sparkle and shine and glitter with our over-one-thousand varieties of colors?' I want to you close your eyes. Picture a world without tinsel. Picture a gray, static life where none of your Christmas trees or holiday decorations or parties have any of the joy or jubilation that tinsel brings. Now picture yourself at your son or daughter's graduation party, or your best friend's retirement party. Everything is covered in beautiful, magical, delightful tinsel. Which world do we want to live in? When you look into the eyes of those you love the most, do you want to tell them that all the tinsel in the world is gone? Or do you want to say, 'Here, here is all the tinsel you need, go and be free.' Tinsel is life. It is happiness and celebration and success. It is the difference between ordinary and walking into a room where unicorns and the pegasus play in a field of fireflies while music fills the air and everyone you love dances. Where superheroes and average citizens have everything in common. Where narwhals peek out of frozen lakes to greet you. What's that sound? It's the call of your heart, asking you for more tinsel."

Mary took a deep breath. There was a soundless moment of contemplation. The investors and her uncles and aunts leapt to their feet in spontaneous, exuberant applause. Several of the investors wiped away tears. A few of them rushed Mary to hug her tightly.

Casper appeared at the doorway with a garment bag. Beside him was a big, burly, white-bearded older man in a red jumpsuit and overalls who waved to Mary as he walked by the conference room.

"Oh my stars, is that Santa?" one of the investors asked excitedly.

"Oh no, that's Mr. Lovett," Mary said. "He works here in maintenance."

"What?"

"Yes, that's Santa." Mary immediately covered her tracks.

Her uncles and aunts privately showered her with congratulations and words of approval. Mary bid each of the board members and investors good day as they began filing out. As they did, Casper scheduled follow-up appointments with each one of them. Mary exhaled, her nerves steadied, left alone with Bright and Joseph.

"That was very impressive," Bright said.

"You're one of those people who says words with nice connotations but the meaning is completely different, aren't you?" asked Mary, only half-kidding.

"I was genuinely touched by your moving tribute to the joy of tinsel. All this time, I thought it was a frivolous product that we can mass produce for way cheaper using robots and cutting-edge technology, but now I know it's love that makes tinsel sell and money is no object. Who needs revenue streams when we can all live on love and tinsel?"

"You're doing it again." Mary cocked her head. "Like one of those sarcastic mean girls who lets you sit at their lunch table so they can talk about you behind your back and how your mom accidentally packed koala nuggets and banana-flavored milk in your *21 Jump Street* lunch box that had lip gloss marks over Peter DeLuise's face because you practiced kissing it in case you ever got a chance to do it in real life even though all the other girls loved Johnny Depp but you were holding out for him because you knew Peter would understand and respect you."

"That was weirdly specific."

"What are koala nuggets?" Joseph asked.

"Exactly what they sound like," Mary said defeatedly.

"Mary," Casper said. "You have a Zoom call with the salespeople in Yemen in five minutes. I can take Bright and Joseph on a tour of the factory."

Casper saved the day once again. There was no Zoom call. Her beloved assistant was rescuing her so she could change out of her hideous outfit and gather herself. She smiled in relief, telepathically telling him, "I love you." He telepathically replied, "I know."

Mary motioned to the door, where Casper formally introduced himself to Bright and Joseph. Before Casper ushered them away, Bright turned back to Mary.

"Joanna Kerns on *Growing Pains*," he said.

"Huh?"

"My first crush. I was eleven and she was the most beautiful woman I'd ever seen."

Mary nodded. Bright smiled and headed off with Casper and Joseph.

Chapter 8

In between Bertha manning the front desk of The Happy Goose, she delivered gooseberry pies to the guests. The inn did steady business, especially with Tinselvania being a popular tourist destination for its Christmas scenery and Tinsel Inc. tours, yet most people stayed in the chain hotels on the outskirts of town.

The bells over the doorway jingled just as Bertha was wrapping up another pie. She greeted the man who entered. He was dressed in heavy winter clothes and a buttoned-up navy blue peacoat. He had a big white beard and appeared to be somewhere in his sixties.

"Hello," she said.

"Hello," the man said. "I'd like a room, please."

Bertha opened up the inn's floor plans on his computer, keys clacking as he typed.

"Would a room on the third floor be acceptable?"

. "I'll take it."

"I just need a credit card and your driver's license."

The man handed her a card and license, noting that his name was Llewellyn Barnes. Bertha noticed what looked like a smear of blood on the man's hand when he handed it to him. When Barnes realized Bertha might have seen it, he withdrew that hand and put it in his peacoat pocket.

"Thank you, Mr. Barnes. Have you ever visited Tinselvania? I can give you several brochures on local eateries, shops, and places to visit."

"Not necessary. I grew up in Tinselvania. I haven't been back in an awfully long time. It looks different but somehow still the same."

"Oh, really? I grew up here too. Our families might have known each other."

"Maybe," the man said, clearly uninterested in small talk.

"Are you here for business or pleasure?"

"There's some people here that I haven't seen in many years. They aren't expecting me. I'm here to surprise them. I've traveled a long way to be here."

"Can I take your bags for you, Mr. Barnes?"

"No, thank you. I don't have any bags."

It was unusual that a guest didn't have any suitcases or luggage with them, but Bertha shrugged it off. She had seen a lot of strange things, met a lot of weird characters, over the years working there. This was simply a harmless old man back in town to reconnect with old friends. Maybe he was independently wealthy and was going to buy a whole new wardrobe while he was there. Bertha didn't know his life.

She handed Llewellyn his room key and watched as the man walked away without any more conversation.

Chapter 9

Mary was finally in her business attire again as she perused contracts and messages Casper left on her desk. She'd drank another five or six cups of coffee by now and was ready for the workday to be over with. She still had to have an official meeting with Bright but let herself relax and recalibrate for a moment.

Mary heard the gurgling noise of the watercooler from outside her office.

"Casper?" she called out.

"Oh, uh," a man's voice said.

Mary looked up and saw a smiling, bearded man in his thirties, dressed in a flannel shirt and dark blue jeans standing in her doorway, crumpling up a paper cup.

"I'm Chuck Brinkerhoff," he continued. "Human resources told me to come by. I started today and wanted to come by and say thank you for giving me the job. I finished my first training shift. That welcome video from 1988 is not as outdated as you'd expect. I particularly liked when the actors playing workers rapped about safety."

"Hello, Chuck," she said. "Come on in. I'm glad someone around here appreciates our cutting-edge, technologically advanced VHS tapes."

"I'm sorry to barge in on you. There's no one at the front desk."

"Yes, that seems to be happening a lot today. It's the Christmas season. We're extra busy and a lot of people take their Christmas vacations around now so we need the help. Are you new in town? Everybody around here knows everyone but you don't look familiar."

"Ah, yes. I'm actually Bertha Havighurst's nephew. I'm staying with her until I find my own place. Apparently The Happy Goose doubles as a home for wayward nephews. Aunt Bertha had some really nice things to say about you and your family. She says hello and that you owe her a visit. She'll make her famous shepherd's pie."

"Tell her I'll be by soon. If there's nothing else, Chuck, why don't you head on home and enjoy the rest of your day? It gets dark here around 4 p.m. this time of year. Tinselvania is a beautiful place to live. You'll love it here."

"I already do."

As soon as Chuck left, Mary stretched and started mentally preparing for her meeting. Her mind raced with thoughts and ideas. She was the little engine that could. She would not be stopped. She summoned her inner She-Ra and Wonder Woman. She opened her desk drawer, where she kept a framed photograph of Dolly Parton.

"Guide me, Dolly," she said.

"Oh God, are you doing that weird thing where you psych yourself up and send for the strength and grace of Michelle Obama, Oprah, and The Golden Girls?" Robin asked from the doorway. Kara and Liza were with her.

"We got you!" Liza said, pushing the "play" button on her iPhone as Whitney Houston's "I'm Every Woman" emanated from the speakers.

Kara, Liza, and Robin joined in with Mary, doing freestyle interpretive dance, their call to the universe for confidence, success, and clarity. Some people prayed. Some went on spiritual retreats and did yoga or practiced mindfulness. Mary and her friends liked to dance it out.

"What in the name of *Solid Gold*?" Casper asked before he joined in.

Casper stopped himself despite how much fun he was having. He gave Mary the cue that she was needed elsewhere. Mary shrugged to her friends, took a big breath, and followed him to the board room, where Bright and Joseph were waiting for her.

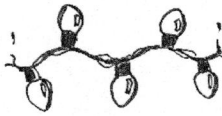

Bright was already seated and looking impatient when Mary arrived. Casper shut the conference room door behind him and escorted Joseph back to his work desk.

"Have you had a chance to take a tour of the facility?" Mary asked. "We actually do on-site tours for guests and visitors year-round."

"Yes, your assistant Casper was very knowledgeable and helpful," answered Bright. "I think he and Joseph are currently comparing the various phone and computer programs they use to schedule our lives. I'll need meetings with your CFO and COO as well. Casper's arranging that."

Mary sat across from him. His face was constantly serious, grim, all business. Mary had dealt with many of these types before, usually older men who thought she was less intelligent or less marketing savvy simply because she was a woman. She didn't get that vibe from Bright. His vibe was one that said, "City life, good; country life, pathetic."

"I have some notes," he continued. "Most of your employees can be replaced by modern robotic equipment that will do the job ten times faster and a hundred times cheaper. You need to get rid of all the extraneous departments that can be handled by outside resources. The cafeteria is completely unnecessary and costly. Let the employees go into town and get their lunches or bring one from home."

"Did you not hear a word I said when I talked to the investors? This is a family business. The people who work here are our extended family. They are Tinsel Inc."

"Tinsel Inc.'s business model and acumen, like this town, is frozen in 1999. I think I saw that *The General's Daughter* is playing at your local movie theater."

"People here really like John Travolta! They're playing *Face/Off* and *Michael* next week."

"You know how business goes. If you don't change with the times, you don't grow and expand. You could be making so much more money if you administered new rules and regulations. Cutting down on employees and labor hours would result in your company's earnings growing exponentially."

"Do you even care about Christmas?"

"Christmas? A made-up holiday with made-up traditions that have nothing to do with religion, goodwill, or actual spirituality. Nothing about Christmas honors any historical legacy. It's all been bastardized beyond recognition. We're forced to buy presents we can't afford for family members we are stuck with for a holiday we can't escape. We tell kids that some fat creep watches them all year long to judge whether they're worthy of gifts or not, when every other day, we tell kids to stay away from fat creeps. It's a holiday invented for the rich to get richer and send people into credit card debt and for companies to make money. Have you ever researched the origins and meanings of Christmas, before the greeting card companies hijacked it? It's terrifying. Christmas rivaled Halloween for a night of horror. Nowadays, it's a soulless, commercial endeavor with nothing genuine or heartfelt behind it. Why do you think suicide rates are highest during the holidays? Christmas makes people feel unworthy, alone, stressed, depressed. And the craziest part? The whole universe celebrates it and tells us we're the outcasts if we don't. It's mind-blowing."

"What I'm hearing is, you asked Santa for a *Sabrina the Teenage Witch* Tamagotchi and he didn't come through for you. It's okay to be bitter."

"We're deluding ourselves, Mary," Bright said. "I'll push tinsel as long as it makes me money, but I will never pretend that I think there is anything honest and virtuous about Christmas."

"I've met so many people like you before. You come in and after one day, you judge and mock the people here and the way we do things. This company has the most cutting-edge technology and equipment available today. We don't need twenty new buildings to make our deadlines or fill our orders because we have dedicated real people with real feelings who come in every day and give this building life. Unlike you, they take pride in their work and value the human aspect of their job. These people give us what machines can't, which is passion for their work and respect for each other and this company and this town. A robot doesn't have a family depending on it. A robot doesn't have a family to feed."

"Machines will be able to do that in a few years, I'm sure. Think about all of the other businesses you could run if you converted to mechanized workers. How about an Arbor Day store?"

"Tinselvania is a Christmas town."

"Or a frozen yogurt shop."

"Ugh! We eat real ice cream here, dairy intolerance or not."

"What about catheters? You could always sell those."

"I'm sure if you did, you'd overcharge so you could make the most profit. Who cares about other people, right? You could stick one in your mouth with all the crap that comes out of it."

"I'm just saying, if the board agrees with some of my findings, you have options."

"Has living in New York City made you so cynical and hardened your heart so much that you don't care about people's lives? Maybe you can't find a Starbucks or a Duane Reade here, but you'll find a lot of people who live honest lives and are good neighbors. Not everybody needs to 'be seen' by the cultural elite."

"If the cultural elite saw this town, they'd burn it down like a bunch of villagers chasing down Frankenstein's monster with pitchforks and torches."

"How dare you, sir! I won't need your services here any longer."

"Unfortunately for me, you didn't hire me. The board did. So I'm here in town until they are satisfied with my findings."

"You couldn't find your butthole with a compass. Not even the kind you need for camping– I mean the one you use for math class!"

"What?"

"Good day to you, sir!"

"Good day to you as well, ma'am!" Bright said, getting up from his seat. "Oh, actually, we'll be seeing each other tonight. Your sister Noelle insisted that I come to her house for dinner tonight. Should I bring my own silverware or will sporks be provided?"

"Fine. I will see you at 7:00. Where we will eat dinner with actual forks. Maybe I'll bring a life-sized Terminator standee so you'll have something else without a soul to talk to at dinner."

Bright gathered all his important files and papers and left Mary alone in the conference room. She stood there, angry at Bright and at herself for letting him get to her.

Chapter 10

Llewellyn Barnes wandered the town of Tinselvania, overcome with waves of nostalgia for the life he had before he left. So many of the old storefronts had been updated but they were still owned and operated by the same families he had grown up with, now run by the next generations.

He walked through the town square, remembering the old decorations and light shows that dazzled the residents. Although the new décor was more modern-feeling, it maintained the echo of Tinselvania past.

He smiled at passersby, watched the people falling and laughing at the ice-skating rink, and ordered a fancy coffee drink at a boutique coffee shop (well, it was boutique for Tinselvania). He didn't have a concrete plan in place yet. He needed to get the feel of the town again.

In due time, he would reintroduce himself to the people he'd left behind. He would revisit the past and make his presence known.

Until then, he would hide in plain sight and observe.

Mary, Casper, and Joseph were waiting for Bright so he could take the official guided on-site tour. He made it in time for the last tour of the day, surrounded by tourists who had come to Tinselvania to admire and photograph their extensive Christmas décor and tinsel factory. Mary steeled herself for whatever challenges Bright may bring, kicking herself that she mistakenly thought she had the rest of the day free from him until the 7:00 dinner at her family's.

Bonnie Payne, the tour guide, loved two things in life– Paul Revere and tinsel. She was a freshman at Clement University in the neighboring town and worked as a tour guide at Tinsel Inc. to pay her bills. She couldn't be in Boston to work at The Paul Revere House and sleep in the same bed as Paul did, so until she could, she'd get to tell visitors all about the magical, whimsical, life-changing world of tinsel.

Today was extra special because Mary Classen, the CEO, was attending the tour. It was Bonnie's chance to shine and show Mary how dedicated, knowledgeable, and enthusiastic she was. She pumped herself by listening to war songs from the American Revolution on her iPhone, the same war her beloved Paul Revere fought in. This was her moment, her chance to shine bright like Paul on his horse warning the minutemen of the impending British invasion.

Bonnie had her best Paul Revere shirt on beneath her beige blazer. She stood before the eager crowd of twenty, plus Mary and her team. Her light brown hair was pulled back in a braid with a pink ribbon. Bonnie added dashes of powder to make it more authentic, like the soldiers and ladies in Paul Revere's day.

Llewellyn Barnes had bought a ticket to the tour and joined the group. He didn't know if he was risking being recognized before he was ready, but he wanted to see the factory again. How it had changed and developed since the last time he'd seen it.

"Hello, everybody! I'm Bonnie, your tinsel tour guide," she beamed, showing off her pearly white teeth as she remembered that Paul Revere worked as an amateur dentist, because he too knew how important good oral health was. "Remember that old show *Pop-Up Video* on VH1? Think of me as your real-life trivia bubble. If you'll follow me."

Bonnie brought the tour group into the factory line, where the tinsel was inspected and tested. She loved the look on the tour group's faces. She wanted to bottle their wonderment, awe, and marvel.

"Tinsel was first invented as early as 1610 in Nuremberg and was originally made of silver," said Bonnie, gesticulating like she was a flight attendant giving a demonstration or the models on *The Price is Right* that showed off the prizes.

"Fun fact: Paul Revere was a silversmith by trade," she continued. "So I like to think that he loved tinsel! And me. What? You're going to be on Santa's naughty list, Bonnie!"

The tour group laughed, their heads in constant motion to see all of the workers, tinsel product, and machinery that surrounded them.

I'm on fire! Bonnie thought. *This stuff will kill at the open mic night I plan to institute at The Paul Revere House! Mary will see that and write me a glowing recommendation when I graduate and move to Boston.*

"The word 'tinsel' comes from the French word 'estincele,' which means 'sparkle.' When it's in long, narrow strips and not attached to any thread, tinsel is called 'lametta' and mimics icicles. France was the number one manufacturer of tinsel until World War I, until Tinsel Inc. and Tinselvania, Maine, became the world's number one purveyor. Archibald Classen, our founder, saw the need and desire for a world filled with tinsel. Like Paul Revere founding the first rolling copper mill in the United States, Archibald Classen created Tinsel Inc. to provide the world with a vital, important, invaluable treasure that no man or woman should ever be without."

Mary and Bright stayed in the back of the crowd as Bonnie spoke. Casper and Joseph gave them space and tried to blend in with the tour group.

"I thought you were done for the day," said Mary.

"The workday is never done," Bright said. "First rule of business."

"The first rule of business is to always stay in business. Did you go to the Michael Scott business school?"

"I did. I learned everything I know from *The Office*. What was the first rule of fight club?"

"There will be no fighting. You are our guest and we will treat you as such. I am at your disposal. Regardless of your feelings about this town and this business, we have to work together and I think it would be beneficial to both of us to make it as pleasant as possible."

"I agree. Listen, Mary, I didn't mean to come across as rude or insulting. I can be very passionate about the things I believe in and tend to have very strong opinions."

"No need to explain. What are we without our convictions?"

"I'm sorry about that, though. I should behave more maturely and in a manner more befitting a professional relationship. I think we may have more in common than we might expect. I think everything your family has built here is quite spectacular."

"We don't frown on business associates becoming our friends here."

"I'm starting to see that," Bright said. His smile was genuine and disarming.

Mary was silent for a moment. Maybe Bright wasn't as bad as she initially thought. She tried to figure out if he was a Jay Gatsby or a Nick

Carraway. She decided he wasn't a Tom Buchanan like she originally assessed.

"Your tour guide really loves Paul Revere, huh?" said Bright.

"And that's how you can make your very own tinsel-embellished Paul Revere body pillow," Bonnie explained to the crowd, followed by their applause.

Mary sighed as they rejoined the tour in progress.

Chapter 11

Mary returned to her office to find Robin at her desk using her computer and eating her secret stash of Little Debbie Vanilla Christmas Tree Cakes. Casper was used to Mary's friends' multiple daily visits, so he didn't even tell her Robin was there. Robin said hello but barely looked up from Mary's computer. Mary stood next to Robin to see she was perusing pictures of musclebound men showing off their hairy underarms.

"Robin! What are you doing?"

"I wanted to check Armpit Addicts and see if there were any new photos."

"Why are you using my computer to look at porn?"

"Because I'm at work and it wouldn't be professional to use my computer."

Mary shook her head, closing her laptop.

"You can go now. Don't you have work to do?" Mary said.

"You know what I was thinking about? Remember in those old *Hustler* spreads, where the girls would put lollipops up their hoo-has? What do they do with the lollipops after the photo shoot is over? Does someone eat it? Or do they just throw it away? Is there some lollipop-atorium where they collect all of them?"

"Oh my god, Robin, I'm going to send you to a sex addiction group."

"I'd just sleep with all of them."

"Please go away and stop corrupting my browser history."

"Oh, Mare, speaking of browser histories. I got a look at yours. It is so, so sad," Robin said, pulling up Mary's recent searches. "Extreme ironing, water tower pictures, adult coloring books, shower curtains, 1980s Martin Hewitt, The Boyfriend Pillow, business rompers, how to get edible cookie dough delivered to your house, when does *Tanked* air. That is the 'lonely lady' starter kit."

Mary threw Robin an "I-don't-have-time-for-your-tomfoolery" look and ushered Robin out the door. She grabbed her storage clipboard and raced to her next meeting.

Bright and Joseph were waiting for Mary when she arrived. Joseph fixed Bright's collar, then read off Bright's schedule to him, making notes on his computer as Bright rattled off a list of who he needed to contact and when. Ethan and Josh joined them.

They were in what the employees called "Frankenstein's Laboratory." It was filled with large spools of chemically-enhanced plastic wrap, coated mylar film, polyvinyl chloride, aluminum and other metals, and the various liquid and solid components that created tinsel. Items like petri dishes, flasks and beakers, alcohol burner, pipets, funnels, thermometer, tongs, and chemical spoons lined long, shiny laminated tables.

The workers wore heavy white lab coats and goggles. Although the tinsel was actually created in a different portion of the factory, Frankenstein's Lab was used for quality control, experiments, and tests on the tinsel. Several boxes of differently colored tinsel were stacked in the corner, mostly unusable, the products of failed inspections. A large, neon-pink high heel shoe-chair brightened up the corner of the room.

Mary went over the mechanics and purposes of the various equipment and implements, showing Bright and Joseph how the tinsel was made.

"Long-term exposure to some of the gases and chemicals used to make tinsel can be harmful to your health, which is why we wear so much protective gear," said Mary. "We're working with some highly volatile chemicals, many extremely flammable, so the 'no-smoking' policy is especially enforced in here."

"Many of the products you see on shelves and boxes here are things we're tinkering with, sort of new ideas to make tinsel more accessible to everyone," she added. "For instance, is there a chemical or smell we can put on it to make it less appealing to your cat or dog, thereby preventing them from eating or ingesting it? I know it goes without saying, but this is a room filled with secrets. So, anything you see here today, you can't share with anyone. We also don't want you to be too dazzled by our brilliance. The workers here put together a lot of the lab equipment themselves to make it more expedient and high-yielding for production purposes, with Ethan and Josh's help."

"You can always tell which ones of us had science kits and those Mouse Trap games when we were kids," said Ethan.

"We watched a lot of *Designing Women* as kids too," Josh said.

Ethan looked at Josh as if to say, "Not now."

"I already signed the non-disclosure agreement," said Bright. "I will never sell you ladies out."

"We strictly adhere to all the governmental laws of safety and quality, as we have for a century," Mary said. "Tinsel Inc. prides itself on its impeccable standards for the best tinsel in the world."

The tour was over and Ethan and Josh went their respective ways. In the hallway, Mary stopped Bright.

"Hey, Bright, I have an online call with your boss later," said Mary. "Any tips or insights you want to share with me into who he is?"

"Well, he thinks he's really funny but he's not really," Bright said. "You might want to practice your fake laugh. Here, you can try it out on me."

"I can't fake laugh. Never could."

"It's going to be an awkward call."

"He's either funny or he's not. That's on him. My laughs are earned. *Wayne's World*, *Clue*, *Tommy Boy*, *13 Going on 30*, funny. Those videos where people play mean pranks on innocent, unsuspecting people, not funny."

"Duly noted. I support this. He's going to hate you, but I have your back."

"I guess he'll have to cry himself to sleep tonight."

"Bright," Joseph interrupted. "You've got a call yourself in five minutes. We need to fix that hair."

"What's wrong with my hair?"

"Never mind, I'm going to take care of it for you. Sorry, Mary. I have to keep this guy looking like Zoolander. Come on, Bright, let's go practice your 'Blue Steel.'"

Mary laughed. "Good luck. If you're hungry later, let's meet up in the staff lounge. There's hot pretzels and cheese sauce." She had an extra skip in her step as she thought of cheese.

Bright smiled and followed Joseph to their office. He chuckled to himself. He wanted to get to know anyone who got that excited over cheese sauce.

Chapter 12

Tinsel Inc. was quiet and still now that the last employee had gone home for the day. Everyone except for Alfred and Balthazar, the father-son chef team, who were making food for tomorrow. Estelle had let them know she was leaving so they had to lock up once they were done. Most of the lights had been turned off for the night, other than the ones in the kitchen.

Alfred stirred the enormous steel pot of potato chowder that simmered on the industrial-sized stovetop. Balthazar was busy wrapping up the day's leftovers to be donated to local shelters and children's homes. Tomorrow the two of them would be on their way to Disney World and Alfred's sous chef would be taking over the culinary duties until his return. He and Balthazar saved all of their vacation days just for this trip, where they'd meet up with old friends and ride teacup rides and eat cotton candy.

"Balty?" Alfred called out. "You almost done back there? We can put this in containers and get home and pack!"

Balthazar didn't answer. He could hear him moving in the back. Clangs of kitchen utensils and doors opening and closing. A multitude of sounds and noises that let Alfred know he wasn't alone, although some of them didn't seem familiar.

The lights went out. The kitchen was cloaked in blackness, only lit by the flame from beneath the mammoth pot on the stove.

"Balty? The automatic lights went off. I gotta go fix them."

Balthazar still didn't say anything back. Alfred wiped his hands on his chef's apron and grabbed a flashlight, then headed out into the darkened cafeteria.

Alfred shined his light over the empty tables and tray station, trying to locate the breaker box on the back wall.

A sudden, skittering movement caught his attention. Someone– or something– had dashed from one table to another, its shadow barely captured by Alfred's flashlight.

"Is somebody there?" he said.

He made it to the main circuit breaker panel and reset the switches. The cafeteria and kitchen flooded with light again.

He did not see the person in the reindeer costume standing behind him, off in the distance, just staring at Alfred through the holes in the reindeer mask.

The speakers turned back on as well, as a song from Jewel's Christmas album flooded the air. Alfred laughed to himself. He couldn't tell you who Jewel was, but he knew every single one of her holiday tunes by heart after hearing them twenty times a day.

When he was back in the kitchen, he called out for Balthazar again, to no avail. He stirred the soup and readied a stack of empty plastic containers to ladle tomorrow's lunch into.

"Hey, Balty, I could use some help here!"

He turned to the back room, waiting for any kind of answer from his son. Shaking his head, he turned back to the pot of soup.

He filled the ladle with some potato chowder and shouted. Balthazar's head popped up, floating in the soup. His lifeless eyes stared at the ceiling as his head bobbed up and down in the hot liquid.

He ran toward the cafeteria, car keys in hand. There, among the tables, stood the person in the reindeer costume. The reindeer was motionless, expressionless, simply glaring at Alfred.

"Who are you?" Alfred yelled.

The reindeer raised a crossbow and fired a shot. It whizzed past Alfred's ear, barely missing him. Alfred turned on his heel and ran back into the kitchen. He'd escape through the back exit.

He made it into the back room and slammed the door behind him. His son's headless body was propped up on the door by several arrows that jutted out of his corpse. Alfred wanted to hug his son, to tell him it was all right, but that was futile now. He ran to the exit door.

He heard the backroom door burst open. When he spun around, the reindeer was gaining ground in a fast walk toward him, the crossbow loaded and ready to shoot.

Alfred was halfway out the back door when he heard the crossbow discharge. He felt the searing pain of the arrow slice through his hand and pin it to the door.

The reindeer advanced, only pausing for a moment to inspect the various sharp kitchen implements stashed away in the back room. It threw down the crossbow, exchanging it for a sharp meat cleaver.

Alfred almost had his hand free of the arrow. He was sliding his bloody hand off of it in order to release himself.

It didn't matter. He didn't have time to scream as the cleaver came down on his face, over and over again. The last thing Alfred saw was the reindeer's mask and the empty eyes beneath it.

The reindeer collected Alfred and Balthazar's bodies and transported them back to Emmett Branscombe's house. Cleaning up the bloody kitchen at Tinsel Inc. was a bitch but it couldn't have people investigating a crime scene. Not yet anyway.

It took all three of the men's decapitated heads and placed them beneath Emmett's tree, their vacant eyes gazing out at nothingness, their black irises illuminated by the blinking Christmas lights around them.

Chapter 13

Mary was in her room, the stress and strain of the day fading away as she changed out of her business clothes and into comfortable jeans and a T-shirt. She could hear her mom and Aunt Elaine chattering downstairs and getting ready for dinner at Noelle's. She wanted to stay home and watch old movies, not have dinner with that obnoxious Bright Harmon. She had to work on a new article for *Tinsel Monthly* magazine and hadn't even started it yet.

She stared out the window into her backyard. It was dark outside but the sky was clear and full of vivid stars. She loved it here. You wouldn't get a view like this in New York City, she told herself. Although she would love to see a Broadway show someday.

Someone in a reindeer costume and mask was in her backyard. Standing stock-still, looking right up into Mary's window. Right at Mary.

She lurched back, surprised. Her phone buzzed, startling her further. It was Liza calling.

"Liza?" she said into the phone.

"Hey, wanna go to the bowling alley this Friday night? I promised the kids I'd take them."

Mary went back to her window and peered out, trying to hide herself from whoever the reindeer weirdo was.

"Mary?" Liza said over the phone. "Are you there?"

The reindeer was gone.

"There was a reindeer outside."

"Not possible. There's no wild reindeer left in Maine. Maybe one escaped from Mrs. Cheevely's reindeer farm."

"No, a person in a reindeer suit."

"Did you hit your head today at work?"

"Oh, uh…" Mary regained her composure. "Yes, tell the kids Aunt Mary is down for bowling."

"Okay. You feeling all right?"

"Yes. Just a long day, I guess."

"You have tinsel on the brain. Call me after Noelle's big dinner."

"I will. Bye."

Mary disconnected the call and stared out the window again. There was nobody there. She shook her head and laughed at herself for being silly and seeing things.

Chapter 14

Dr. Sylvia Post contacted her team with the news of Chester Persimmons' escape and probability of repeating his previous massacre. Within the next hour, she had assembled Frances Boggs, Willa Pataki, and Belle Mulvaney, her lifelong friends. She had grown up with all of these women, as they supported and loved each other through triumphs and tragedies, marriages and divorces, children and grandchildren, and everything life had thrown at them. She knew she could always count on them, no matter what.

To their friends and family, they were sweet, affable older ladies who got together for bridge club and quilting bees. But the four women had skills and talents that only few people who required their assistance truly knew of. Frances had retired from her long career as an FBI agent and profiler. Willa was a former CIA operative and national security expert. Belle's career as a jazzercise and physical fitness expert masked her karate and ninja training.

Sylvia had called on them in the past to locate and immobilize escaped mental patients or violent threats to society. Knowing how grisly and gruesome Chester Persimmons' rampage had been two decades ago, she needed her team.

Her driver Pike, a strapping man in his early thirties who said and needed very little, drove her to Frances's farmhouse in the deep woods. Frances had made her home away from the noise and chaos of the cities surrounding her thirty-acre estate.

Frances brought the women downstairs to her furnished basement, taking the colorful tapestry off the back wall to reveal a hidden chamber. Once she typed in the code and her retinal scan was identified, access was granted and the metal door opened to reveal a fully stocked weapons armory. Various instruments of battle, from assorted guns and knives to grenades, nunchucks, axes, drills, and the like, lined the inside of the arsenal. Frances handed the ladies a GPS locator, tracking device, camera equipment, audio apparatuses, and a myriad of paraphernalia and hardware designed to hunt down and apprehend an enemy.

"I never really liked guns," Belle said. "I prefer more hand-to-hand combat."

"Take this then," said Frances, handing her a self-defense baton and a stun gun. "I'll take the Uzi. This baby got me out of a really bad jam in Montreal once. Poutine factory was a front for a money-laundering operation. That's all I can say."

"Where did you tell your kids and grandkids you were going?" asked Willa.

"They think we're all going to Dollywood," Sylvia said, inspecting the shotgun Frances handed her.

"All these years and none of our kids ever suspected a thing," Frances said. "I once had an illegal broccoli-trader kingpin show up at my house with his goons at dinnertime pretending to be an air-conditioning repairman. I took him and all his bodyguards out without anyone in the house noticing. Sometimes I'm relieved that the kids never caught on, but the other part of me wonders, 'Did I raise stupid kids?'"

Once they had their weaponry collected and packed, Sylvia showed Belle, Frances, and Willa the files on Chester Persimmons.

"Here's what we know," Sylvia said. "Chester Persimmons, now in his sixties. Born and raised in the town of Tinselvania, Maine. Lived there until he moved his family out to Nevada to start a new life. After a few years in his new location, without any warning or signs that anything was wrong, he went on a two-year murder tear. It was later discovered that he was deeply in debt, which he kept hidden from his family and business associates, after he opened his own small tinsel company that not only went under but caused him to lose all of his savings. That was the only motivation I could come up with for what would have set him off."

"His killings were vicious. Most were planned ahead, judging from the massive murder kit the authorities found in his house. When he carried them out, they were frenzied and berserk, almost animalistic. He targeted neighbors, strangers, even his own wife. His two young sons, Garland and Shepherd, walked in on him murdering their mother– Chester's wife– Noreen. They escaped to the neighbor's house, and Chester went on the run, where a statewide manhunt eventually found him, after he had brutally murdered a family of five for their station wagon. He never confessed to the crimes or gave any sort of explanation as to why he did what he did. He was declared insane and unable to stand trial and housed in The Calista Asylum for the Criminally Insane until it closed, then he was moved to a different mental health facility. Now he's escaped and is on the run, and my guess is he'll go to the one place that he associates with happiness, before his savage instincts took over his psyche. Tinselvania."

"So what's the plan then?" asked Belle. "We show up and pound this guy into ground chuck or what? Bag him and tag him?"

"I called local law enforcement to warn them of my theory," said Sylvia. "I spoke to a deputy named Nash, and just as I suspected, he dismissed my call as baseless flights of fancy and unsubstantiated conjecture. I think we go there, have a look around, catch this maniac, and save the town from a senseless slaughter. The man Chester Persimmons was disappeared long ago. All that's left is predatory rage and a desire for inflicting pain on innocent people."

"Just once I wish we really were going to Dollywood," sighed Belle.

Chapter 15

Ethan Classen and his wife Heloise, who worked as a marine biologist in the next town over, arrived home around the same time. The remnants of their daughters' snow angels in the front yard were fading, and the salt from the salt trucks had cleared up most of the ice in the driveway.

They had four daughters: Georgina, sixteen; Dulcie, twelve; Maisie, eight; and Eugenie, six. Georgina watched the other girls after school, before Ethan and Heloise returned home from work. Ethan had grown up as a latchkey kid and didn't want his daughters to do the same.

The house was a hub of commotion as usual. Georgina was on the computer or her phone with all of her girlfriends instead of doing her homework. The *You, Me and Dupree* Advent calendar Heloise had bought for the girls had already had every flap for each day opened, with all of the chocolates already eaten. That day's chocolate piece had been Owen Wilson shaped.

Ethan and Heloise barely had time to put their coats and work bags down when Maisie announced she needed help with her Christmas diorama for school. She had arranged a scene using household items like popsicle sticks, magazine cutouts, fuzzy pipe cleaners, and colored construction paper to depict the elves making presents in the North Pole. A sickly looking green-and-gray blob with tentacle-like arms and red eyes, fastened out of cardboard colored in with markers, loomed over the elves, who had expressions of terror on their faces.

"Maisie, what is that in Santa's workshop?" asked Heloise.

"It's the Cloverfield Monster!" Maisie said proudly.

Ethan and Heloise didn't argue it. They weren't going to stifle their daughter's creativity or imagination. They were also way too tired to reason with an eight-year-old on why the Cloverfield Monster had no cause to attack defenseless elves. They would set stricter parental controls on the television later.

"Pizza?" Ethan asked, his cell phone already out and finger ready to press "send" on his speed-dial. Heloise agreed, flipping through the mail.

"Postcard from your folks," she said, holding it up. "They're in Montreal having poutine and hanging out with the Mounties."

"Mom!" Dulcie said, rushing into the kitchen. "I need help running my lines!"

Tinselvania High School was putting on *Jaws: The Revenge: The Musical*. Dulcie had been cast as Swimmer #3. Heloise hugged her daughter and said a silent prayer that this year's show was better than the previous efforts, like the interpretive dance version of *Trainspotting*, the slam poetry version of *Maid in Manhattan*, and the ill-conceived Kabuki theater version of *No Country for Old Men*.

Heloise held the script in her hands while Dulcie focused on an imaginary spot in the distance, raising her arm and pointing her finger as she delivered her impassioned line.

"Sh-sh-shark!" cried Dulcie, fully in character.

Ethan ordered extra pizzas since his brother Josh and he had to go over accounts and paperwork for their meeting with Bright. Josh and his family were on the way over. Heloise looked around her house, at what a mess her kids had made, and shrugged. It was as clean as it was going to get at that moment. She considered grabbing the Dustbuster and doing a cursory vacuum but realized it wasn't worth the energy. Like her mom used to say, it would be like polishing a spatula while the house burned down around her.

Josh and his wife Susan arrived right after the pizzas did with their two sons– Hewney, eleven, and Kyle, seven. Susan was the manager of Virgil's Videos, located in the neighboring town. Whereas most video stores had long gone out of business, Virgil's Videos remained a popular staple amongst the citizens of Tinselvania and its sister towns. It was an institution, nestled in a strip mall in the center of town square, alongside a car wash, launderette, antique store, and various other restaurants, eateries, coffee shops, and patisseries. Josh and Susan fit into the same category of "typical, but not basic, small-town family" that Ethan and Heloise did.

The grown-ups rounded the kids up to eat. Heloise, Ethan, Susan, and Josh sat back and let the kids chatter. It was entertaining for them. They had given up years ago on owning a magical remote control that turned the volume of their kids down.

"Can you help me with my piccolo lesson?" Maisie asked.

"I want to show you the tricks I can do on my yo-yo!" said Kyle.

"Mom and Dad got us giant Jenga and a ping-pong table!" Eugenie said.

"I got a job working on a paper route," Dulcie said.

"I want to go as Holly Hunter in *Living Out Loud* next Halloween," said Hewney.

"We're going on a whaling boat on Sunday to go see whales!" said Maisie.

"Mom and Dad, will you get us a dune buggy for Christmas?" asked Kyle.

"Is Snuffleupagus real?" Eugenie asked.

"Why does corn always look the same when it comes out as it did when you ate it?" asked Hewney.

"Okay, guys, eat your dinner. Don't make me call the gypsies to come take you away," said Ethan. He leaned down to whisper to Hewney. "*Living Out Loud*? What are you and Aunt Mary watching when she baby-sits you guys?"

Maisie and Kyle bristled at the thought of pizza so Heloise made Dino Buddies chicken nuggets for them. Ethan and Josh ate with their families then adjourned to Ethan's study to workshop ideas for their presentation. Heloise rounded up the kids to play Chutes and Ladders and Hungry Hungry Hippos in the living room. Susan had brought *A Christmas Story* and *A Diva's Christmas Carol* from the video store.

Georgina protested and went back to her room to online shop for a dress for the upcoming Christmas dance. She put on her Panic! At the Disco Spotify station and texted her friends how her dad, without irony, asked what had caused the "panic" at the disco. She and her friends, known as "The Heathers" in school, were online having an Amazon watch party. Heather #1 chose *Chopping Mall*. Georgina hated scary movies but didn't say anything. She'd be sleeping with a nightlight on later.

Meanwhile, in his office, Ethan laid out a stack of paperwork and clicked on one of the twenty-five tabs on his computer to reveal a spreadsheet. Numbers upon numbers, company names, bank accounts, investor information, all accounted for and summed up tidily on one page.

Ethan and Josh's father Cobden had sold his stakes in Tinsel Inc. to his brother Bernard with the caveat that Ethan and Josh would be guaranteed high-ranking positions in the company. Bernard agreed, as it had always been his plan to keep the company in the family. Bernard, Mary's father, had a similar relationship with Cobden as Ethan had to Josh. Bernard and Ethan were the older brothers who looked out for their younger brothers.

Josh had always looked up to Ethan. Even when they were little, Josh wanted to go everywhere with Ethan and emulated all of his interests, pastimes, hobbies, and ideologies. When Ethan grew his mustache out to be like Tom Selleck on *Magnum, P.I.*, Josh did too. Josh joined The Society of American Magicians after Ethan did. Heloise called Josh "Ethan's shadow." Ethan never minded. Josh was his best friend.

While the menfolk discussed business, the kids insisted that Heloise and Susan play "the watermelon game" with them, where they pretended they were watermelons and their moms had to chase and catch them. The next couple of hours consisted of watching Kyle demonstrate his yo-yo skills while they ate pepperoni pizza and watched *The Greatest Showman*. The kids starred in an outfit-modeling movie montage, where they tried on all of their clothes (and some of their parents') and walked down an imaginary runway while the Kidz Bop Spotify channel played.

They paused to eat some cotton candy grapes and attempted to convince Heloise and Susan to let them watch *60 Days In* (the answer was "no.") They wore Socker Boppers and had a fake boxing tournament against their Spider-Man Bop Bag. They set up their bubble machine and turned the playroom into a mini-nightclub as they had a bubble dance party. Heloise and Susan broke the bad news that it was time to get ready for bed. The objections were swift and immediate.

After negotiations ended, Heloise and Susan finally got them all settled on the couch, sharing a big comforter as they watched television. The ladies went to the kitchen to have some coffee as the kids dozed off.

"This is my favorite part of the day," said Heloise. "Five minutes of quiet. I love those kids and I'll do anything for them, but sometimes I fantasize about running away and becoming a Dress Barn supermodel and marrying Tom Hardy, Hugh Jackman, George Clooney, Colin Farrell, Mark Ruffalo, or Ryan Reynolds– any one of them will do."

"Our children will never know the struggle of holding your cassette tape recorder up to the radio just to record a song you've been waiting all day to hear, only to have the DJ talk over the beginning and the end of it," Susan said. "We've done our jobs well."

"Mom? Aunt Susan?" Georgina said quietly. Her expression was serious and concerned.

"Hey," Heloise said. "What's the matter?"

"You should look outside," said Georgina. "In the backyard."

Georgina brought Heloise and Susan to the backroom window overlooking the backyard. The house's rear motion lights shone brightly yet couldn't reach the object Georgina directed her mother and aunt's attention to. At the edge of where the illumination met the darkness stood a stationary figure.

A scarecrow, most likely stolen from the Millers' farm down the road, had been hoisted up and hung on a makeshift stand in their backyard, barbed wire wrapped around its lifeless torso to hold it in position. It was dressed in tattered, ripped clothes, with its stuffing and straw bursting out. Beneath its straw hat, covering its face, was a smiling, red-cheeked plastic Santa Claus mask.

Georgina filmed the scarecrow on her phone. Heloise and Susan inspected the stuffed figure closely. Ethan and Josh came out when they heard their wives calling for them.

"Okay, nobody have a whack attack here," said Heloise.

"Mom, nobody says 'whack attack,'" Georgina said.

"That Rock Miller," Ethan said. "He's getting us back for when we put Spice Girls shirts on all his scarecrows last summer. He's probably sitting at home, patting himself on the back and calling himself a diabolical genius."

"Yeah, it's definitely Rock," Josh seconded. "He did stuff like this when we were all in high school together too."

"What kind of sick, sad deviant doesn't love the Spice Girls?" Heloise said, shaking her head sadly.

"This is a little darker than his usual pranks," said Susan. "Maybe he's having a mid-life crisis."

"Am I the only one totally freaked out by this?" Georgina said.

"Yes, Georgina," said Ethan. "It's a stupid prank pulled by Rock Miller. Wait til I see him at church. I'm going to put a fake spider in his pocket."

"Good one, Dad," Georgina said, her eye-rolling visible from space.

"Don't be so sarcastic or maybe Mr. Scarecrow will end up under your bed tonight," Ethan said to Georgina, waving his fingers in an attempt to be spooky.

Ethan gave the scarecrow a playful slap. Josh followed suit. Georgina shook her head at her parents and went back inside. Ethan gave Josh the nod that they had to get back to work. As they made their way back into the house, Heloise and Susan lingered for a moment to observe the disheveled, demented-looking scarecrow.

Chapter 16

Mary rode to her sister Noelle's house with her mother Alvinia and Aunt Elaine, who sang Christmas songs the entire ride. Even though it was at most a five-minute ride, she hoped to never hear Perry Como's "Winter Wonderland" ever again after listening to the screeching and squawking that passed as their singing voices.

Aunt Elaine was Alvinia's sister. She had been married twice and widowed both times. Her children had moved away years ago, which was a rarity in Tinselvania, especially for Mary's family. Unlike most people who moved away, Elaine's children and their families hadn't come back yet. Aunt Elaine was a robust woman who wore lots of flowy, garish layers, garments, and baubles. Alvinia's style was more muted. If Aunt Elaine was neon pink and plaid, Alvinia was beige.

Mary was Alvinia's oldest child. Her two younger sisters, Noelle and Glory, lived in Tinselvania. Noelle's house was a large, charming colonial-style that was typical of the neighborhood. A plastic snowman stood in the front yard beneath twinkle lights in the trees illuminating all of the Christmas decorations.

Noelle and her husband, Jed Kubiak, were setting up the dining room table for dinner. Noelle was head of the packing and shipping department at Tinsel Inc. All orders went through her, from origination to inspection. She and Jed had been married for over a decade now. They met when he visited Tinselvania on a vacation from his home state of Colorado, where he made his own soaps and hemp clothing. He moved to town to be with Noelle and opened his own vegan food store in town, Vegan Visions.

Jed dressed like he was getting ready to follow Phish all over the nation— hemp clothes, beaded necklaces, and Teva sandals. Mary wasn't even sure he owned a suit. Noelle dressed more like a schoolmarm, usually covered in big, fluffy sweaters and long skirts or pleated slacks. She rarely took her long, dark hair out of banana clips or scrunchies. They had two children, Dashi and Acorn. Dashi, a boy, was eight; and Acorn, a girl, was seven.

The television was on, tuned in to a channel with a yule log burning in a fireplace as Christmas music played in the background.

"Noelle?" Alvinia said. "Why don't you just use the actual fireplace?"

"We don't burn firewood," Jed said. "When you do, you can hear the wood screaming. It's the sound of it crying because it's in pain. We do not want to participate in deforestation and the destruction of natural resources."

"I brought fruitcake!" Aunt Elaine announced.

"That was perfectly timed," Mary said, feeling like she was surrounded by fruitcakes.

Noelle gave Mary a glass of wine then went to the table to make sure all of the silverware and plates were uniform and equal distance from each other.

"Symmetry," Noelle said, proud of herself.

"Why did you invite Bright to dinner tonight?" Mary asked.

"Well, he's a guest in our town and doesn't know anybody. Shouldn't we welcome him? Not to mention, if he gets to know us all, he'll see us as people, not just as numbers and placeholders at work. It's psychology."

"If he has dinner with us, he'll see us for the crazy weirdos we are and then he'll most certainly try to get rid of everyone."

Noelle poured something into a cobalt blue gluggle jug.

"Is that eggnog?" asked Mary.

"No, it's wheatgrass and kale juice, from Jed's store."

"Yeah, that'll definitely win Bright over."

Glory, the youngest of the sisters, put her arms around them. She worked in the art department with Mary's friend Kara at Tinsel Inc. Glory had always been the most carefree of the sisters, which drove Noelle crazy, but Mary rather admired. Glory was never as bothered or worried as the rest of the family was about anything. She married her high school sweetheart Cotter Ellis and they had a sixteen-year-old daughter, Ivy. Glory and Cotter were one of those couples who always seemed so madly in love, even after all these years, something else Mary admired. Cotter worked in the packing and shipping department with Noelle, but as a driver.

Glory looked more like Mary than Noelle did. Glory had long, wavy blonde hair and wore lots of band T-shirts, which matched how Cotter dressed. Cotter seemed like he walked right out of an Average Joe catalogue of brawny, affable men.

"How many drinks do you think it'll take for Aunt Elaine to be drunk enough that we can throw her abominable homemade fruitcake into the trash but convince her tomorrow that we all actually ate it?" she said.

"Jed made vegan candy-cane mint brownies for dessert," Noelle said.

Glory and Mary exchanged unimpressed glances, both ready to laugh.

"Don't start," Noelle said.

"I brought some firewood in for you guys," Cotter said, taking Glory's wine glass and having a sip.

"Don't bother," said Mary. "Firewood has feelings. The TV will keep you warm."

"Mary!" Alvinia called from the other room. "Your guest is here!"

"My guest," Mary said to Noelle accusingly. "My guest. You invited Thanos to dinner and it's my guest."

Alvinia took Bright's coat for him, smiling widely and assessing his snappy suit and good looks.

"This is a nice coat," she said. "Is this polyester?"

"Uh, I think it's wool and cotton," said Bright. He held up the bottles of wine in his hands. "I didn't know what you like to drink, so I brought white and red."

"I usually just have some Yellow Tail and I'm good. These are very fancy. Thank you."

"Hi," Mary said, not wanting Bright to feel too welcome. He could eat with them and hang out but there was no way she was advocating for it.

"Hi, Mary," he smiled. "Thanks for having me."

"Mary, stand up straight and stop making that face you make before you're going to fart," Alvinia ordered.

"I'll hold it in," Mary remarked. "I think Jed needs you in the kitchen."

Alvinia left to go assist Jed as Bright chuckled at Mary's discomfort. She took the wine Bright had brought with her.

"Is your mother embarrassing too?" she asked.

"Uh, actually, my folks passed when I was little," Bright said. "I grew up mostly in foster homes and orphanages."

"Oh, I'm sorry."

"No, no, it was a long time ago. Almost a whole other lifetime."

"Is Joseph with you?"

"No, I think your assistant is showing Joseph the town tonight. Those two might have made a love connection."

An awkward silence hung in the air between them. Mary stood on the balls of her feet then clapped her hands together.

"Well, I guess you should meet the rest of the gang."

Noelle and Jed were setting the dinner table with platters of food and side dishes. Every time Jed placed something down, Noelle rearranged it so it conformed with her aesthetic table vision.

"Everybody, this is Bright Harmon from the Yule Love It Christmas Corporation," Mary announced.

Her family waved and greeted him as people began taking their seats.

"Mom!" Dashi shouted, running into the dining room. "Ivy said Santa is going to put shit in our stockings!"

Mary and Glory stifled laughter as Noelle sighed heavily. Dashi and Acorn came running to her for hugs.

"To be fair, they asked what would happen if they were bad this year," Ivy said as she entered. Ivy always reminded Mary of herself at that age. They were both driven and smart, socially conscious, and not interested in doing things simply because they were trendy or popular.

"I don't want shit in my stocking!" Acorn cried out.

"Well, most shit is vegan so your parents won't mind," Glory said.

"Santa isn't going to poo in your stocking," Noelle said, giving Glory a death glare. "You guys have been good all year, haven't you? Santa is going to bring you lots of fun stuff. And what did I tell you about saying the brown word?"

"Ivy said it," protested Dashi.

"Snitches get stitches," Ivy said.

"Can we just have a nice, normal meal without any poop talk for once?" Aunt Elaine asked. "Everybody sit down so we can enjoy this beautiful dinner Jed made for us."

"Oh, Bright, you sit there," Alvinia said, pointing to the empty chair next to Mary.

"This looks wonderful," Bright said as he situated himself. "Thank you for having me."

"Who would like to say grace?" Aunt Elaine asked.

Nobody answered. Aunt Elaine looked around the table disparagingly.

"Bright, would you like to say grace?" she persisted.

All eyes landed on Bright. He shifted uncomfortably in his seat.

"Um, okay," he said. Everyone bowed their heads. "Dear God, thanks for the food and the company and the ramparts we watched that were so gallantly streaming…uh, and the rocket's red glare and bombs bursting in air and…um, don't be fooled by the rocks that I got because in the shallow, the shallow, we're far from the shallow now. Amen."

Aunt Elaine wasn't impressed, though everyone else at the table was about to burst from stifling their laughter. She chose to eat rather than publicly scorn Bright's toast.

"That was beautiful," Mary said to him.

"What are we having?" Bright asked, ignoring Mary.

"It's tofu spaghetti," Jed said proudly, his feng shui bracelets clacking together as he passed a plate of okra to Noelle. "It's good for you, made with squash. My friend Kerri gets great squash imported to her and she brought us some. We also have zoodles, which are zucchini noodles."

"Tomorrow night we're going to eat cardboard," Glory joked.

"Everything is cruelty-free and just as delicious as whatever regular spaghetti you've had," said Jed.

"Is this the house that gives out raisins on Halloween?" Bright said quietly to Mary.

"Have some lima beans, Mary," Alvinia said, spooning a heaping portion onto Mary's plate.

"God, I hate coming here," Mary said, louder than she expected.

"Hahaha yeah, sure. Everybody make fun of the vegan hippies," Jed said mockingly. "You've all been coming here for ten years and still complain that there's no real pepperoni or cheese on the cauliflower pizza we make, or we have baba ganoush as a main course and not a snack. We can't all be high-powered executives like you."

"I was just teasing, Jed," Mary said, feeling guilty. "Really, I'm sorry. Look, I love my lima beans. I'm going to eat them all. Without butter, since you don't have any in the house because cream is murder, and even though butter is delicious and would make the lima beans more palatable, I love them anyway."

"Smooth," Bright whispered to her.

"Eat your squash, guest," she hissed back.

"What is an 'isthmus'?" asked Dashi.

"What's 'figgy pudding'?" Acorn said.

"It's a narrow strip of land with sea on either side, forming a link between two larger areas of land," Ivy said. "Isthmus, not figgy pudding."

"Welcome to The Island of Misfit Toys," Glory said to Bright. "The family that we make."

"Are you saying we're all broken, damaged, and irregular?" Aunt Elaine asked.

"Dashi, Acorn," said Mary, trying to redirect the conversation. "What do you want Santa to bring you for Christmas this year?"

"Elmo and Minions and anything with music or puzzles or art. I like *Frozen*. Olaf is a snowman," Acorn said. "And *Toy Story*."

"What does Buzz Lightyear say?" asked Noelle.

"To infinity, let me on!" Acorn said.

"I told Santa to bring me glowsticks, a Magic 8-Ball, mood rings, Shrinky Dinks, slap bracelets, Colorforms, candy necklaces, and the headset and special goggles for my virtual reality *Win a Date with Tad Hamilton!* video game," Dashi said. "Oh, and a red panda. I wrote Santa a letter. His address is still the North Pole, right?"

"A real red panda or a stuffed animal red panda?" asked Bright.

"A real one!" said Dashi.

"We'll have to see what Santa says, my little zookeeper," Jed said.

Everyone ate quietly for a minute. Jed, Noelle, Dashi, and Acorn happily devoured their dinner. The rest of the group struggled a bit but sucked it up for the sake of family.

"So, Bright, what is New York City like?" Alvinia asked. "You must not be used to how quiet and tranquil Tinselvania is."

"I haven't really gotten to see much of the town yet," he said. "Everybody definitely has Christmas spirit here."

"More Christmas, less hookers and crack addicts," Aunt Elaine said. "Tinselvania is a respectable city. We value traditions and family, unlike the heathens in big cities."

"The hooker who works the corner near my building is very friendly," Bright joked. Aunt Elaine practically clutched her pearls.

"Do you have a girlfriend?" Alvinia asked.

"I did," Bright said, clearly uncomfortable, hiding it with a laugh. "Not anymore."

"Oh really?" she said, her eyes directly on Mary. "I'm so sorry. What happened?"

"Candeeee and I wanted different things. I wanted her to be faithful to me and she wanted to sleep with all of my friends."

"What a shame," Alvinia continued, not meaning a word of it, as her plan was hatching. "You know, there's a lot of very intelligent, beautiful, successful, amazing women in Tinselvania. I bet they'd love to meet a catch like you. A guy who wears wool coats. And what nice teeth you have."

"I'm only going to be in town for a little while," said Bright.

"That's what I said too," Jed said, putting his hand on Noelle's. "Life had different plans for me. Our chakras aligned and I've been here ever since."

"Why Mary, if I remember, you haven't gone out with anybody since that nice boy Ralph," Aunt Elaine said. "You always found the funniest reasons to dump men. You didn't like that one guy because he always talked during *Elementary*. And the other one you dumped because he always wore that Members Only jacket. Oh, whatever happened to Ralph? You guys were such a handsome couple."

"Ralph was selling his jizz socks online, so I wasn't super excited to commit to a life with him," Mary said.

"What's 'jizz'?" Dashi asked.

"Jazz!" Noelle said. "She said 'jazz.' You know, like 'jazz hands' or 'all that jazz' or 'Aunt Mary would never say a bad word in front of my kids so clearly she said jazz.' Like scatting. People who scat when they're playing jazz."

"You know, 'scatting' has a different meaning," Ivy began.

"And that's the end of that sentence," Noelle cut her off.

"How much money was he getting for the socks?" Cotter asked. Glory playfully smacked him.

"You know that we would love you if you were a lesbian, Mary," Alvinia said. "I would watch *Bound* with you. I love you no matter what."

"For the eight millionth time, Mom, I'm not a lesbian."

"I'm just saying, there's nothing wrong with it. I run into April Fleming at the grocery store all the time and she always asks about you."

"Why me?" Mary said, looking to the ceiling.

"Tinselvania is a very inclusive town," Alvinia continued. "There's no prejudice or hate here. We accept everybody. Even Mr. Drexler, and he married his tractor."

"It was a lovely ceremony," Aunt Elaine agreed.

"Maybe I'll just marry Mr. Drexler then," Mary said.

"Oh, he'd never look at you the way he looks at that tractor," Glory interjected, completely loving this roast. "We're opening the closet door here for you, Mary. Come out! Don't you want to be who you were meant to be?"

"I mean, at your age, you're more likely to be eaten alive by a pack of rabid beavers than get married," Aunt Elaine said.

"Aunt Elaine, everyone who isn't married is not gay!" Mary almost-shouted, before she adjusted the volume of her voice. "This is my coming out party, and I'm coming out as straight and not willing to settle just because my crazy mother and insane aunt think I'm going to shrivel up and die without a man!"

"Well, that's a little dramatic, don't you think, dear?" Alvinia said.

"A little help here," Mary pleaded with her sisters.

"Nah, you're doing great." Glory waved her away.

"The floor is yours," Noelle chimed in.

"It's like watching a hot air balloon without a pilot," Cotter said. "Just floating up, up, up and away into the sky."

"You know what?" Mary said. "At the next county auction, you can just put me up for sale to the first guy who has enough cows for my dowry."

"Hmm." Aunt Elaine mulled it over.

"That wasn't a serious suggestion, Aunt Elaine."

"Is anyone else sad that *Sealab 2021* didn't predict the future?" Jed interjected, trying for some levity. It didn't work.

"Please don't write about this on the neighborhood watch forum, Mom," said Mary. "This is a conversation that doesn't leave this dinner table. Okay? I have embarrassing stories about you, too, dearest mother. True story. My beloved mother thought LOL meant 'lots of love' so when Bootsie McCallister's husband died last May, she sent a card that read 'Thinking of you. LOL. XOXO.'"

"Don't you go telling everyone my secrets, young lady!" Alvinia said. "I know things too. Your Aunt Elaine saw a report on *Oprah* that said that nutmeg can be used as a drug now, so she wouldn't let any of us buy it for the house. That's why when we have eggnog at Christmas, we have no nutmeg."

"They use it to make hallucinogens!" Aunt Elaine insisted. "You know they take nutmeg and watch *Flubber*. Pardon me if I don't want all the neighborhood kids staring at lava lamps, all jacked up and seeing Rainbow Brite floating on the ceiling. This is just like high school. You're all a bunch of mean girls. Somehow I'm not invited to the cool kids party."

"I only want you to be happy, my smart, beautiful daughter," Alvinia said. "I always tell you the same thing I told Noelle and Glory. You don't need another person to feel whole. You are already complete. You need to meet someone who will add to your life."

"Oh god, this is my genetic legacy," said Mary. "And you were the one who bought me *Microwave for One* last Christmas!"

"Oh, Mary, your love life always required orange cones and that yellow caution police tape around it," Aunt Elaine said. "You'd rather beat the boys at business deals than date them. Robin set you up with one of her firefighter friends and you didn't like him because he said 'ax' instead of 'ask.'"

"Which is ironic for a firefighter," Mary said. "He also said 'upmost' for 'utmost,' and pronounced the 'L' in 'salmon,' to be fair. Don't you want me to feel magic and see fireworks when I fall in love? He wasn't even really a firefighter. He was a dancer in an all-male revue and that was his costume. He also did kids' parties using the same costume, which leaves me with lots of moral and ethical questions."

"I want you to be happy, dear," Alvinia said. "I'm not that old-fashioned. Just stop acting like the Unabomber, all alone in the wilderness. I worry that someday we're going to find some crazy manifesto you wrote in your garment drawer. I'm just saying, maybe you could entertain the idea of settling down and having some babies."

"This claim is disputed," Mary grumbled.

"What about this handsome fella here?" asked Aunt Elaine, pointing to Bright. "Why don't you marry this one? He's a nice boy."

"Subtle as a shark attack," Mary said. "Contrary to popular belief, men and women can be just friends."

"That's not what *When Harry Met Sally* tells us," Alvinia said.

"Think of your ovaries," said Aunt Elaine. "They must be dust by now."

"We just don't want to see you turn into one of these crazy cat ladies who die alone in their rocking chair and then when someone finally realizes, your cats have eaten you," added Alvinia in a helpful tone, though her words were hardly helpful to Mary.

"There's a really rundown assisted living home five states away with both of your names on it," Mary said, pointing to Alvinia and Aunt Elaine. "I'm putting the deposit down tomorrow."

"I think it's cool that you don't get married for tradition's sake, Aunt Mary," Ivy said. "Women don't need men to have careers or lives of their own. We only need them for breeding purposes, and there are special facilities you can go for that."

"Where?" Acorn asked.

"The mall," Noelle cut off Ivy before she could answer.

"I'm actually doing my senior science paper on the difference in how stress affects a woman's brain compared to a man's," Ivy said. "The school is letting me go to the university and observe the on-site testing of subjects so I can collect data for my thesis."

"Nerd alert," Cotter told her.

Glory and Cotter shook their heads, laughing at themselves, so proud of Ivy but in constant shock at how intelligent and enterprising she was.

"We don't know where she got it from," Glory said. "She didn't get it from us. I think someone switched our babies at birth and some super-nerdy couple has a hillbilly redneck baby and we have their genius wunderkind."

"Half this town is hillbillies," Ivy said.

"What's a 'hen-bennies'?" asked Dashi.

"Chickens," Jed said. "We don't want any stray chickens showing up, do we? They're terrible houseguests. Make messes and never clean up after themselves. They don't even do the dishes. Not even a thank-you note after they leave."

"What's 'irony'?" asked Acorn.

"It's when an old man turns ninety-eight, and then wins the lottery, and then dies the next day," Mary said. Acorn seemed sufficiently satisfied with Mary's answer.

"Oh, Grandma," Ivy said. "Can I invite Betsy, Ellie, and Stacy to the *Family Stone* party?"

"Of course," Alvinia said. "Tell them no phones during the movie, though. I know we're lucky to live in an age with so much technological advancement, but that's special family time. Too much social media just means too much misinformation and bad news spreads too quickly and it turns into an information assault."

"Great, thanks," said Ivy, instantly texting her friends from the dinner table.

"And the one who always says 'no offense' and then says something mean afterwards," continued Alvinia. "Explain to her that saying 'no offense' before insulting someone's curtains does not make it less impolite. No one says 'no offense' unless they're going to say something offensive."

"Okay, Grandma," Ivy answered, still texting.

"And you, young man." Alvinia turned to Bright. "I insist you attend our party. Every year we have a family and friends gathering to watch *The Family Stone* and be grateful for the blessings in our lives. You will attend and I will not take 'no' for an answer. Mary will fill you in on the details."

"Yes, ma'am," said Bright, unequipped to battle her.

"Grandma, can I bring Rudy?" Acorn asked.

"Who's Rudy?" answered Alvinia.

"He's the reindeer who hangs around outside and sometimes hides in my closet and scratches at the door at night," said Acorn.

"That's her imaginary friend." Noelle smiled and turned to Acorn. "We'll probably leave Rudy at home for the night. Reindeer don't really care about movies."

"He's not imaginary!" Acorn insisted. "He's real. He talks to me. He used to live in Tinselvania but someone new lives in his house."

"Okay, sweetie," Jed said, patting her hand. "Will you use your Jedi Knight superpowers and help me clean up all the dishes?"

"Yes!" Acorn said. Dashi jumped up as well, both kids eager and willing to help clear the table.

Noelle got up and headed into another room as Jed, Dashi, and Acorn began collecting the dirty plates. They were in and out, making several trips.

"Thank you so much for dinner and for the company," Bright said.

"Oh, you're not going anywhere yet," Alvinia said. "We still have to watch the *Ally McBeal* Christmas episode where Robert Downey Jr. sings 'River.' 'Tis the season."

"Aunt Elaine, why don't you let me make you a Hinge profile?" asked Glory. "That way you can meet some nice gentleman to take you to bingo on Mondays."

"Oh, this shop is closed," Aunt Elaine said. "Two husbands, four children, and six grandchildren. I'm not interested in a date unless there's a handsome, ghostly old sea captain out there who wants to play Scrabble with me. Not a euphemism."

"Aunt Elaine, you did date a sea captain once," Noelle said. "It was between husband number one and two. He really liked you. Remember him? What happened to him?"

"He died," Aunt Elaine sighed.

"He was lost at sea," Alvinia said. "They never found any of the crewmen. He was part of a *Gilligan's Island* fan club that reenacted the show and, well, weather on the ocean can be unpredictable. We were never sure if one of the overeager fan club members purposely wrecked the ship and they've all been living on some deserted island ever since."

"They did find a wooden figure that looked just like me, but as a mermaid, washed up on the beach years later. He had carved 'Elaine + Hayden' on the bottom. I like to picture him like Tom Hanks in *Cast Away*, counting down the days until he can make it back to me. He liked it. He just never got the chance to put a ring on it."

"Speaking of, I love that Helen Hunt, don't you?" Alvinia said.

"Who's Helen Hunt?" asked Dashi.

"She's the lady in that movie you like with the flying cow in the hurricane," said Noelle.

"Oh my God, now I know why you wouldn't go with us to see *Cast Away*," said Glory. "Or *The Life Aquatic with Steve Zissou*."

"Is that why you wouldn't watch *Boat Trip* with me?" Cotter said.

"No, that's because *Boat Trip* is a garbage film that should be used for toilet paper or torture techniques to get criminals to confess to their crimes. That had nothing to do with Aunt Elaine's missing sailor," Glory said.

"Glory!" Alvinia said. "Have some sensitivity. That was the love of your Aunt Elaine's life and he's probably stranded on an island in the middle of the ocean with a volleyball for a best friend."

"Sometimes I put on the Carpenters and a candle in the window to light his way back home to me," Aunt Elaine said forlornly. "Our safeword was 'clams casino.'"

A general "ugh" and "eww" spread over everyone at the table.

"I'm going to Betsy's," Ivy said.

"Home by eleven," Glory said.

"Yes, Mom," Ivy said, kissing her mom and dad and then hugging everyone good night. "Betsy lives three minutes away. I'm not going to be abducted."

"They'd return you as soon as they got to know you," Cotter teased her.

"Emmett Branscombe lives next door to Noelle and Jed," Alvinia said to Bright. "His grandfather was one of the men who started Tinsel Inc. with my husband's grandfather."

Noelle returned with a giant, life-sized cardboard cutout standee of Arnold Schwarzenegger as The Terminator.

"Hey, Mary, what do you want me to do with this?" she asked.

Mary gave an embarrassed glance over in Bright's direction. He was smiling.

"I'll grab that on my way out," Mary said.

"We're making hot chocolate for everyone!" Jed said from the kitchen. "Everybody go get comfortable in the family room and we'll bring it out for you."

"It's amazing to have a smart daughter, but at the same time, sometimes I think it's good for her to get out of her head once in a while," said Glory. "Ivy reminds me of you, Mary."

Cotter was sidetracked by Aunt Elaine, who asked him to flex so she could feel his muscles. Glory barely noticed and leaned in to chat with Mary.

"He's having a hard time dealing with the fact that Ivy's going to be going off to college next year," Glory whispered, gesturing to Cotter. "You know that Nestle Tollhouse Cookie commercial, where the mom comes home and the kid baked cookies because he got his acceptance letter? Waterworks, every time. He says it's just his allergies. But the other day, he was in the garage working out, listening to that song 'Don't Cry Out Loud'– that Melissa Manchester one– and lifting weights as he cried. Our browser history is filled with articles on how to adjust to empty nest and how to say goodbye to your college-bound child. I can't have a husband who just looks up porn on the computer like a normal person."

"Ah, everything is so much funnier when it doesn't happen to me," Mary said.

"Aunt Elaine, stop that!" Glory slapped Aunt Elaine's hands away. "You're a walking sexual harassment lawsuit waiting to happen."

Chapter 17

Mary sat on the bed in her sister's guest room, drinking the last of her wine. She didn't even bother to turn all the lights on, instead settling on the dim glow from the vintage lamp on the bedside table.

She scanned the framed photographs that lined the walls. Her, her sisters, her parents, Tinsel Inc., the house they grew up in, their extended family– all represented in the pictures that hung, now only memories of Mary's childhood. She thought about what a happy childhood she'd had, how much fun her sisters were, and how it always felt like Christmas in their house. Sometimes she missed that innocence, that naivety, that hope for what the world had in store for her. Now she was middle-aged and a lot of that life had passed by. She wished her father were here. The holidays were the hardest time to be without him. She remembered her parents taking them all to the tinsel factory when Mary was twelve. They were delivering Christmas presents to each and every employee. Her father turned to her and said, "One day, this will all be yours."

"I thought only serial killers sat in dark rooms all alone," Bright said from the doorway. "Your mom sent me up to keep you company."

"I'm avoiding all of my deranged relatives," she said.

"In your mind? Are they invisible? Are they here in the room with us right now?"

"No, they're downstairs probably discussing how many cats to get me so I won't grow old alone since my lady bits apparently give off radioactive waves. I'm officially the cat lady in the family to them now. I don't even own a cat! And who cares if I did? Cats are nice. I'm hiding. Besides, most serial killers sit alone in barns."

"I admire your bravery and courage. Why are you hiding from them? Do you owe them money? Do they have compromising video of you and the milkman and are threatening to post it to XTube? Do they want to take your organs and sell them on the black market? Oh, can we trust them?" Bright mocked her playfully. Mary cracked a smile.

"No, none of the above. The way my crazy family barges into my life. It's like I'm fifteen again. Wait. Why am I telling you this? What's happening here?"

"I think what you consider 'deranged,' other people would see as people who love you so much that they worry for you and want to help you. We are always toughest on the ones we love. You can't tease anyone that aggressively unless they're family."

"I see what you're doing here."

"I never really got to know how great it was to have a family. The way you guys all talk to each other. They all love each other so much. It's really awesome. It was nice to be a part of something like that tonight," Bright said as he stepped inside the room.

"Ever notice how after you turn twenty-one, you always tell people what you do for a living and your marital status? Like somehow it defines you? Like it's all you are? It's so depressing. Like it's the only thing you have to talk about. Well, I have the career, now my mom and aunt obsess over my love life."

"Yeah, I get it. I spent most of my life in foster care. No families that I ever really felt like I was a part of. I had to work for everything I have. All these things other kids were just handed, I struggled for. I was a busker, I washed dishes, I shoveled shit, all to save enough money for college. Meanwhile, all the rich kids in school had jobs lined up for them once they graduated because of who their parents were. I had to work my way up. I worked at the Enigma Enema company for years and didn't get anywhere while nepotism guaranteed my less-qualified coworkers would move up and I'd stay stagnant, always relegated to the penalty box. I started in the mailroom at Yule Love It and never slept, never gave up, worked my ass off, and became a high-powered executive."

Bright was looking at all of the photos on the wall.

"Is this you?" he asked, pointing to a picture of young Mary in a snowsuit.

"Yes. I think that was 1987. That was right before I won the school's big spelling bee and then the boys all stopped talking to me."

"What was your word?"

"My word?"

"The word that won you the championship."

"*Archaeologist*. Thankfully I had read lots of books about Margaret Murray, one of the most famous women archaeologists in history."

"That's both incredibly cool and one of the dorkiest sentences anyone's ever said to me."

Bright stopped at another photo.

"Is this your dad?" he asked.

"Yes. He was a really happy guy and a good dad. He loved this town. He and my uncle and his best friends all ran Tinsel Inc."

"It must be big shoes to fill."

"Sometimes. I have no idea where he found the time and energy to accomplish so much with the factory and be a devoted husband and doting father. He bought me my first briefcase. He loved Christmas. He would never let us have a fake tree. Every year, we would go on a grand adventure to find the perfect real tree. I miss that."

"He sounds like he was a great man. Do you mind if I ask how he died?"

Mary took a deep breath. Even though he had been gone for a while now, it was still hard for her to talk about.

"We used to go to this golf course at a country club. My dad was an avid golfer. It was a beautiful, sunny, happy day. My dad had bought new golf clubs he wanted to try out. There were several games going on and Dad was on the ninth hole. There was a golf ball machine that was being repaired on the practice course. The machine malfunctioned while it was being fixed. All of a sudden, errant golf balls came flying out of nowhere at lethal speed and velocity and hit him on the left side of his head. At the same time, there was a wedding reception in the grand hall of the club and someone had shaken up the champagne bottles. When the bottles were opened, a hailstorm of corks came flying onto the golf course and hit my father on the right side of his head at the exact same time as the golf balls were hitting the left side. His head exploded. And then a wild pack of coyotes came out of the surrounding forest and ate him."

"I'm so sorry, Mary. That's horrible. I don't know how awful things like this are allowed to happen."

"Bright," Mary said, trying to choose her words carefully. "What happened to your parents? If you don't want to say, that's okay."

"I was only seven when it happened. My father and mother went on a trip to Mount Everest. They were going to climb to the top while we waited for them at one of the lodges in town."

"Oh my god, they were killed on Everest?"

"Oh no, after they climbed back down, they went to the local galleria with my siblings and grandparents and were killed in a stampede of people trying to get Cabbage Patch Kids."

Mary was silent for a moment.

"1983," Bright said quietly. "The year it all changed. After that, the only person watching out for me was me."

They were quiet for a moment. Bright wanted to fill the gap in conversation, so he said the first thing that popped into his head.

"A few nights ago, I couldn't sleep, so I watched *Brokedown Palace* and *Vacancy*. How come every time Kate Beckinsale leaves home, something bad happens to her? It keeps me up at night."

"Oh, Bright. You're not going to end up in a foreign prison, making drink koozies and at-home anal bleaching kits. Just think of Kate in *Serendipity*."

"She was so happy then," Bright said wistfully.

Alvinia peeked into the room.

"Don't mind me!" she sang, setting up candles on the dresser and lighting them. "Just a little mood lighting for you!"

"Good grief," Mary said.

"We're so happy to have you here, Bright," Alvinia said. "You smell so manly and musky. What is that?"

"Probably just my Old Spice deodorant," he shrugged.

"Hmm, Old Spice," Alvinia said excitedly, looking over to Mary and then back to Bright. "It's nice to see Mary taking an interest in something other than tinsel. She needs a little excitement around here."

"How are we related?" Mary asked.

"Don't forget, Bright," Alvinia said. "Church with the family on Sunday."

"Yes, ma'am," he said. "Aunt Elaine said I need Jesus."

Alvinia ducked out, leaving Mary and Bright chuckling.

"You are so welcome to this family if you want it," said Mary.

"Oh, I think you secretly love them."

Mary shifted in her seat, ready to get up and join the rest of her family.

"Listen, I'm sorry for coming off as judgmental and condescending," Bright said. "Tinselvania is a really nice town. The people are friendly here. I think I just have the big-city attitude. I hope I wasn't too rude or unpleasant. You've done amazing things with the factory. You've all made me feel very welcome here. You are a very impressive, intelligent woman, Mary."

Mary saw Alvinia hiding in the hallway, peeking into the room. Bright did not see her. She was mouthing the words "Kiss him!" and waving her arms for Mary to get up and make a move. Mary tried to shoo her mother away without Bright noticing.

"I completely understand," Mary said. "It's business. Anything you would like for me to help make your job here easier, you just let me know."

Mary stood. Bright was facing her. It was like he was seeing her for the first time as a person and not as a business associate or sexless, robotic colleague. There was a strange electricity between them.

Mary's mind envisioned Bright running toward her in slow motion, in a lush field full of colorful flowers, as Roberta Flack and Peabo Bryson's "Tonight, I Celebrate My Love" played over the speakers of her imagination.

Bright's mind envisioned he and Mary spinning around in slow motion, in the middle of a glorious spring in Central Park, as Chaka Khan's "Through the Fire" played over the speakers of his imagination.

"Aunt Mary, will you read me a bedtime story?" Acorn said from the doorway.

Mary and Bright both snapped back to reality.

"Yes, of course," said Mary, suddenly embarrassed and awkward, averting Bright's eyes.

"I want you to come with us too, Bright!" Acorn smiled.

"How can I refuse that invitation?" he said, also averting Mary's eyes.

Chapter 18

Acorn was all tucked in underneath her *Trolls World Tour* and *Kung Fu Panda* comforters in her twin bed, clutching her plush reversible octopus. Mary and Bright were on the end of the bed, at the end of the book Mary was reading from.

"…and they all lived happily ever after," said Mary. "The end."

Mary closed the book softly, hoping Acorn's droopy eyelids would close all the way. As she and Bright gingerly got off the bed, Acorn's eyes sprung back open.

"Wait!" Acorn said. "Bright didn't tell me a story."

"What book do you want to read?" he asked.

"I don't want you to read me a book. I want you to tell me a story, please."

Bright paused, thinking. He didn't know any kid's stories. He couldn't remember any from when he was a kid. The last time he heard a bedtime story was when he was seven, before his family died. He was never even around kids.

"Okay," he said, decided. "Many years ago, in 1997, my friends and I were involved in a drunk driving accident and thought we had killed someone, so we disposed of his body in the local river. A year later, I got a note in the mail that read, 'I Know What You Did Last Summer!' A fisherman in a black slicker used a giant hook to kill everyone except for me and Jennifer Love Hewitt. It was scary!"

"What is wrong with you?" Mary whispered to him through clenched teeth. Acorn didn't seem that fazed or scared by Bright's ridiculous recap of a slasher movie.

"Aunt Mary!" Acorn said. "Check the closet for monsters."

Mary opened the closet door, looked in, and inspected it quite seriously for Acorn's benefit.

"Nope," she said. "No monsters here. They know they're not allowed to stay here. We gave them a letter of eviction. They moved somewhere else."

"Are you sure?" Acorn asked.

"I'm sure. We met the people whose house they moved to. They said the monsters are very happy there. They didn't like it here anyway. They said you were too brave and strong for them."

"You have to do the monster dance," said Acorn.

Mary hesitated. Bright was looking at her, the imaginary bubble above his head asking, "Monster dance?"

Mary started to shimmy and shake, flailing her arms and legs around like she'd lost control of herself.

"Monsters no! You need to go!" she chanted. "Why? 'Cause I said so! Monsters flee! Leave me be! Why? You don't scare me!"

Bright suppressed his laughter. Acorn was sufficiently convinced that her room was a monster-free zone. Mary kissed her good night.

"Door open or closed?" she asked.

"A little open," Acorn answered, on her way to sleep.

Mary and Bright started to make their exit quietly.

"Bright?" Acorn's tired little voice said.

"Yes, Acorn?" he whispered.

"My Aunt Mary is really cool."

"Yes, I've noticed."

Mary and Bright left the door open a crack as Acorn rolled over to finally fall asleep.

"*I Know What You Did Last Summer*?" Mary said to him in the hallway.

"I panicked," he said.

Chapter 19

Ivy left Betsy's house, adhering to her parents' curfew of home by eleven. It was 10:45. She'd be home in five minutes.

The night was cold, still, and quiet, like many of the nights in Tinselvania. People here went to bed early. The houses on Betsy's street had their porch lights on but most of the people inside were already in bed for the night.

As Ivy got to her car door, keys in hand, she thought she saw something off in the distance. Much farther down the street, in between the already-sparse streetlights. Someone was standing in the darkness between the wooden light poles. She couldn't make out any definitive features but she saw the outline of someone there. She felt their eyes looking in her direction, at her.

She got in the car and started it up immediately, the chill running through her from the temperature outside and the uneasy feeling that gripped her. She double-checked the locks on the car doors.

There was a box on the passenger seat next to her. It was wrapped in shiny, colorful paper, with a large, ostentatious bow on top. Ivy sighed. Betsy had probably left a present for her even though they decided they wouldn't get each other anything for Christmas this year. She knew that Ivy hated opening gifts in front of anyone. It made her feel self-conscious and embarrassed.

Ivy unwrapped the box, removing the lid. It was stuffed with lime green tissue paper sheets. She dug around inside and stopped when her hand felt something.

Something cold. And wet.

Ivy pulled the item out of the box. It was an ornament for a Christmas tree. On the side of the silver ball was a painted picture of the Tinsel Inc. factory. "1990" was inscribed in calligraphy underneath the illustration. It was one of the old Christmas ornaments her family would give to the employees at the factory every year.

Part of the bulb was smashed inward and warped. It was covered in a sticky, smelly red substance. Ivy knew it wasn't red paint. She instinctively threw the ornament back in the box and drove away.

She didn't see that the reindeer-costumed person had advanced on her car. It had almost gotten all the way to her passenger side window, slowly and methodically, making sure it was hidden among the shadows, when she pulled out of Betsy's driveway.

It stood in the middle of the road, briefly lit up by the red glare of the car's taillights, watching Ivy ride away into the distance.

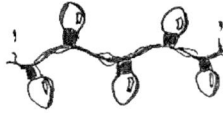

Acorn was sound asleep when the tapping at her window stirred her awake. She sat up in bed, the light from the hallway illuminating her room enough for her to see clearly.

She rubbed her eyes, the insistent tapping faint but pointed. She turned to her window and saw her imaginary friend outside.

He was tapping his hand against the glass. He must have climbed up to the second-story roof above the porch to see her. She trotted over to the window excitedly.

"Rudy!" she said quietly.

She knew it was him because he was her reindeer friend. He put his hand up on the glass and she put hers up against his, separated only by the windowpane.

Acorn slid the window open as Rudy the reindeer climbed inside her room. She was so happy to see him, practically jumping up and down.

Rudy looked her up and down then crawled over to her closet, making himself comfortable inside. Acorn followed him, standing at the closet door and watching him.

"Shh," Rudy whispered, putting a finger to his lips. He shut the door.

Acorn hopped over to her bed and went back to sleep.

Chapter 20

Ivy jumped on a Zoom call with her best friends Betsy Scofield, Ellie Branscombe, and Stacy Fuller as soon as she got home. They had all been friends since they met in kindergarten. They were inseparable most of the time and even joked that they'd started to look alike.

"You didn't leave that weird ornament in my car, Betsy?" Ivy asked again. Though Ivy and Betsy were the best of friends, Ivy's commitment to school couldn't have been farther from Betsy's complete disinterest in anything academic. Betsy was as smart as her friends but didn't apply herself. Ivy worried that Betsy would be stuck in Tinselvania forever while she planned to make it a reflection in her rearview mirror.

"I swear to you, I didn't," she answered. "I was with you the whole time you were at my house. How could I have?"

"I bet it was Chip Wilson," said Stacy, Chief Fuller's daughter. Stacy, like Ivy, was a serious student. Both of them cared more about their grades and friends than almost anything else. "He told me he was going to ask you to the Christmas dance. He said he left a gift and a note in your car for you."

"Chip Wilson?" said Ivy. "I'm not interested in guys who giggle any time the teacher says 'Uranus.' And that was a disgusting gift. A broken ornament covered in fake blood? Thank you, next. I can do better than Chip Wilson."

"And make sure you lock your car doors, Ivy," Stacy said. "My mom will give you a mind-numbingly condescending lecture on carjacking statistics and safety precautions if she ever finds out."

"Ugh, what's worse?" Ellie said. "Someone stealing your car or your mother giving you one of her monologues? We get it, Iola, there's no crime here. Because we live in the middle of nowhere."

"Maybe she should give a speech to Chip Wilson about leaving creepy, crappy gifts in girls' cars," Ivy said.

"Speaking of middle of nowhere," said Betsy. "Why did I choose Iowa as my state project for Geography class? The only fun fact I've learned is that they have laws against drunk surfing and water-skiing even though they're landlocked."

"John Wayne was from Iowa," Stacy said.

"That's helpful," sighed Betsy. "If I want to give the presentation to my racist grandparents."

"Speaking of grandparents," Ellie said. "My grandpa left for his annual cabin in the woods trip. He said we can hang out there if we want." Ellie had always been close to her grandfather Emmett. Even though he had retired, he wanted Ellie to work at Tinsel Inc. like so many of their family did. To carry on their family legacy, begun by the Branscombe, Classen, and Persimmons families, who founded the tinsel company together.

The girls were distracted by unusual grunting noises and flashes of unclothed skin coming from the television set behind Betsy. Her head blocked most of the action.

"What are you watching, Bets?" asked Ivy. "I can see part of your TV in the background and it doesn't look like good, clean, wholesome programming."

"*Dawson's Crack*," Betsy said.

"*Dawson's Creek*?" asked Ivy. "Were we even alive when that show started? My mom loves that show."

"No, *Dawson's Crack*," Betsy corrected her. "I was watching ASMR videos on YouTube because it helps me relax sometimes and clicked a link and this came on."

"Betsy Alexis Scofield!" exclaimed Stacy. "I'm calling your mother!"

"How is it?" Ellie asked, intrigued and trying to get a better look at the TV in the background of Betsy's Zoom call.

"Great storyline, convincing acting, and a very moving ending. No pun intended. I've learned a lot. Did you know that if guys ask each other for help with homework it's code for 'sausage party'? The more you know," Betsy said, as she waved her hand across an imaginary line in the sky, imitating the old NBC commercials.

"And knowing is half the battle," Ellie said.

"This was linked to an ASMR video, you dirty strumpet?" Ivy laughed, doubtful of Betsy's origin story.

"Hey, do you think I'd make a good internet whisperer?" asked Betsy, leaning into the computer's camera lens and lowering her voice as quietly as she could before speaking into the microphone. *"Dawson's Crack."*

The girls chatted for a little longer, then called it a night around midnight. It was a school night, after all. After Betsy threatened to put Nair in Stacy's shampoo if she told her mother what she was watching, they all signed off.

Ivy wondered what she would do next year when she had graduated. She could picture a life outside of Tinselvania but was stricken with melancholy and sadness that she wouldn't see Betsy, Ellie, and Stacy every day anymore. The realization of change was sinking in. It was her last year there.

She hoped it would be a happy and eventful one.

Chapter 21

Mary was in her bedroom at her desk, trying to stay focused on the important business papers spread out in front of her.

She could hear her mom and Aunt Elaine downstairs having drinks and watching *Stop! Or My Mom Will Shoot* and laughing, while working on flyers for the upcoming Christmas Jamboree. She heard them whisking something in a bowl, probably a sweet confection they'd eat when they were drunk enough so Aunt Elaine could go on Chat Roulette and scold all of the naked people on there, telling them that God sees everything.

She moved back into her childhood home after her father had died so her mom wouldn't be alone. So her mother would have someone to take care of her. But it was Mary who seemed to end up alone most of the time. Her sisters had families of their own. So did Liza and Kara. Robin's social calendar was continually full. Somehow her mom and Aunt Elaine both had more of a social life than Mary did.

She knew and loved tinsel. She understood tinsel. She had never understood crushes or dating. She didn't even want to admit that her thoughts kept turning to Bright and his warm smile. Or that the front he puts up in order to be a successful, driven businessman was a disguise he used to hide the fact that he might actually be a kindhearted, interesting guy. She didn't want to go down that road. She would not entertain the idea. She had done this before and it never worked out.

Then why was she acting like a schoolgirl with a crush? She needed to recalibrate and stop behaving like she was giggling over the dreamy pin-ups in *Tiger Beat* magazine. She had work in the morning and had to get through these important business papers. She wished Kara or Liza were up so she could text them and ask them for advice. She knew Robin would be awake, but she also knew Robin would tell her to jump right in. Don't ask too many questions and take your clothes off, that was Robin's motto. It had worked well for Robin, but it wasn't Mary's style.

Mary felt desperate. Against her better judgment, she texted Robin about her night. After a few minutes, Robin responded.

Just tell him you have something on your vagina that you need him to check out with his face.

Mary knew she walked right into that one. Thanks anyway, Robin. She texted back to say they'd talk tomorrow. Mary laid down on her bed, looking up at the ceiling. She wasn't going to get anything else done tonight. She closed her eyes and drifted off to sleep.

Noelle and Jed were sound asleep in their bed, oblivious to the world around them. Dashi and Acorn had been asleep for a while. All of the houseguests had gone back to their respective homes for the night. The house was quiet and dark. The only noises were the house settling against the wind from outside.

Neither one of them stirred as the reindeer stood at the end of their bed. It stared at them, watching and observing. Not making a single move. It stood straight up, as if contemplating something, taking in the sleeping forms before its eyes. It blended in with the darkened room, undetectable in the blanket of night.

Noelle and Jed were none the wiser.

Chapter 22

The Happy Goose was the only inn in the entire town of Tinselvania. Thankfully for Sylvia, there were enough rooms available for her and her friends. Pike offered to sleep in the van but she insisted he take his own room and get some rest.

It was almost midnight when they arrived in town. As the ladies unloaded their bags and gear from the car, they passed Casper and Joseph, who were at the end of their date. The women took no notice of the smiling twentysomething men, who were jolly after their fabulous night out. Sylvia, Frances, Willa, and Belle were on a mission.

Bertha assisted the ladies in bringing their things to their respective rooms. The ladies decided to get settled in first and then reconvene in Sylvia's room in thirty minutes to go over strategy and game plans.

Sylvia unpacked her things, storing the more lethal items in a locked case that she hid under her bed. She put pictures of her husband and family on the desktop. If she couldn't physically be with her family, she liked to at least be able to see their faces while she was away.

She thought about Chester Persimmons. A colleague and friend had emailed his files and crime scene photos for her to scrutinize. Sylvia wondered if she could have done more for him when he was her patient. He had been a good man once. What was the catalyst for his violence and would it continue now in Tinselvania? She didn't know. All she knew was they were going to stop him.

Chapter 23

Orson McGarrigle enjoyed being retired. He had worked at Tinsel Inc. on the assembly line almost his whole adult life. Nowadays, he spent his time on his new hobbies, like cooking exotic foods such as miso salmon and pot stickers or playing Minecraft against a bunch of faceless tweens on his computer. His wife Estelle hadn't been ready to retire yet, and he respected her for that. He knew her work was important to her and gave her a sense of purpose.

He was snuggled under a big comforter on the couch in front of the television, Estelle snoring soundly beside him. It was way past their bedtime but they'd stayed up later to catch *It's a Wonderful Life* on cable. He didn't have the heart to wake her. She worked so hard.

Neither he nor Estelle noticed the thing standing behind them as they lounged on the couch. The reindeer-costumed entity stood silently, so close it could reach out and touch them, watching them in their contented obliviousness. It was barely visible with the only light in the room emanating from the TV set.

He got up to go to the bathroom. He went to the kitchen afterwards to get himself some string cheese and a cream soda. The sound of jingling, clinking, and clunking diverted his attention from his snacks. He walked to the front hallway, his attention immediately drawn to the staircase.

Glittery, shiny ornaments were scattered and broken all over the steps on the staircase, spilled out onto the bottom of the stairs. Orson looked to the top of the stairs. He saw someone turning the corner into the bedroom, but it was so quick that he couldn't make out the figure. He couldn't remember if he or Estelle had left a box of ornaments at the top of the steps. Maybe Estelle had woken up and knocked it over in her sleepy state on her way to bed.

"Estelle?" he called out.

There was no answer. Orson felt uneasy but couldn't place his finger on exactly why. Tinselvania was an incredibly safe place to live. The chances of an intruder were almost none. He scolded himself for being silly, grabbing a broom and butler out of the closet to sweep up the shattered ornaments.

After he cleaned up and threw all the shards in the trash, Orson made his way back toward the TV room. As he walked, he noticed the blinking Christmas lights coming from that direction. The Christmas tree was in the den, so there was no reason for the colorful flashing lights unless Estelle had started decorating in the past thirty minutes.

Orson couldn't shake the feeling that something was wrong. Silently, he approached the TV room, unprepared for what he found.

The glimmering, flickering Christmas lights had been wrapped around Estelle's body. She was still positioned on the couch. Several candy canes, the strabes made into deadly sharp points, were sticking out of Estelle's body. One was lodged up to the curve, jutting out of her neck. Her eyes were wide open, frozen in a blank stare of death. Her clothes and the couch were soaked and splattered with her blood.

Orson gasped and stumbled back, disbelieving what he was seeing. He felt his back press against something.

The reindeer was right behind him. Orson didn't have a chance to scream out or plead for mercy when the reindeer raised something in the air. Orson recognized it right away. It was the tree topper from the Christmas tree, a large white star adorned with sparkles and glitter.

The reindeer brought the tree topper down on Orson, over and over, slicing and stabbing him with the razor-sharp point of the star. The killing blow came as the reindeer jammed the star into Orson's gut, ripping it open, spraying blood everywhere as Orson's innards plunged to the floor.

His last thoughts were of the trips he had always hoped to take with Estelle. That would never happen now. He thought about how much he loved his children and grandchildren and hoped that they wouldn't be the ones to find his and Estelle's bodies.

Chapter 24

Bonnie Payne was high on life. She had a great night with her fellow Revere-philes at a Paul Revere Fan Club meetup in Boston. Almost a dozen other people from New England got together for their bimonthly meetings to talk about anything and everything related to their icon and hero. Bonnie got to debut her one-act historical-fantasy-romance play, where Paul falls madly in love with a local farm girl named Connie. She felt alive and understood. Those were her people. The people of Tinselvania were kind and caring, but she loved getting to be a part of a group who shared her interests and didn't give her cockeyed stares over her passions for Paul. Afterwards, they hit up the twenty-four-hour buffet in the suburbs and Bonnie stayed out too late, drinking egg creams and loading up on potato skins and chipped beef.

She listened to her Paul Revere biography audiobook, scolding herself for getting so caught up in the dazzle of her fan club that she didn't consider the fact that now she only had six hours before she had to be to work. The road home was lonely and quiet at 3 a.m. Bonnie got off the highway a few miles back and was on the desolate stretch of country roads leading back home. She hadn't seen any cars for almost half an hour. The road ahead was empty and dark, lit up only by an occasional streetlight. Farmland, grass fields, and trees surrounded her on either side, along with intermittent bucolic houses located at the end of long driveways whose porch lights were only specks in the distance. She kept a watch out for deer, moose, and bears, which had a habit of milling about late night in the middle of barren roads.

Bonnie eased off the gas pedal when she saw it. A car in the middle of the street up ahead. Driver's side door wide open, taillights blinking, stopped at an obtrusive diagonal angle. Some kind of accident. Beside the car, on the road, was an unmoving figure. A person, facedown on the asphalt. It was too dark for Bonnie to make out any of the static figure's features or state. She slowed down, the car creeping up on the bizarre sight.

What if this was a dead body? What if this person needed help? Bonnie's mind raced with possibilities. She didn't want to leave a defenseless, wounded person out in the open to die. But something about the whole situation felt off to her. Like it was staged. A feeling of dread and trepidation gripped her insides. She debated pulling over, getting out of her car, checking on whomever this was. Her instincts screamed for her not to. She was alone in a remote area with no cell phone reception.

She slowly maneuvered the car around the body in the road. Between the darkness outside, the position of the body and her viewpoint in her car, and the blinking taillights, she couldn't discern any specifics. No details or identifying marks. She stared out the passenger side window, half-expecting the body in the road to suddenly jump up and bang on her window.

As she pulled past, putting distance between her car and the body, the red glow of her taillights illuminated the prostrate figure. She had her phone in hand, intending to dial 911 as soon as her phone had bars.

Her car was separated enough from the body, now a dot in the background of her rearview mirror. Even with the lack of proper lights from her vantage point, she saw it stand up. The figure in the road got to its feet, facing the direction she was driving away. Bonnie hit the gas and sped away as fast as she could. She didn't slow down until she saw the sign welcoming her to Tinselvania.

Chapter 25

Kara, Liza, and Robin all met at Mary's house in the morning to walk to work together. Mary heard Robin call from downstairs that it was "coffee time," signaling they were all waiting for her. She hurried up, still getting dressed for the day. It was her own fault for giving them all keys. Mary's mom and Aunt Elaine weren't awake yet. Mary guessed that they were sleeping off the drinks from the night before.

The weather was unseasonably warm as the ladies walked toward the factory together, chatting and laughing. The snow from the previous days had mostly melted away, revealing more patches of grass.

"What is that smell?" asked Liza, sniffing the air.

"Oh, it's the grape soap that Jed and Noelle make," answered Mary. "I used it this morning."

"Do grapes have a smell?" Liza said.

"I don't know," Mary said. "I mean, orange is a smell and a fruit. The soap was purple. Does purple have a smell?"

"I hope it's not the same as that soap," said Robin.

"So how was dinner at Noelle's?" Liza asked Mary. "Did you have to eat fake-meat sausage made out of tears and feelings? You were supposed to text me afterwards."

"You were already asleep by the time I got home," said Mary. "I resorted to asking Robin for advice, which was as helpful as a monkey throwing its poo."

"Hey," said Robin. "I was trying to turn that vacant landing strip into a busy airport. Who cares about dinner anyway? What happened with Bright? Did you play 'UPS delivery man' where he has a 'big package' to deliver to your 'mail slot'?"

"Robin, I wish you would stop being so shy and just come out of your shell already," Liza laughed.

"We all just want what's best for you," said Robin. "You can have the great job, awesome family and friends, and a terrific man by your side. You don't have to choose. You can have it all."

"I can have it all!" Mary shouted to the ether, doing an exaggerated twirl and spin.

"I've seen you eat chicken out of a can," Kara said. "You can do anything."

"When you're starving and can barely cook well enough to heat a Hot Pocket, you'll eat chicken in a can and thank your lucky stars someone thought of putting chicken in a can. Every coin has many sides."

"Coins have two sides, Mary," said Liza. "Not multiple sides. How did you get to be a high-powered executive?"

"Well, sometimes I wonder, but I think it was nepotism," Mary sighed. "I was born on third base and tell everyone that I hit a triple."

"Mary Classen, don't you ever let me hear you talk about yourself like that ever again," Liza scolded her. "You were valedictorian of our high school. You were the only kid to go to class on senior skip day. When the rest of us were at the drive-in, you were reading books about famous business leaders and how to take over the world. You graduated in the top one percent at Harvard Business School. You earned your spot here."

"Agreed," Robin said. "Without you, I would never have studied. All I cared about was looking fabulous but you made me study, so now I look fabulous and am a killer PR specialist with her own upcoming human interest feature story in *The Tinselvania Herald*, which has a readership of like 237 people."

"I don't deserve you guys," Mary said.

"Yes, you do," said Kara, putting her arm in Mary's.

The ladies waved to Tyler Dawkins and Mike Hudson, friends they had grown up with. They were waiting in the distance for the ladies by the factory entrance.

"Remember growing up with Tyler and Mike?" asked Robin. "They were always the nicest guys but I had no idea they were gay, let alone now gay with each other. We were all so clueless. Mike took me to the Paula Abdul and Bette Midler and Madonna concerts and I always wondered why he never made a pass at me."

"I think you answered your own question," said Liza.

"Mike told me about this game he and Tyler play," Robin said. "It's called 'prison shower.' Whoever drops the soaps loses– or wins, depending on your point of view."

"I'm putting you in a time-out, Robin," said Kara. "It is way too early for the fire in your crotch. We just had breakfast."

"We all can't spend our lives putting popcorn on strings and sewing pillows with sayings like 'Live Laugh Love,'" said Robin.

"I made gingerbread houses and watched *A Very Brady Christmas* with the girls last night after they did their math homework and it was really fun," Kara said. "You were invited, Robin, but I believe you said you had to see a man about opening the gates of Mordor."

"Math homework," said Liza. "If I were in a *Saw* movie, my trap would be math questions. I graduated top of my class at law school and have yet to use the Pythagorean theorem."

"Oh, wait," Robin said, taking out her cell phone. "I didn't even tell you guys. I got a super creepy voicemail last night."

Robin pulled up her saved voice messages, put it on speaker, and pressed play. A cacophony of voices, some shrill and tinny, others deep and commanding, moaned and groaned over various shrieks, squeals, screams, and howls. A few words and sentences could barely be deciphered amongst the static and bombardment of noise.

"*Ring out false pride in place and blood*," the voice screeched and hissed. "*The civic slander and the spite.*"

"That was the only sentence I could make out," said Robin. The message ended abruptly. Robin shrugged. Kara, Liza, and Mary were quiet for a moment.

"That's a Tennyson poem," said Mary. "I can't remember the name."

"Those voices," Kara said. "Was that one person?"

"Are you sure it's not just Angus playing a prank on you?" asked Liza.

"Angus has never read a Tennyson poem," Robin said. "Although I have heard him make some of those noises."

"Should we call the police?" asked Kara.

"Yes, I'm sure they'll send their top detectives, Kara," Robin laughed. "There's probably an anti-poetry unit in the Tinselvania police force that will trace who left the message. The call is coming from inside the house!"

"How did they get your number?" Kara said, her eyes filled with worry.

"It's on the wall at every truck stop bathroom from here to California," said Liza. Robin smacked her playfully.

They reached the factory. Tyler and Mike greeted the ladies. They had been a couple for several years now and had been Mary's date for many events over the years. Tyler was a giant, squishy teddy bear of a man, while Mike was more classically handsome, with a chiseled jawline and runner's physique. Tyler worked in the metal and PVC (polyvinyl chloride) department and Mike worked in the electrical and mechanics division.

"Hey, Mary," Chuck said, arriving to the entrance door at the same time and introducing himself to everyone.

"Hi, Chuck," Mary said. "Are you ready for day two?"

"Yeah, I wore my lucky *National Lampoon's Christmas Vacation* socks," he smiled, showing them off.

"Hello, Chuck," Robin said, brushing past him. "I have to get inside and get all of these layers off. My boobs are so sweaty and need some air."

"As always, Robin," laughed Tyler. "Graceful and delicate like a meteor shower."

"That new hire is rugged and handsome like Paul Bunyan," said Robin. "He looks like he could chop down a tree with one swing of the ax. He probably has one of those big, amazing '70s bushes."

"Has anybody seen Estelle?" asked Mary. "She's never late."

Everybody entered the building to get ready to start work. Mary stood outside the entranceway, looking around for Estelle.

Chapter 26

Pike drove Sylvia, Belle, Frances, and Willa to the Tinselvania Police Department and waited in the car for them.

The ladies approached the front desk. Deputy Leland Nash was making a log all the calls and reports that had come in since last night. The usual small-town concerns— power lines and trees that were down, missing pets, and potholes that needed to be filled. Of note was the panicked message from Bonnie Payne about a strange man and broken-down car in the road, but since it was a county over, Nash directed Bonnie to call the neighboring police station.

Deputy Nash, a middle-aged man with salt-and-pepper hair, had worked for the Tinselvania police for over two decades, vigilant and dedicated to the safety and protection of its citizens. He was a survivalist, hunter, fisherman, and avid outdoorsman; though he built his own underground bunker in his backyard, he did not like being thought of as a "doomsday prepper," but rather as someone prepared and aware.

"My name is Dr. Sylvia Post," said Sylvia. "I'm here to speak with Chief Fuller."

"Is there anything I can help you with?" asked Nash.

"No, thank you," Sylvia answered, remembering his unwillingness to hear her out on the phone earlier. She couldn't blame him really. If she had gotten a phone call from some stranger claiming an escaped lunatic was headed for town, she'd probably have thrown it into the wacko pile too. "If we could see Chief Fuller, I'd appreciate it."

"Sure thing," Nash said, almost feeling left out. He knocked on a closed wooden door in the back of the station, saying something the ladies couldn't hear once he got the okay to open it.

Deputy Nash headed back to the women with Chief Iola Fuller in tow. Fuller was a lifelong resident of Tinselvania, like Nash. She had worked for the police station since she was eighteen, almost thirty years ago. Now she was chief of police in Tinselvania. Since she was a little girl, her dreams were of being in law enforcement, solving mysteries and catching bad guys. While the other kids in her class were playing dodgeball and hide-and-seek, Iola was playing cops-and-robbers with her parents, arresting them for their fake crimes of burglary and general maleficence.

She kept photos of Nancy Drew, Pam Grier in *Foxy Brown*, Frances McDormand in *Fargo*, Geena Davis in *The Long Kiss Goodnight*, Agent Clarice Starling, Buffy the Vampire Slayer, Veronica Mars, Agent Dana Scully, Captain Olivia Benson, and Drew Barrymore, Cameron Diaz, and Lucy Liu in *Charlie's Angels* on her bedroom wall at home, calling on their strength and intelligence every day as she prepared for work.

Sylvia introduced her squad to Fuller, who brought them back to her office. Fuller wasn't tall or imposing yet had a stern and serious demeanor that radiated off of her. She kept her dark hair cut short— that way, if she ever had to catch a perp, they couldn't grab onto her hair. She looked over the files and crime scene photos as the women explained the situation to her.

"We are not trying to be alarmists here, Chief Fuller," said Sylvia. "I worked at The Calista Asylum for the Criminally Insane for many years. I'm not– we're not– a bunch of crackpots screaming that the sky is falling. I'm still waiting on some information and records from some of my contacts, but we have enough intel to hypothesize that he's on his way here."

"I know your work," said Fuller. "I read your paper on psychopathic versus sociopathic deviance in murderers who are impacted by neglected childhoods and undiagnosed mental disorders."

Sylvia watched the chief's expressions and movements, unable to stop herself from psychoanalyzing her. Fuller came across as stern but earnest. Her walls were decorated with various commendations and medals. Sylvia was relieved to see that she was taking their conversation and theories seriously.

"Chester Persimmons was both a serial killer and a collector," said Sylvia. "He kept the heads of all of his victims as trophies. He kept them in a trunk filled with Christmas decorations."

"What makes you think he'll come back here?" Fuller asked.

"I know he will," Sylvia said. "He was my patient for many years. He can't risk seeing his children now. He'll know the police are watching. He'll come back to the only other place he knows. He has happy memories here."

"And you think after all of these years, all of the therapy he's had, he'll devolve back into his violent tendencies and bloodlust?"

"We wouldn't be here if we didn't, Chief Fuller. What I know is that sometime last week, the asylum he was at went into lockdown during a false fire alarm. Persimmons used that to overpower and kill a guard and escape by putting on the guard's clothes and stealing his car. There are reports from several states on the path from upstate New York in this direction of home invasions and murders where money, clothes, and cars are taken. We think it's him. He's breaking into people's houses, killing the homeowners, and switching vehicles as often as he can. He's taking over the identity of the last person he killed. Every crime scene on the map is connected by the fact that at least one of the victims is a male in his sixties, around the age Persimmons would be. You can follow the path on a map. It's leading to Tinselvania."

Sylvia showed Fuller the news reports, police reports, and red dots on her phone's map that pinged where each crime scene had been. It started in New York and tracked toward Maine.

"We have to factor in the possibility that there are crime scenes that haven't been discovered yet, or that he's hiding out somewhere," said Willa. "He avoided detection and capture for many years during his original killing spree. He's good at this. He doesn't look like a monster but a gentle older man. He could be using that to his advantage and gaining the trust of his victims before he kills them."

"What kind of authorization do you have from the police department to be a part of this investigation?" Fuller asked, not a challenge but for understanding.

"We aren't working with the police," said Sylvia. "You could say we're unauthorized. But we also have connections of our own. We're looking into visitor and call logs from the psychiatric facility Persimmons was housed at, to see if there's any associations we can question. We're trying to find his former roommates in the many units he's been incarcerated in, as well as business and personal associates from his life here in Tinselvania and down in New York. There's a multitude of people and areas that need to be covered."

"There may be some other law enforcement officials and possibly FBI headed this way," said Frances. "They'll be looking for him too, in a formal capacity. We're not the bureaucracy. We're more like the surprise, sneak-attack, raggle-taggle crew."

"Tinselvania is a small town," said Fuller. "I doubt we're high on their priority list. I haven't heard anything about Chester Persimmons until you ladies showed up. I don't want to be disrespectful here, but you're all working on a hunch here, not actual proof, correct?"

Sylvia, Frances, Willa, and Belle exchanged glances. Yes, they knew they could be completely off-base here. Yes, they may just be doomsayers who erroneously cry that the sky is falling. But Frances, Willa, and Belle knew Sylvia. If she thought there was a real chance that Chester Persimmons was on his way to Tinselvania to begin a murderous rampage, her word was all they needed.

"Chester Persimmons was moved from Nevada, after his killings, to Maine to specifically be under my care at The Calista Asylum for the Criminally Insane," said Sylvia. "I've dedicated years of my life studying him and people like him. I know how he thinks. I feel that the rage he carries inside started here."

"Okay," Fuller said. She had a good feeling about them and if everything they were saying was true, she could use the extra hands. "What can I do for you?"

"We'd like to see the house he grew up in," Frances said. "It's likely he'll go back there, and if there's a family living there, they could be in great danger."

"Well, I haven't seen anything out-of-the-ordinary or out-of-place the last couple of days," Fuller said. "But I'd rather be safe than sorry. I need you to keep this between us. I don't want the people of this town in a frenzy over any perceived threat. We haven't had a murder or violent crime here in over a century. I'd like to keep it that way."

"Are there any places you think he'd want to visit here?" asked Belle. "Places with sentimental value to his childhood or the town itself? Things with history that would have been here when he was growing up? Maybe places that would have been special to him because of his sons Garland and Shepherd."

"We don't have a large staff at our disposal," said Fuller. "It's me, two deputies, and three officers for the whole town. That's it. I'll send my deputies out on patrol. I'll accompany you to some specific places I can think of where Persimmons might have some sort of emotional connection. I remember the news when he was caught. I had only been working here for a little while then. My parents knew him. So did everybody in town. They said he was a genuinely nice, friendly man. It doesn't look like it to me, looking at these pictures. I'll take you to the

Wilsons' house first then we'll check out any of his relatives still in Tinselvania."

Fuller instructed Deputy Nash and Officer Barnaby Cogan to go on neighborhood watch with Officer Cord Jennings, the most recent member of the police team (he was hired five years ago, but the turnover for police in Tinselvania was incredibly low). Their day would be spent identifying anything suspicious without alerting the general population that there may be an intruder in their midst. Deputy Darcy McCloskey and Officer Kenny Buchanan would stay back at the station while Fuller and the ladies went investigating. She wasn't completely convinced that Chester Persimmons had returned to Tinselvania, but she intended to make sure every member of the community would be safeguarded and secure if he had.

Chapter 27

Mary's workday had been busy and eventful as usual. Casper gave her all the details of his date with Joseph. She was happy to see Casper so excited. Like her, he rarely met anyone he was interested in, although unlike her, he went on lots of dates. Estelle's son had called and left a voicemail to inform her that she and Orson were extremely sick and wouldn't be into work for the rest of the week. She had Casper place an order for a "get-well" flowers and chocolate delivery to Estelle's house.

She visited the various departments to oversee the day-to-day operations. She made sure all of the tinsel was up to code and specs had been met, chose which colors and lines would be featured in the national advertisements and news articles, reviewed the packaging for boxes, double-checked the receiving lists before they were loaded onto trucks, discussed chemicals and elements with the scientists in the PVC department, went over the plans for the Christmas Jamboree, took around thirty-seven phone calls, and then hid in the bathroom so she could eat a Snickers bar alone.

She hadn't seen Bright all day. He was visiting all the departments himself, but he was doing so to see where corners could be cut and money could be saved. Mary started to feel foolish that she had been so attracted to him the night before. This was business, and he was here to make changes that she didn't want. She wouldn't put her own romantic interests over the health and security of the factory. She was embarrassed that she had misread Bright's intentions. She promised herself she would make a more concerted effort to stop believing her life could be a romantic comedy.

At lunchtime, she joined Kara, Liza, and Robin for potato chowder as *Home Alone* played over the cafeteria's television screen. She wasn't going to think about Bright. She couldn't date a client or someone who did business with Tinsel Inc., she reasoned with herself. She would use that as her wall of protection the same way Bright used his as if he were an alien in a human suit trying to act like a person. She made up her mind. That was that.

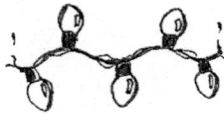

Bright wondered why Mary hadn't come to check in with him all day. Maybe he misread what he thought were sparks between them. Ever since he broke up with Candeeee, he didn't know what he was doing. Mary was nothing like Candeeee. He liked how upfront and genuine Mary was. She loved business but didn't believe it meant whacking down people like weeds to get it done.

Yule Love It was an atmosphere of fear. Bright lived in constant terror that he'd be replaced at any moment. Any minor mistake or change in the wind could be the catalyst for it. There were so many younger executives rising up the ranks, who could do everything faster and cheaper. Bright was starting to feel like a relic. He didn't really notice until he got to Tinsel Inc. When he heard the way the employees spoke so positively about Mary as a boss and saw how much pride and care they took in their work, Bright realized he hadn't felt any kind of enthusiasm or excitement for his job in a long time. He was a cog in the wheel, a rat running around a maze made by wealthy businessmen who had inherited their wealth. Bright was a number, a replaceable android in their eyes. Sure, he made great money and lived in an amazing city. Then why did he feel so hollow inside?

He knew all about fear. It was his constant companion from growing up in foster homes and orphanages. It figured he'd select a career that thrived on the same feeling. Fear was the emotion he was most familiar with. Getting to be a part of Mary's family time last night was just a fantasy, a glimpse at a life he'd never have. It was like the Grand Canyon– he knew it was there, that it existed, but he didn't get to experience it very often.

He was angry at himself for being so silly. Mary was just being friendly and welcoming, like everyone here was. His misconstrued her good nature for the spark that could set off the fireworks. He would be completely professional from this point on. He was here to take over her company, after all; to learn its secrets and weaknesses so he could take advantage of them and allow Yule Love It to acquire it. There was no room for butterflies and romance.

3

He did feel a little jealous when Joseph told him all about his great date with Casper. He realized he didn't ask Joseph anything about his personal life in the two years Joseph had been his assistant. He'd certainly never seen Joseph float into a room like his feet weren't touching the floor like he did today. For years, Joseph looked at him like he was the only man for him, and now Bright didn't even have that.

He would maintain a polished, businesslike composure for the rest of his stay, however long that would be for.

Chapter 28

Bonnie Payne had told several coworkers about her strange encounter the night before, but most of them dismissed it as a bizarre anomaly and simply asked if she reported it to Chief Fuller. She replayed the incident in her head over and over, wondering if she should've stopped. What if the person was really hurt and she had overreacted and imagined things to be scarier and more threatening than they were? Then again, what if she was right and she narrowly avoided an encounter with a nefarious person, like Paul Revere did when he was in the Massachusetts infantry? He'd been a part of the military but thankfully didn't see much in the way of battle. That's how Bonnie rationalized her decision to keep driving.

When she went to lunch and sat by herself as she always did, her eyes caught sight of the new guy at the factory. Later she found out his name was Chuck Brinkerhoff. She watched him get his food and walk around, stopping to flirt with Robin (as all the guys did), then leave. There was something about the way he moved, the shape of his build, that sent a shudder through Bonnie, like she recognized his face. That face, illuminated by her back headlights as she drove away from the figure in the road the previous night.

Or was she just being silly, just convincing herself that by some minuscule chance he was one and the same person? He was new after all, and maybe her mind was playing tricks on her, associating his unfamiliar presence with her frightening encounter? She looked down at her potato chowder and wished Paul Revere were sitting with her. He'd understand.

Wally Wilson was taking advantage of the melting snow and cleaning out the leaves that had accumulated in the gutters around his house. He chipped away at the ice that hadn't melted yet with an ice pick and hammer. He had taken two extra days off from Tinsel Inc. to go snowboarding with his family. That was the plan anyway, until he realized how many things around the house needed fixing. Wally prided himself on being handy.

Their house was the last one on Santa Claus Lane, closest to the nearby woods and farthest from the main street in town. Wally liked the quiet, the fact that nature was all around them, the big yard to play badminton and have barbecues in. He smiled as he looked at the giant snowman with the carrot nose and coal eyes they had made the day before. It was still thriving, even in today's warmer weather.

His wife Heddy was inside the house with their two teenaged sons, Doug and Chip. Their twin boys were seniors at Tinselvania High School and would be off to college next year, so Wally wanted to make sure they all spent time together while they could.

Heddy came out from the house carrying snowboarding equipment and waved to Wally on the ladder. She threw the instruments in the back of the truck and yelled up to him.

"I made some chocolate chip cookies with the boys. Why don't you come on down from there and we'll watch *The Muppet Christmas Carol* and have some family time?"

"I'll be done soon," he said, grunting as he hammered at ice that was blocking the drain spout. "Save me some cookies."

Wally and Heddy turned their attention to the police SUV that pulled into their driveway. Chief Fuller stepped out of the vehicle, accompanied by four women that Wally and Heddy had never seen before.

"Good afternoon, Heddy, Wally," said Fuller.

"Is everything okay, Chief Fuller?" asked Heddy. Wally climbed down the ladder and joined his wife as Fuller introduced everyone.

"I would appreciate your discretion on this issue," Fuller said. "I don't need everyone in town creating a panic or mass hysteria. Your home was formerly owned by Chester Persimmons, correct?"

"Yes, but that was decades ago," said Wally. "Is there a problem? We have all the paperwork for the house. My family purchased it legitimately."

"Yes, I know, Wally," said Fuller. "That's not why we're here."

Sylvia looked at Fuller, waiting for the nod of approval for her to take over the conversation. Fuller conceded.

"Chester Persimmons is a former patient of mine," Sylvia said. "He recently escaped from a high-security psychiatric facility. We have reason to believe he's headed back here, and to your house in particular."

"Why?" asked Heddy. "We never did anything to him. We knew him when we were younger. We went to school with his kids."

"We don't believe you're his target, but this house may be. Have you noticed anything suspicious or disconcerting in the past few days?" asked Sylvia.

"No, nothing," Heddy said.

"No footprints in the snow that weren't yours, or strange cars that were on your street, or unexplainable noises or evidence that someone else might be in your home?" Frances said.

"We don't want to alarm you," added Belle. "We feel that in this situation, it's likely that Tinselvania is his ultimate destination. We wanted to make sure you were safe and secure. Do you have any friends or family you can stay with for the time being, just until he's caught?"

"I guess we can stay with my family in Neve," Heddy said, looking over at Wally worriedly. "We were headed out of town this weekend anyway."

"Mom, Dad, is everything okay?" Doug called from the front porch. Chip stood next to him. They both had concerned expressions on their faces.

"Would you mind if I went and spoke with your children, see if they saw or heard anything weird?" Willa asked. Heddy and Wally agreed. Willa and Belle headed toward the porch to talk with the young men.

"You think he's coming here?" Heddy said.

"We can't be sure," said Frances. "His trajectory indicates that he's making his way here. He's armed and dangerous. He's eluded authorities so far."

"Chester Persimmons," Wally said. "I remember those murders. Never once would I have thought he would do something like that. It's horrible."

"May we have permission to do a sweep of your house?" Sylvia asked. Again, Heddy and Wally agreed and brought Sylvia, Frances, and Fuller inside.

After an extensive search of the house, none of the women found signs of a break-in or unlawful entry. No broken locks or windows, no disturbed dust in the attic or basement, no indication that any intruder or stranger had been trespassing in the Wilson home. All money, jewelry, clothing, and personal items were exactly where they'd been left. Nothing under the beds or in the closets.

Fuller and the women thanked the Wilsons for their time, letting them know to call her immediately if they needed anything or felt unsafe. As they got back into the police SUV, they shared a perplexed and determined energy between them.

"Does this mean he hasn't gotten here yet or that he's somewhere other than the Wilsons' place?" asked Fuller.

"He doesn't have any direct personal connections to the people in this town anymore," reasoned Frances. "He's been gone for almost three decades. His parents and brother have passed away. There's no evidence that any extended family still here has ever visited him or even written or called. So, it's doubtful he has any dedicated family here to hide him."

"You mentioned family before, though, Chief Fuller," said Willa.

"Bertha Havighurst was married to Chester Persimmons once," Fuller said. "Chester's family didn't approve of Bertha and she was his first wife so she has no ties to him, and Chester's children stopped speaking to their father when they learned about the murders. One of his sons lives out west, the other in Chicago."

"I ran criminal background checks on Chester's sons," Frances said. "They're all clean. I spoke with them separately on the phone and with the authorities in their respective areas, and everything checks out. They have no idea where Chester is."

"We need to speak with Bertha then," said Sylvia. "She might not know they're here and they may not have any idea that Chester is on the run but they could be targets."

Fuller hit the gas and headed for The Happy Goose.

Chapter 29

The school bell at Tinselvania High rang as all of the students rushed into the hallway to their lockers, cheering that their school day was done.

Ivy waited for her friends by the front lawn. Floods of students exited the high school, running to catch their busses or jump in their cars. Betsy, Ellie, and Stacy joined Ivy and they started walking down the street towards their neighborhood.

"You know how Gloria Estefan sings that song 'Rhythm Is Gonna Get You'?" said Betsy. "You ever wonder what she really meant by that? Like, why does it want you and what is it going to do to you once it has you? Should I be afraid? Is it a conspiracy? What does it want? Is Janet Jackson in on it 'cause she sings 'We are a part of a rhythm nation'? Is it a whole global movement designed to slaughter us? Do you think other musical artists are in on it? Adele? Lady Gaga? Vampire Weekend? Fleet Foxes? The Judds? Oh man, my mom is going to be so upset if Michael Bolton is part of it."

"Is your brain like the inside of a claw machine?" Stacy asked.

"Hey, what are you writing your senior thesis on?" Ivy asked.

"Either whether or not the Keebler Elves are real or the reasons why calzones are just pizzas that are lying about who they are," said Betsy. "What about you?"

"Have you ever heard of Lady Krampus?" Ivy said. "You know about Krampus obviously. We all watched *Krampus* at your house last year. But Lady Krampus is different from him. She finds men who have wronged or mistreated women and steals them away into the night and punishes them for their horrible misdeeds."

"Oh, can we be friends with her?" Betsy said.

The trees were barren and their branches clacked together in the slight breeze. The weather was still much warmer than Decembers past. They walked together down the wet sidewalk, passing by the two-story houses that made up the area. Every house was decorated and adorned with Christmas lights and holiday décor, from the outside façade of the home to the yard.

"Hey, you guys haven't responded to my Evite yet," said Stacy. "It's our annual scary Christmas movie marathon sleepover. The original *Black Christmas*, the 2006 *Black Christmas* remake, *Gremlins*, *Night of the Comet*, *Silent Night Bloody Night*, and all the Christmas episodes of *The X-Files*. I need your RSVPs."

"This is the whole group, Stacy," said Ellie. "Right here. We don't hang out with anybody else. We don't even like anybody else. This is the gang. We'll all be there."

"Who sends Evites to things anyway?" asked Betsy. "Should I bring an abacus and a cell phone the size of a shoe and we'll all pretend it's 1996?"

"I still require your RSVPs," Stacy insisted. "It's called courtesy."

The girls laughed and chatted as Ivy looked at the street ahead. A few houses down, partially hidden by leafless sticks that used to be hedges and brush, was someone in a reindeer costume. It stared down the street at the girls, watching them silently.

"Hey, who's that?" Ivy asked.

Her friends looked toward where Ivy pointed. The reindeer was gone.

"I don't see anything," said Ellie.

"Some weirdo in a reindeer costume was staring at us," said Ivy.

"It's probably just one of the neighbors in a Brony roleplay outfit," Betsy said. "I read all about it on the *My Little Pony* adult fan website. They're into that stuff."

"You won't read the biography of Alice Paul for the book club I want us to start, but that website you read," Stacy said.

"Sometimes being friends with you and Ivy is like being friends with a teacher," said Betsy. "I worry when I come over that you're going to give me a pop quiz on hydrothermal vents."

"Be quiet or I'll make you write an essay on *Animal Farm*," Stacy said.

"Animals? Cute!" Betsy sounded happy. "Are there dolphins?"

"It's not a picture book," Ivy interjected. "It's a critique and analysis of the history and rhetoric of the Russian Revolution."

"Also, I know you've seen farms before," said Stacy. "Do you recall any dolphins on farms, my sweet special blueberry?"

"Siri!" Betsy said into her phone. "Google 'Best places to hide your annoying best friend's body.'"

The sound of a police siren startled the girls. Across the street, Deputy Nash had stopped his police SUV and tried to get their attention.

"Hey, ladies!" he shouted from the driver's seat. "Stacy, your mom wants me to drive all of you home."

"We're not that far from our houses," Betsy said.

"Chief's orders," Nash shrugged. "You'll have the best police escort in town."

Stacy looked at her friends in disbelief. They knew it was futile to argue or push back.

"Sometimes I wonder if my mom is overprotective or if she really believes she's Jessica Fletcher on *Murder, She Wrote*," said Stacy.

The girls piled into the back of the car. Deputy Nash had been a part of Stacy's life since she was a little girl. She felt comfortable and safe with him, and also knew that he'd catch hellfire if he didn't follow through on her mom's directives.

Chapter 30

The Wilsons had packed up their car and were ready to go. After their visit from Chief Fuller and her associates, their sense of safety and security had been shaken. They double-timed their efforts to close up the house indefinitely and take what they needed with them on their impending trip.

"Doug! Chip!" Heddy called out from the bottom of the staircase. She hadn't seen Wally or her sons in a few minutes. She'd been in the basement making sure the water pressure regulator and fuse box panelboard were in working order. She had heard them moving around and packing things in the distance earlier, but now everything was too quiet.

"Wally?" she said as she ascended the basement steps into the first-floor hallway.

She listened for a moment, shivering against the draft that hit her. She made her way to the source of the air. Someone had left the back door wide open.

She heard a sound she couldn't identify. It was a squeaking, straining noise, back and forth, fading and rising in repetition. Back, forth, quieter, louder, back, forth, quieter, louder. It was coming from the backyard.

The breeze outside brought in cool air but the day was temperate and sunny. Sunset would be there soon and Heddy wanted to get on the road.

The noise persisted, like the sound of a something loose being whipped by the wind.

It wasn't something loose.

It was Wally.

He was hanging from the rooftop, his neck and body wrapped in the Christmas lights that decorated the exterior of their house. His body was covered in blood, his face blue. His legs swung aimlessly, nowhere near the ground. The ice pick he had used to clean the gutters was jammed into his head. The claw of the hammer he had used was lodged in his chest. His neck had a gaping wound running the length of his throat.

Whenever the breeze blew, the sound of the cord from the Christmas lights, enveloped around Wally, rubbed and groaned against the gutters that lined the house. Back, forth, quieter, louder. Wally's lifeless corpse was the origin of the sound.

Heddy didn't scream. The horror overtook her body but she couldn't stop herself from staring at Wally's body. As if the reality hadn't sunk in yet. She knew what she saw but the flood of emotion and terror had gripped her so tightly that she couldn't react.

The reindeer stepped into view from the side of the house, where it had been waiting. Heddy began to back away and emitted small cries. She watched as the reindeer raised his arm, reached for the belt around Wally's waist, and pulled down on his hanging body.

Wally's body crashed to the ground, his severed head landing right next to his headless corpse. Heddy turned and ran. She screamed, having found the ability to vocalize her fear. She locked the back door behind her.

The reindeer stood calmly at the back door, its black eyes staring back at her through the window. It raised a costumed hoof and smacked it against the glass.

Heddy screamed out for her sons. She ran up the stairs to their rooms. She heard the sound of the door being forced open downstairs. The reindeer was in the house.

Both of her sons' rooms were empty. She remembered the gun in her bedroom. She would get the gun, call Chief Fuller, and find her boys.

She saw her sons as she passed the spare room, which was used for gift wrapping and hiding presents. Among the wrapping paper, ribbons, bows, unwrapped presents, and boxes were her two sons, slumped against the wall. Both of them were headless.

They had been propped up next to each other, their fingers intertwined as if holding hands. They were posed amongst the colorful backdrop of the gift room, positioned as if they were a part of the festive ambience. The room was saturated in their blood.

She heard the reindeer's footsteps getting closer. There wasn't time to grab the gun. Heddy slammed the door to the gift wrap room, trapped inside with the mutilated corpses of her sons.

She saw the giant commercial-grade paper cutter on the desk. Heddy hastily unscrewed the handle with the large blade, a makeshift weapon to defend herself.

The doorknob rattled. The reindeer was on the other side. It banged against the door, slamming its weight against the wood. The door cracked open against the pressure.

As soon as the reindeer burst into the room, Heddy swung at it with the dislodged paper cutter blade. The reindeer sidestepped the attempt.

Before Heddy could make another advance, the reindeer pushed her with both hands, sending her lurching backward. She stumbled over the bodies of her sons and crashed through the glass of the closed window behind her. Her body fell to the ground below and landed with a wet thud and a crunch.

The reindeer looked down at Heddy's body below, leaning out from the smashed window. Shards of glass had embedded themselves in her neck. The snow beneath her was sprayed with her blood. She had landed at an unnatural, twisted angle.

Feet away from Heddy's body was the snowman she and her family had made. Its head was on the ground, melting away. The heads of her two sons, Doug and Chip, their eyes wide open and faces frozen in expressions of terror, sat next to each other atop the snowman.

Chapter 31

Mary's workday was almost over and she had barely spoken with Bright. Her tasks for the day were not complete but were as finished as they were going to get for the time being. The employees had all started to leave for home. The factory emptied out as Mary looked through a few last-minute emails.

"Mary?" Casper said. "This just came for you."

Casper handed her a small package before he got the okay to call it a night. As he gathered his things, she saw that Joseph was waiting for him to get off work. She felt a slight pang of jealousy but smiled, happy to see Casper getting to enjoy himself for once.

Mary opened the package, sorting through the crinkle-cut shredded paper atop its contents. She started taking out each individual item. They were plaster-cast figurines, the kind someone would use for a miniature Christmas scene. Small statues of Santa Claus, Mrs. Claus, various elves in colorful outfits, and assorted townspeople.

They were all missing their heads.

Mary stared at the white plaster where the heads had been severed. She rummaged through the rest of the box. Their heads, though broken off, were nowhere inside the package. There was a note, written in red.

All through the house, a creature is stirring.

She didn't know whether to laugh or be afraid. Tinsel competitors had sent her threatening mail before, from voicemails and e-mails to ripped-up photographs of her family. This was new. Headless Santa and associates. Mary shook her head.

"You're coming ice skating with us," Mike said from the doorway.

"Are you redecorating?" Tyler asked. He stood next to Mike and pointed at her collection of headless mini-statues. "Is this slasher movie Christmas chic? I have some old *Teenage Mutant Ninja Turtles* action figures you can defile if you want them. You won't win first place in the Christmas Jamboree holiday-scene competition, but maybe Tinselvania has a goth subsection we don't know about that you can befriend."

"The tinsel business is ruthless," said Mary. "Stuff like this happens every year around this time. Not this extreme, but it's safe to say there's a lot of assholes out there."

"Get up," Mike said. "Go home and change into non-high-powered executive clothes and get your skates. I won't take 'no' for an answer. We're getting pizza and watching *The Holiday* and *Just Friends* after."

"Mike," whined Mary. "I have so much work to do at home."

"There's always work to do," Mike said. "Life is happening! Get on board. We'll meet you in ninety minutes. Don't make me call your mother!"

Tyler and Mike left to get ready. Mary collected her things and dumped the broken statues in a big blue plastic trash bin.

Mary peeked into the various rooms to make sure they were empty and that everything had been properly shut down for the night.

She did not see the reindeer pass by the open doorway behind her. She headed down the hallway toward the exit, unaware there was a presence watching her.

The lights in the building turned off, leaving Mary standing in total darkness. She fumbled for the flashlight on her phone. She paused when she heard the sound of someone walking behind her, accompanied by various bangs and creaks she couldn't identify.

She got the flashlight on and spun around, shining it down the hallway. She was alone. She heard every noise around her. Various whirs, moans, groans, clicks, some simply the building settling. The others she couldn't identify.

Beyond the length of light her phone produced was a dark pocket at the other end of the hallway. Mary squinted as her brain identified a human shape standing there.

"Hello? Who is that? Can you get the lights back on?"

Her questions were met with no response. Mary shifted between her feet nervously.

"Is someone there?"

No reply. Mary spun around and rushed down the connecting hallway to the exit. As she passed one of the workrooms, Chuck stepped out and startled her.

"Oh, hey, Mary," he said. "Did I scare you? I'm sorry."

"No, no," she said, composing herself. "I think I scared myself."

"I do that sometimes too."

"What are you still doing here?"

"I had some last-minute things to take care of. I'm headed over to Robin's house for dinner tonight. She and her friend Angus invited me over since I'm new in town and all and don't know anybody. She said it'll be a threesome."

Mary chuckled to herself, knowing Chuck didn't fully understand Robin's definition of "threesome."

"I'm sure you'll have a fun time," Mary said. "Don't work too late, okay? I'll let security know you're still in the building."

Chuck smiled and waved as Mary exited the factory. The night had gotten much colder. Darkness was setting in. Mary put on her scarf and gloves, then headed toward her house. She paused when she saw the man standing beneath one of the streetlights.

Llewellyn Barnes, who Mary didn't know, was staring at the factory. He saw Mary leave the building and stop when she noticed him. She had to walk past him in order to get to her house. He gave her a tip of his hat as she approached.

"Evening," he said.

"Hello," Mary said cautiously. "Can I help you with something?"

"Just out walking and stopped to reminisce."

Mary felt uneasy around this man. She knew everybody in town for the most part but didn't recognize him, and the tourists didn't usually skulk around the factory when the sun had gone down. She wondered if he was a spy sent from a competing tinsel company.

"You're Alvinia and Bernard's oldest, aren't you?" Llewellyn asked.

"Yes. Do I know you?"

"Oh, not really. You were very little the last time I saw you. You wouldn't remember me."

"What's your name? I'll tell my mother you asked for her."

"I'm nobody. Just an old friend. I'm just passing through. I have some unfinished business in town to attend to. I might stop by for a visit later. Have a good night now, Mary."

Llewellyn tipped his hat again and then slowly walked past Mary, down the street away from the factory. She speed-walked home, perplexed and slightly unnerved, checking over her shoulder every few seconds to make sure the man was gone.

Chapter 32

When Mary arrived home, her mother and aunt were at the dining room table creating their annual Christmas cards. They made them by hand, using woodblocks, fancy Strathmore printing paper, and ink. Every year featured a new Christmas design and handwritten messages inside. There were codes imposed by Aunt Elaine rating each Christmas card recipient from how much she liked them to her level of disdain toward them.

Alvinia and Aunt Elaine had a coding system for the cards. Anyone whose name had a red sticker next to it was not getting a Christmas card, according to Aunt Elaine's penchant for holding a grudge. Alvinia tried to convince Aunt Elaine to ease up on her restrictions. Mary listened as she put her things down.

Aunt Elaine's list of infractions and/or things that could prevent the arrival of a cheerful holiday card included but was not limited to people who showed up at parties with uninvited guests, hipsters, youths, Uber and Lyft drivers who wanted to make conversation, people who left their laundry in the washer or dryer, anti-vaxxers, people who rushed on to the elevator or subway before they let anyone else off, people with bad tattoos, keyboard warriors, people who blasted their music out loud instead of listening to it on headphones, slow walkers, bad tippers, people who called others "big guy" or "chief" or "boss" or "buddy," rude people, stupid people, entitled people, people who used "pens for women," and most people in general.

"What about Rhonda Pippenger?" asked Alvinia.

"She doesn't think that science is real," Aunt Elaine said.

"She's a teacher," Alvinia said, dumbfounded. She refocused. "Darren Rexroth?"

"He called my spinach puffs 'dry' at the church bazaar."

"The Abrahamsons?"

"They said *Die Hard* isn't a Christmas movie."

"Beulah Thacker?"

"She doesn't put her shopping cart away at the grocery store. She just leaves it wherever she wants."

"The Becketts?"

"They wear Ed Hardy gear. Even at Christmastime."

"But we're sending one to Ben Bailey from *Cash Cab* yet again?"

"He's going to write me back one day and realize we were meant to be together."

"Elaine, Christmas is a time of forgiveness and peace on earth. Letting go of petty grievances and spreading joy and happiness to others. For family and giving, love and understanding, togetherness, rebirth, and renewal of the soul. Don't be such a Scrooge."

"Christmas forgiveness can eat my queefs," Aunt Elaine said. "I don't know how you do it. You're always so positive. I have eight new people I hate before breakfast. Remember that movie *Scanners*? If I could have one superpower, that would be it. We would just be walking through people's brains all over the streets. Why is it called common sense, common decency, and common courtesy when it's not common at all? I'd take care of that. If I had the power to vaporize people with my thoughts, the population of Earth would be 250 max."

Alvinia sighed and resumed the list. "The Callaghans?"

"I don't like how they're always smiling. What are they hiding?"

Mary said hello. Alvinia and Aunt Elaine looked up and smiled, the madness interrupted. Dashi and Acorn ran past her. Dashi had a big jug of wine in his hands. He held on to it with all his might, headed to Alvinia.

"I've got your Grandma juice for you!" he announced proudly.

"I wanted to give Grandma her juice!" moaned Acorn.

"Thank you, sweetheart," said Alvinia as Dashi tried his hardest to pour the wine into her glass. She took the jug for him. "I've got this."

"Are the Christmas cookies done yet?" asked Acorn.

"We'll go check on them in a minute," Alvinia said. "Did you say hello to your Aunt Mary?"

Dashi and Acorn waved. Dashi mimed something in his hands and gestured as if he were putting a fictitious item in his mouth.

"Those were my marshmallows!" Acorn yelled at him.

"They're mine now," Dashi said as he pretended to eat them.

"Dashi stole my imaginary marshmallows!" cried Acorn. She grabbed at Dashi's empty hands in an attempt to steal back her invisible marshmallows.

"Why don't you just make some new pretend marshmallows?" Mary suggested to Acorn.

"I want those ones!" Acorn shouted.

"Are they in a bag or are they loose?" asked Mary.

"A bag, Aunt Mary," Acorn said in a "duh" tone.

"Okay," Mary said. "Dumb question."

"Dashi, give your sister back her imaginary marshmallows," said Noelle. She appeared from around the corner, her hands full of fabric and sewing equipment.

Dashi groaned and gave Acorn the make-believe marshmallows. Acorn took them and proudly trotted to her mother.

"What are you doing here?" asked Mary.

"I'm making the kids their costumes for the Christmas Jamboree," Noelle said. "Mom has enough old cloth and crafts to open her own Hobby Lobby."

"Oh, Mary," Aunt Elaine said. "There was a delivery for you earlier. We put it in the living room."

"Hey, guys, why don't you show your aunts and Grandma your song for the Christmas concert?" said Noelle.

"Oh no, that's okay, they don't have to," said Mary. She did not want to witness whatever atrocity the kids were being forced to perform. She tried to sound easygoing and breezy.

"Why don't you wait and surprise us?" Alvinia said, also not in the mood.

"Show them," said Noelle happily. "You rehearsed all week and you did so well!"

Noelle went to Alvinia's computer and queued up New Kids on the Block's "Funky, Funky Xmas." As soon as the music began, Dashi and Acorn launched into their dance with enthusiasm and determination. They did their best. However, it was two under-ten-year-old kids who flailed and thrashed like two giant inflatable tube men outside of a used car dealership whipped by the wind. They sang along off-key to the lyrics.

"Sometimes talent skips generations," Aunt Elaine said when it was over.

"Do you guys want to go watch a movie while your grandma does her cards?" Noelle asked Dashi and Acorn. "I have more stuff to go through."

"*The Prince of Tides*!" Dashi and Acorn said in chorus.

"No, how about a Christmas movie?" said Noelle. "*Simpsons, Garfield, Christmas at Pee-Wee's Playhouse, Emmet Otter's Jug-Band Christmas, Mickey's Christmas Carol*?"

"*The Prince of Tides*!" Dashi and Acorn persisted.

"They couldn't sleep one night and *The Prince of Tides* was on," Noelle said. "I knew I shouldn't let them watch it."

Noelle ushered Dashi and Acorn out of the room, the kids making their case for their movie choice the whole walk away.

"How was work, sugar?" Alvinia asked.

"It was fine," said Mary. "I have to go meet Tyler and Mike at the ice skating rink. What are you guys doing tonight?"

"We have our Cher circle later," Aunt Elaine said.

"Share circle?"

"No, Cher circle," Alvinia corrected her. "We get together and talk about how much we love Cher. Tonight we're watching *Mermaids*."

"How much Grandma juice have you two had today?" asked Mary, as she pointed to the various alcoholic beverages before them. "I'm starting to worry you're hanging out with a bad crowd. What have I told you about giving into peer pressure? Your real friends will like you for who you are. I don't want those Cher circle ladies to be bad influences on you. I haven't even met these ladies' parents. Do they come from good families?"

"You're not the boss of us!" Aunt Elaine said.

"We've only had a jug and a half of wine today," said Alvinia. "And I've seen you drink before, young lady."

"I learned it by watching you!" said Mary in her most faux overdramatic voice. "Remember, if you have too much to drink, you call me and I'll come pick you up. No questions asked. I'd rather have you home safe and sound than dead in a ditch because you drove under the influence."

"I made a Christmas yule log cake," Aunt Elaine said, pointing to the brown oval dessert on the counter in the kitchen.

"It looks like a gigantic T. Rex turd," said Alvinia. Aunt Elaine gave her a knock with her elbow.

"On that note," said Mary. "I have to go get ready. You ladies on your best behavior tonight! Don't shame the family, you boozebags."

Mary grabbed the large package in the living room and brought it to her room. Someone sent her a gift. She thought about the headless statues and shivered. She didn't know if she wanted to open this.

She did anyway. It was a beautifully crafted, wooden rocking chair and a big fluffy bathrobe. There was a note inside.

Just some helpful items for your journey on becoming a cat lady. From Bright.

Mary smiled and held the note. She was happy. She tried to control her excitement as she changed and grabbed her ice skates. Noelle peeked in to chat and noticed the rocking chair and Mary's smile. Mary didn't notice at first, too consumed with her blossoming joy.

"Major Tom to ground control," Noelle called out, reading Bright's note on Mary's desk. "That's a present from the big-shot city slicker? Maybe he's not the Grinch we think he is. It's like a Nora Roberts novel."

"It was definitely unexpected," Mary said. She didn't want Noelle to see that she was interested in Bright.

"These fancy city boys," Noelle continued. "They think their money and flashy clothes cover up the fact that they're humanoids. Is it working?"

"You think everyone from the city is bad," said Mary.

"I'll admit, I'm impressed. He better treat my big sister right."

"I'm not running off and marrying the guy. I don't know if he's putting out an olive branch or trying to tease me and stab it in my back."

"It's okay to be happy about meeting someone, Mary. Life isn't all about work."

"What if he is one of those flat-earther people? Or is into Bigfoot erotica? Or has a room at home full of balloon animals that he talks to like they're alive? That he hosts mock United Nations meetings for? While he builds his cosplay Kevin Spacey outfit from *The Negotiator*?

What if he goes in those chatrooms for people who think there's a race of reptilian lizard people? They look just like you and me."

"Lizards are reptiles, so that's redundant. And did you ever think, what if he's none of those insane things and might be worth stepping outside of the walls of the high-security compound you've built around yourself? What would Dolly do? She'd put on something sparkly and make Bright sing 'Islands in the Stream' with her."

"Relationships don't usually go well for me. Maybe the idea of someone is the most I'm meant for."

"That's nonsense. It's Christmas. Anything is possible."

Noelle spread imaginary fairy dust in the air, like they used to do when they were kids.

"The magic of Christmas," Noelle emphasized.

Chapter 33

Bertha was left shaken after Chief Fuller showed up at The Happy Goose Inn and asked if she could answer some questions. Fuller and the women she was with– Sylvia, Frances, Willa, and Belle– had asked her questions about her first husband Chester Persimmons.

When was the last time she'd talked to him? Seen him? Heard from him? Had he ever shown violent or unstable tendencies while they were married? Did she know his whereabouts? Had anyone that struck her as unsavory or unseemly checked into the inn recently?

She answered them as honestly as she could. Her marriage to Chester was over three decades ago. It was brief and buried deep in her past. They weren't married for long. They were in love but Chester's family thought Bertha and her family were poor trash. Chester gave in to their demands and caved into the pressure his family put on him to leave her.

After they divorced, she never thought she'd recover. Her heart was broken and her faith in the world was shattered. She moved to California for a year because she couldn't even face Chester or his family, not to mention the gossip of the town. When she returned at the behest of her family, she never spoke to Chester again. He had already met someone new at that point anyway.

Once her interrogators left, she went back to her room to compose herself. She pulled out an old photo album and flipped through the pages, reminiscing about Chester. They were so happy then, for a fleeting moment in time. She loved her second husband very much and they had wonderful children, but if Bertha was completely honest with herself, she knew that Chester had been the love of her life.

She wasn't ready to admit that to herself yet though.

Stacy was used to making dinner for her and her mother. Chief Fuller usually didn't get home until late on a normal weekday, so Stacy wasn't surprised when her mom came home even later than normal. It was already dark outside and the moon hung in the air outside as Stacy's mom sat at the dinner table where Stacy was doing her homework.

Stacy had made Salisbury steak and mashed potatoes with gravy. Fuller sat across from her and piled some food on her plate.

"Long day at the office?" Stacy asked.

"I just came home to check on you and have dinner together," said Fuller. "I have to go back out and patrol a little tonight."

"What's going on, Mom?"

"I don't want you to worry. I don't have all of the facts yet. I'm putting something together."

"It's kind of obvious that you're worried about something."

"Why do you say that?"

"Mom, you sent Deputy Nash to pick me and the girls up from school. That was kind of a dead giveaway."

Fuller sighed. She didn't know how much she wanted to share with Stacy. She knew that her daughter would understand but she didn't want her to worry. It had always been just the two of them. Stacy's father had taken off when she was very young, leaving Fuller to raise her alone. They were lucky because she had friends and family who helped whenever they could, but in the end, they were a team.

"You're too young to remember but there was a man who used to live here. Years ago, he hurt a lot of people and I have information that he may be here in Tinselvania," Fuller said.

"So are you sad that he's not here yet or that for the first time in your life, there's the possibility of some real action around here?"

"Stacy! I'm not some fiend filled with bloodlust. I want everyone in this town to be safe," said Fuller. She sighed. "Okay, maybe I was a little excited to solve this mystery and be a hero. The most exciting thing that happens in this town is when Mr. Harcourt takes shrooms and pees on the picture windows at The Malt Shoppe while people are having lunch."

"My piano teacher does that?"

"Oh yes, my baby, he's a real tweaker," said Fuller. "Listen, do I tell you enough how proud I am of you? How smart you are and how hard you work? I know you spend too much time alone and it's always just been us. But you're an amazing, accomplished, smart, wonderful young woman. I want you to know that."

"Mom, don't be weird. Why are you talking like this? Like something bad is going to happen to you?"

"Promise me that you will triple-check every lock on the windows and doors tonight before bed. And that all of the outside lights are on. And all the curtains are closed. If anything looks out of place or suspicious, you call me immediately. Don't let anyone in this house unless it's me or one of the officers. Do you promise?"

"Yes, Mom. Of course. You didn't raise an ignoramus."

"You want to go over some of the self-defense techniques I taught you?"

"No, Mom, I remember. And I remember the S.I.N.G. scene from *Miss Congeniality* you made me watch a thousand times."

"And if Betsy or Ellie or Ivy are coming over, you wait inside at the door for them and let them in quickly? And set the security alarm. Okay?"

"Okay, Mom. I promise. What's this guy's name?"

"Who?"

"The one who has you so spooked."

"Chester Persimmons. This is classified information, by the way. It stays in the vault."

"Do you want to watch a little bit of *Elf* before you have to go back out?"

"Yes, that would be very nice, baby."

Fuller squeezed her daughter's hand. She wasn't sure if she had any real reason to be worried, but a nagging feeling of dread and foreboding she had told her to stay alert.

Chapter 34

Tyler and Mike waited for Mary by the benches near the entrance to the ice-skating rink. Townspeople were out and about, admiring the decorations and lights in town square. The rink was at half capacity, which left plenty of room for them to skate. Pentatonix's "God Rest Ye Merry Gentlemen" played over the loudspeakers aimed at the rink. People waved and smiled at Mary, Tyler, and Mike as they passed by.

Mr. Lovett, dressed as Santa, rang bells on the corner for the Christmas collection. People dropped their change and extra cash into the donation bucket beside him. Christmas carolers walked up and down the street, stopping outside of businesses and crowds, singing "Good King Wenceslas" and other well-known holiday songs. Workers prepared for the upcoming Christmas Jamboree in the square, securing lights and decorating the mammoth tree with elaborate, ostentatious ornaments and homespun, handcrafted trimmings and accessories. Stage parents and construction workers assembled a platform for the Little Saint Nick pageant, where the kids in town dressed in Christmas costumes and performed songs and skits.

Mary was lacing up her skates as she chatted with Mike and Tyler. She noticed someone standing near her. When she looked up, she saw Bright smiling at her, his hands shoved in his coat pockets like a bashful schoolboy.

Mary's mind envisioned herself on a majestic, regal steed as REO Speedwagon's "Can't Fight This Feeling" played over the speakers of her imagination. She burst on to the battlegrounds of a war between Vikings and their enemies. Bright was on the battlefield, sword in hand, slicing and dicing at his foes. She approached, the galloping hooves of her horse beating like thunder against the ground, her hair flowing behind her in the wind. She swept him up with one arm and threw him on her steed as they fought against their opponents together and rode into the sunset.

Bright's mind envisioned Mary dressed up as a giant cheeseburger as Celine Dion's "If You Asked Me To" played over the speakers of his imagination. He was dressed as giant French fries in a red container. They saw each other and held out their hands. They skipped together through a large park toward a picnic, where they joined their friends Grilled Cheese, Taco, Chicken Nugget, Bacon, and Waffle.

"Oh, hey, Bright!" Mike said, instantly bringing Mary and Bright back down to earth. "What are you doing here?"

"You guys invited me," he answered. "Remember? You said to meet you here."

"Oh yeah, I must've forgotten," said Mike unconvincingly. "Glad you could make it."

"You said you'd put exploding dye packs around my hotel room if I didn't."

"Well, what's important is that you're here now and ready to skate," Mike said as he avoided Mary's clenched-jaw stare.

"I've never been ice skating before," said Bright. "I don't know how."

"Oh, really? Well, Mary, you've been skating your whole life!" Mike said. "You can be Bright's skating buddy."

"I don't really know how I feel about embarrassing myself in front of the locals," Bright said.

"There's nothing you can do that would be more embarrassing than the stuff we all know about each other," Tyler said as he pointed toward Mike. "This one used to be in a sad emo rock band."

"Torrential Downpour was not sad emo!" protested Mike. "It was the greatest undiscovered industrial band of our time! We were beloved by tens. I looked so cool on stage. Like Nicolas Cage in *Ghost Rider*. I never did get my leather skinny pants fixed."

"The local paper called them 'more depressing than watching climate change happen,'" said Tyler. "We used to go see them play at these divey, dumpy hole-in-the-wall bars."

"We were fine until one night while we were playing a cover of Culture Club's 'Do You Really Want to Hurt Me?', our drummer Killdozer had an on-stage meltdown," said Mike. "He decided he was Helen Hunt in that *ABC Afterschool Special* where she takes PCP and jumps out a second-story window. He told us all to eat a bag of fried dicks and went careening out the bar's front windows. It was hellacious. But a little funny too."

"How did I forget that guy?" Mary said. "I was there that night. He always wore lederhosen and a fanny pack and would read haikus to the audience. What ever happened to him?"

"He works for Congress now," Mike said.

"I used to think there was a monster inside the car wash," said Bright. "I'd scream and cry whenever my foster parents would take us through one. I still can't go into one."

"What?" Mary, Mike, and Tyler asked in unison.

"Sorry, I thought we were telling embarrassing stories about ourselves. I didn't want to be left out."

"Okay then," said Mike. "See you two on the ice."

Mike grabbed Tyler by the hand and they skated on to the rink. Bright smiled awkwardly at Mary. She shrugged and tried to act normal. She knew she was failing.

"Tyler and Mike like to believe they're on Cupid duty," said Mary.

"I noticed. You know, it smells different here than it does in the city. I used to think it was the smell of all the dead hopes and dreams of people who lived in small towns, but I'm starting to change my mind."

"I love the quiet here at night," Mary said, standing. "Small town people aren't all rednecks and closed-minded bigots. There's lots of beauty and incredible things to be found here."

"There is," he said as he looked directly at her.

Mary blushed. She and Bright inched their way to the rink. He was like a wobbly newborn deer. She put her arm on his shoulder and helped steady him.

"You can do this," she said.

She glided out onto the ice. Bright tried to balance himself, holding on to the rink's railings. His knees buckled and his legs teetered. Mary skated over to him, taking him by the hands. Bonnie Payne skated past them, her ice skates accessorized with photos and symbols of Paul Revere. Bright hugged the wall of the rink as people soared by.

"Ice skating is like a business deal," she said. "You have to focus. You don't show weakness and you don't back down. You're negotiating with the ice. The skates are your bargaining chips. You don't go into a business meeting and accept defeat, right? You make that meeting your bitch. That's what you're going to do with the ice."

Mary held on to Bright as she pulled him out on to the ice. He laughed in spite of himself, embarrassed that he looked so incompetent in front of her. Yet he felt like he was having fun.

"You take all of your problems and worries and you let them go on the ice," Mary said.

Bright steadied himself and took a few medium glides forward. He felt his confidence build. He was doing it. He was ice skating!

Mary let go of his arms as he managed a few more strides and crashed down to the ground. She skated to him and reached her hands out to help him up.

As Bright was trying to rise and gather equilibrium, he fell back down again. This time, Mary came with him. She landed on top of him, her face right near his. They both laughed then got quiet.

"I'm not very good at this," he said softly.

"You're learning," Mary said.

Mary saw Tyler and Mike giving her the "thumbs-up" in the background. She turned back to Bright. Carnie and Wendy Wilson's "Hey Santa!" played over the speakers. Bright looked into Mary's eyes. Mary was ready for their first kiss. He shifted. She closed her eyes for a moment.

Bbbblllrrrraaaaauuuuggghhhhh!!!

Mary and Bright were interrupted as an ice-skating little boy stopped right next to them and vomited his cherry Sno-Cone all over the rink. They both jumped up as quickly as they could, getting splattered by the upchuck.

"That sounds about right," Mary said.

They skated over to the concession stand, wiping themselves off with napkins.

"I think I've had enough fun for tonight," said Bright. "Are you hungry? I haven't eaten dinner yet. Would you like to join me?"

"Eating is definitely on my top-ten list of favorite things to do. Sure. Why not?"

They said their good nights to Tyler and Mike and headed off toward Minnie's Diner. None of them saw Llewellyn Barnes watching them leave, standing amongst the crowd of people at the park.

Chapter 35

Deputy Nash reached out to Sylvia, Frances, Willa, and Belle and welcomed them into his bunker. They used the giant whiteboard on one of the walls to set up a timeline, complete with pictures, paperwork, notable dates, and the details of Chester Persimmons' life.

Nash ordered pizza and they ate as they shared theories and bounced ideas off of each other. The women admired Nash's underground fortress, stocked with canned goods, water, its own plumbing and electrical systems, furniture, and impenetrable vault door hidden beneath a trap door beneath the grass in his backyard.

"Are you worried that the end is nigh, Leland?" asked Frances as she looked through the shelves of books, CDs, and DVDs Nash had stockpiled. "You'd tell us if you were in a cult, wouldn't you?"

"No, they thought I was too square," Nash said. "We do have a cult around here, since the '70s. They worship a guy they call Lord Cephus, whose name was really Murray and used to be a traveling encyclopedia salesman before becoming a guru. They wear man-kinis and ride mechanical bulls and play Croatian kazoo music. They have group movie nights where they watch *I Now Pronounce You Chuck and Larry* and make glitter portraits of each other. They believe that when you die, you get to go to a glorious and enchanting spooky luggage factory."

"And you've got jokes," Sylvia said.

"Benjamin Franklin said, 'By failing to prepare, you are preparing to fail,'" Nash answered.

"You're a real odd duck," Frances said. "I dig it."

"I'd rather never need this place than regret needing it and not having it," he said.

"Do you think that everybody has regrets at the end?" said Willa. "Like, no matter what good things happen to you, or what life path you choose. Does everyone look back on their lives and say they wish they had done things differently?"

"I regret not becoming a train hopper," said Belle. "And that I've never seen a centaur."

"I regret that I never finished my Michael Bublé scrapbook," Willa said. "Or never being a contestant on *Card Sharks*. You ever wonder why they call it that? Sharks don't play cards."

"I regret never telling my dad I loved him before he died," said Nash seriously.

"Well, that got dark fast," Sylvia said, moving to the whiteboard. "Let's focus so we can go back to the inn. I'd rather be in bed watching reruns of that old *Harry and the Hendersons* TV show in German. *Harry Und Die Hendersons*."

"You know how you can block people online rather than deal with them?" Willa said. "I wish I could do that in real life right now."

"Then we go door-to-door, canvassing the neighborhood and checking inside every house in town," asserted Frances, as she polished her gun.

"We can't go busting people's doors down without proof or probable cause, Frances," said Belle. "I know you want to go full Rambo, but you're going to have to take it down about three hundred notches."

"We knock on their doors and tell them we're pet psychics," Frances said. "Gets us in the doors, one of us pretends to read Fluffy's mind, and the rest of us search the house. In and out."

"Is there any kind of neighborhood watch in the community?" asked Sylvia.

"More of an online community, I'd say," Nash said. "There's never been crime here, so it's mostly people getting together for book club or backgammon and drinking wine."

Sylvia pointed out certain dates and locations on the map. Her mind spun as she tried to put all of the pieces together. She, Nash, and the ladies recounted the timeline.

Chester Persimmons' family lived in Tinselvania for generations before he was born. He married Bertha Havighurst then divorced her, remarried, and had children with his second wife. He worked at Tinsel Inc. until his family's share was bought out by the Classen family. He moved to Nevada, where he started his own business, which failed. After personal and professional losses, he committed several murders. He was caught and sent to The Calista Asylum for the Criminally Insane, where Sylvia was his doctor. The asylum closed and he was moved to a psychiatric unit in New York, where he escaped from. His latest path of violence indicated he was headed to Tinselvania.

"What are we missing?" Sylvia asked. "We haven't been able to properly vet or interview his former associates from the asylum or business life. Is someone helping him or is he on his own? What angle are we not seeing?"

"The Morning Light Cemetery," Nash said. "If he's really here, wouldn't he visit the graves of his relatives?"

Sylvia exchanged impressed looks with the ladies. Nash could be on to something.

"It doesn't hurt to check it out," Sylvia said. "Do you have a contact that can get us in?"

"I'm on it," Nash said as he took his cell phone out.

Chapter 36

Chief Fuller and Deputy McCloskey rode around town in one of the police SUVs. Fuller didn't know exactly what she was looking for. Something, or someone, out of place in their tiny town. Any kind of sign that things weren't "right."

"What's the course of action if Persimmons is here?" McCloskey asked. She had agreed to come on the ride-along with Fuller since Nash, Jennings, and Buchanan all had kids at home. It was an unspoken agreement she'd made with herself. The officers with children should wake up the next morning with their parents there. She knew Fuller had Stacy, but she also knew Fuller would go out to canvas regardless. Like Fuller, she tried not to be excited at the prospect of some real adventure in their small town, but it was much more thrilling than the usual calls about property lines, neighbor disputes, and cats stuck in trees.

"We have to assess his mental state at the time," Fuller said. "We know he's armed and has killed, but I don't want to use excessive force if we can help it. I want him to face justice for what he's done. I don't want this to turn into a red Christmas."

"All the years I've been an officer, I've never fired my gun at someone."

"Me either."

"How do you sleep at night? Knowing you've killed people. Knowing you've taken lives and destroyed the lives of the people around them. I could never reconcile myself with that. Sometimes I wonder if there's more bad people in the world than there are good."

"That's why we're on this side of the law. I remember being in high school and making a citizen's arrest when a girl in my grade shoplifted from the convenience store. Let me tell you, it made me super popular with all of the other kids. None of them spoke to me again."

"It's a calling. You know, when I was a kid, my dad told me all kinds of stories about these woods. There's all kinds of urban legends and folklore about creatures and cryptids that live in there. He told me this one story about the ghost of a drowned woman in the river who would rise up from the water and sink her nails into your shoulders as you slept and drag you into the water with her."

"It's not ghosts and beasts that scare me. I've seen the things that humans do to each other. Nothing is scarier to me than other people. Animals kill for food. They say people only kill for three things– love, revenge, or money. But that's too simplistic. Man does it for power, control, jealousy, lack of empathy for human life, the hate in his heart. Sometimes for no reason at all. I'd take a river ghost lady over a person any day."

They drove to the county woodland and park, a sprawling and popular forest and rest area for denizens and tourists alike. The park unfolded near a bridge overlooking an iced-over river that connected Tinselvania to the next town. The path to the trees started right before the bridge's entrance and down a slight hill next to the river. It led to the wobbly bridge, a bouncy walkway that opened into the woods. The suspension bridge was held up by cords and high tensile-strength cables, its bottom made of wood.

Fuller and McCloskey noted Colton Bornheimer's truck parked across from the bridge and made their way over the wobbly bridge into the barren trees and slightly snowy ground. They heard voices laughing and shouting from within the woods.

They walked for almost a half an hour, following the direction of the echoing voices. Fuller and McCloskey headed off-path, deep into the thick of the foliage. This was a part of the forest that most people didn't travel.

They passed an abandoned, rundown ice cream truck, covered in branches, leaves, moss, and flora. A giant faux ice cream cone topped the truck, cracked and chipped. The colors on the truck sides, once lively pastel and warm and welcoming, were now faded and grayed. Nobody knew how it got out into the woods, but it had been there for ages, sort of a trail-marker whose origins were a local folktale.

They made their way toward the faint light in the distance. They followed the glow as it got bigger and brighter. Fuller and McCloskey came to a camping site. A big orange fire blazed. Two tents were pitched around it. There were four people hanging out. They didn't notice Fuller and McCloskey approach.

Colton Bornheimer, a local in his thirties who worked in the trucking department at Tinsel Inc., danced around the fire dressed only in his underwear and boots. A beer in one hand and a cigarette in the other, he shouted and howled into the night.

Colton's girlfriend Wendy McKenna sat in a lawn chair next to Colton's best friend Devin Hutch and Devin's girlfriend Camilla Parr. Wendy, Devin, and Camilla were all employed at Tinsel Inc. as well.

"Chief Iola! Deputy Darcy!" Colton said as soon as he noticed them.

"That's Chief Fuller and Deputy McCloskey, Colton," McCloskey corrected him.

"Nobody calls me Colton," he said. "Everyone calls me 'Beef.' That's what I go by."

"What are you guys doing out here?" Fuller asked.

"We're doing a little snipe hunting," said Beef. "We haven't caught any yet."

"Are we in trouble?" Wendy said.

"We're just having a campout Christmas celebration," said Beef. "Blowing off some steam with friends. You want a beer?"

"You should step back from the fire if you're drinking," said McCloskey.

"I have amazing balance," Beef said, standing on one leg. He wobbled and shook more than he noticed. "Steady as a rock. I'm ready for the Olympic balance beam gold medal."

"Have we broken any laws?" asked Devin.

"No," said Fuller. "Just be careful, please. It might just be safest to go home."

"We're just having some fun, Chief," Beef said.

Wendy and Camilla stood up and walked over to Fuller and McCloskey.

"We'll keep an eye on them," said Camilla.

"Well, you don't have a face tattoo yet so I'm guessing you all haven't gone full K-hole," Fuller said. "Girls, I hope you're making your men use protection. You don't want STDs or babies. We've got enough of those in this town as is. Devin Hutch and Beef Bornheimer? You could do better."

"Is that official police advice?" asked Wendy. "We're not all destined to be spinsters, Chief Fuller."

"I'll have you know that enjoying a quiet night at home knitting and chatting online about the latest episode of *NCIS: New Orleans* doesn't make you a spinster. Don't knock it," said McCloskey.

"Do you know the real meaning of the word 'spinster'?" Fuller asked, trying her best to be informative without sounding condescending. "In the Middle Ages, wool was a lucrative trade good. The women who spun wool were called 'spinsters.' So these women made a buttload of money without having to depend on men, not only giving them autonomy over their own independence, but freedom from having to be married against their own wishes."

"You just make sure you put that fire out properly before you leave, okay?" said McCloskey.

Fuller knew that Beef, Wendy, Devin, and Camilla weren't bad people. Part of her wanted to leave them alone. They were just enjoying themselves. She was young once, though she never partied. The other part knew that she wouldn't sleep if she didn't warn them. She couldn't give too much away. She didn't want to start a panic or an unnecessary public frenzy.

The only major crime they'd had in Tinselvania was when Old Man Boswell disappeared. It turned out he had won big on a scratch ticket and abandoned his family and job at the auto shop to start a new life in Montana. That wasn't even a crime, but for a moment it was a missing persons case that sparked rumors, distrust, and mass hysteria amongst the residents. Fuller didn't want a repeat of that.

"Will you please call us if you see anyone else out here? Any strangers?" said Fuller. "I can't make you go home, but since this is Tinselvania, at least I know you have guns."

"I was about to show Wendy my gun before you guys came along," Beef said.

"All right, Beef, enough of that talk," McCloskey said. "See you at church on Sunday."

"Stay warm and be safe," said Fuller. "No guns or drinking near that fire, you got me? Anything looks weird or suspicious, you go on home. Don't worry about your stuff, just go."

Fuller and McCloskey left the quartet, on their way to walk some of the other trails and investigate campsites in the area. They couldn't stay in the woods all night. These woods were vast, dense, and seemingly endless. There were too many other areas and neighborhoods to patrol.

"Well, that was some good policing," Fuller said, laughing at herself. "I think we really got through to them."

Beef drank another beer while he stood over the fire. Wendy started to look worried.

"Do you think we should go?" she said.

"They're just trying to scare us into being good Stepford residents," said Beef. "Conform and obey and be good robots. Not this guy."

"Why would they be out here patrolling if something wasn't wrong?" asked Camilla.

"Chief Iola and Deputy Darcy just want to feel all fancy 'cause there's never really anything to do in Tinselvania," Beef said. "Goddamn, it's cold! My nipples could cut glass."

"I don't want my face to end up on the side of a milk carton," said Wendy.

"I'll protect you," Beef said, flexing his muscles. "Hulk smash!"

Beef approached Wendy and shook the front of his undies in her face.

"Speaking of things to do in Tinselvania," he said suggestively.

Wendy pushed him away as they all laughed. None of them heard the footsteps that circled the campsite. The footsteps that didn't belong to Fuller or McCloskey.

Chapter 37

Mary and Bright were at Minnie's Diner in a corner booth. She ordered mozzarella sticks, fish and chips, and a bacon cheeseburger with a Diet Pepsi and a strawberry milkshake. Bright had a turkey club sandwich. He was impressed with her ability to eat several meals in one sitting. Wham!'s "Last Christmas" played over the loudspeakers.

"I was going to order the side of asparagus but I didn't want my pee to be stinky," Mary said. She regretted it immediately. As usual, she was kicking herself for being terrible at flirting. Asparagus pee?

"Yeah, I hate when that happens," laughed Bright.

"I never said 'thank you' for the gifts," she said, trying to change the subject. "It was really thoughtful of you."

"You're welcome," said Bright. "It was the least I could do after our rocky start. I know first impressions are important, but I was hoping for a reboot."

"You've got nothing to reboot. I understand. You're no scrub. A scrub is a guy who can't get no love from me," Mary said, then again wanted to crawl underneath the table for saying something idiotic and ridiculous.

"So you thinking I'm hanging out the passenger side, trying to holler at you? I ain't no hollaback girl, Mary."

"Can you tell I don't go on many first dates? Oh, I don't get out much."

"You hide it very, very well. Is this a first date?"

"If it is, I promise to save my really good bodily fluid stories for our third."

"I don't know if I can wait that long."

"Did you know that Jupiter is twice as massive than all of the other planets combined?" Mary said. "And that the numbers one through 999, when spelled out, don't contain the letter 'A.'"

"No, I didn't know any of those things, but those facts certainly come up in conversation often so now I'm informed."

Why am I being such a weirdo? she scolded herself. *You're giving him Trivial Pursuit facts. Stop being an awkward dink! Get it together, Mary!*

"A 'jiffy' is one-trillionth of a second!" she blurted out.

The waiter came by to check on them. He gave Bright the once-over, as if checking that he was good enough to be out with Mary.

"You really do know everyone here," Bright said in amazement. "I have next-door neighbors I've never spoken to."

"When I went to college, I lived in Cambridge. It took me a few weeks to get used to how fast everybody moved and talked. But I loved it. The day I left for school, my mom and dad stood on the front lawn and played 'Massachusetts' by the Bee Gees and cried."

"Everyone should have family that cares about them that much."

"What would you do if you weren't in business?"

"I wanted to do something with the ocean. Live in an underwater research facility and study the marine life and live in a house on the beach when I'm not working. How about you?"

"This is all I ever really wanted to do. It's all I've known. I grew up at my family's business. Noelle and Glory weren't into it the same way as I was. Glory wanted to be a singer but she wasn't really a particularly good singer unfortunately, and Noelle wanted to be a professional organizer but I think we were all predestined to work at Tinsel Inc."

"Childhood dreams rarely come true. Between my family dying around Christmastime and the horrible foster homes I bounced around in, I don't think I've ever had a good Christmas."

"Maybe this year will be different."

Bright paused. He didn't know what was happening, but Mary struck him as so beautiful and smart and fiery. It was awakening something inside of him.

"I think it already is," he said. "I've only been here for two days but I feel like I've somehow always been a part of this town somehow."

"How long are you planning on staying around for?"

"A week, maybe. I have some papers to go through and then you and I can talk about the business and figure out what you want to do."

"Maybe you can stay long enough to be a part of the Secret Santa at work. You could get a really nice snowglobe out of it."

"Well, then I have to stay. Hopefully I'll be here long enough to take you to see *Broken Arrow* at the little theater in town. What are the other nine things?"

"Hmm?"

"You said eating is one of your top-ten favorite things. What are the other nine?"

"Oh. Well, my family. My friends. Tinsel. My job. This town. Movies, music, and television shows, which I guess sounds corny, but I love getting to watch a good movie on the couch under a big comforter. Travel, though I never do it. Board games. Castles. The beach. Books, though I usually only read work orders and emails these days. Being an aunt. Scary movies. I love scary movies. Is that nine yet? These aren't very interesting."

"No, they are," said Bright. "More than you know."

"What about you? What makes you happy?"

"I've been asking myself that since I got here. I love the city. I do. I'm starting to realize, though, that there might be other places I could belong to."

"It's Christmas all year round here. Could you stand that?"

"One family I lived with when I was growing up used to buy Christmas gifts for their biological kids every year. The Perkins' family. I had to sit in the basement as they opened them. I wasn't allowed to be a part of it. I wasn't their kid. I was a way for them to make money. They would lock me down there for the whole day, through their Christmas dinner and celebration. Then they'd let me out when it was time for them to go to bed."

"Bright, that's so wrong and you never should've had to experience that. That's not your fault. That was cruel, horrible people who hurt an innocent boy."

"I'm not wallowing, even though it probably sounds like I am. It's time for me to make new memories and stop letting my past have so much control over me. It's harder to do than it seems."

"We're made up of our experiences, right? Tinselvania is one big family. You're a part of that history now. From now on, when you hear Andy Williams sing 'I'll Be Home for Christmas,' you'll think of us."

"Peach cummerbunds," said Bright. "Those make me happy. Apple orchards. Bioluminescent plankton. *Mork and Mindy* reruns. Corn mazes.

Anything about the ocean or outer space. Elton John. Exploring abandoned places. That moment when you get home and take off your work clothes and feel free."

"Yes, that's my favorite part of the whole day."

"Hockey. I was a really great hockey player in school and I thought for a minute I could have a career in it. I blew out my right knee in a game, though, and I never played the same again. But someday, if it's okay, I could take you to a game."

"I would love that. I know nothing about hockey, but I think it would be fun with the right company."

"I also love karaoke. If this town has a karaoke bar, I want to go."

"Karaoke is one town over, but that's a date. Would you like to join me and the girls for cosmic bowling tomorrow night? You can hang out with Kara, Liza, and Robin and their significant others and respective kids. My niece Ivy and her friends work at the bowling alley so we get the best lanes. You don't want to miss an opportunity to wear bowling shoes that have been worn by the citizens of Tinselvania."

"Yes. That would be a shame. I have a feeling you're an extremely competitive player."

"I was going to say the same thing to you."

"I'd love to. Should we make a bet? If I get the highest score, I get to watch a movie on the couch with you under a big comforter?"

"Okay. And if I win, you get to watch a movie with me on the couch under a big comforter."

"Deal."

"Do you have a go-to karaoke song?"

"Actually, yes. 'Dangerous' by Roxette. Years ago, on the subway, there was this guy sitting by himself, just belting it out to no one in particular, just in his own world. It was so random. While I despise people who play their music out loud or sing out loud without regard for the other passengers, because what kind of tool does that, there was a huge part of me that was inspired by his blind confidence. He was living out loud and didn't care what everyone thought. In a weird way, although he blows for being so inconsiderate, he's also my spirit animal."

Bright tried not to think about the way Mary smiled at him, listened to him. He needed to stay the course. He came to Tinselvania to get a job done. There he was, looking at Mary, thinking about what a beautiful and interesting woman she was. He didn't want to get distracted from his purpose, but he couldn't help himself.

The waiter ame to clear the plates.

"Do you have any cake?" Mary asked, her eyes laser-focused on the dessert counter.

"We may have a slice of the birthday cake left," he said.

"Oh, it's okay," Mary smiled. "I would definitely need more than one piece. No worries. I'm sure there's something else I'll want."

Mary ordered banana cream pie and butterscotch pudding for dessert. Bright ordered a coffee. She smiled at him and he felt his heart grow two sizes.

Chapter 38

Kara and her husband Nick sat on their daughter Eve's bed, flanking her as she was tucked underneath her covers and blankets. Eve, their oldest, was six. Their other daughter, Astrid, was turning three soon, sound asleep in her own bedroom.

Kara read *'Twas the Night Before Christmas* to Eve, whose eyes were almost closed. Once the story was over, Kara quietly closed the book and they tiptoed out into the hallway.

Nick worked at Tinsel Inc. in the trucking department. He was a real-life Mr. Fix-It, who enjoyed working with his hands and any excuse to break out his massive collection of tools and machines. Kara called him Inspector Gadget. He always had a flannel shirt and work boots on. Even his pajamas were flannel. He was currently building an addition onto their modest two-story home.

They made themselves comfortable on the couch. They were watching *Bad Santa* for the fiftieth time, one of Nick's favorite movies.

Boom!

A loud bang from the opposite side of the house, where the addition was being built, caught their attention. Kara paused the movie. They listened.

"What was that?" she asked.

"Probably some equipment that fell," said Nick. "Nothing to worry about."

Kara shivered against the cold. There was a draft blowing through the house.

"Did you leave the back door open?" she said.

Clang!

Another sudden, jarring noise from the other room. Kara looked at Nick with worry. He didn't seem too concerned.

"I'm just going to make sure everything is locked up," she said, getting up. Nick got up with her, not wanting his wife to have to go alone.

They passed the various rooms on the first floor, peeking in. They tried to discern where the draft originated from. They turned lights on and off, inspecting each room. The windows were all securely locked and nothing was out of place.

They reached the toy room, where Eve and Astrid's stuffed animals and various games and playthings were stored. Kara turned the light on. She and Nick stopped.

All of Eve and Astrid's stuffed animals, at least three dozen of them, had been arranged around the room in various positions and poses. It was deliberate and pointed, not the usual chaos and disorder of two little girls' toys scattered haphazardly.

"What?" Nick said.

The breeze blew by again, this time harder and colder. Kara left Nick in the toy room and went to the back door that connected to the unfinished addition.

The back door was slightly ajar, swaying back and forth with the wind. She pushed it open.

The addition was under construction. Tools, lumber, ladders, and blueprints were spread out all over the room. Plastic sheets that hung from the ceiling rustled and crackled in the breeze.

Kara saw a shadow behind one of the plastic sheets. It was gone as soon as she caught sight of it. The shadow dodged out the back door.

Kara ran to the back door, looking out into the darkness. There was nobody there. She saw the tree line and the backyard of her next-door neighbor's house. Most of the lights at the Frosts' house, their neighbors, were off. There wasn't enough light to see far. She flipped the back porch light switch. No light came on.

She saw the set of footprints on the ground that trailed from the back door toward the woods. Next to it was a shattered lightbulb. The lightbulb that once was in the fixture facing the backyard.

She slammed the door shut and locked it.

"Everything okay?" Nick asked. He was behind her now.

"I think someone was in here, Nick," she said.

"Maybe it was a ghost. Angry because I'm renovating his former home."

"Don't say that."

"It was probably Fisher. I took his level earlier and forgot to bring it back."

"Why wouldn't he come in and say hello? Liza would have texted me if Fisher was stopping by."

"I don't know. Maybe he was in a hurry or they didn't want to bother us. Don't get nervous. I probably forgot to lock the back door. You know I never remember stuff like that."

"There's footprints in the snow leading to the forest."

"I went for a walk with the dog earlier, remember?"

He rubbed Kara's arms. She nodded, not entirely satisfied with the reasoning. She knew Tinselvania was a safe place to live. It was dark in that room, so she conceded that her eyes could have been playing tricks on her.

"What about the toy room?" she said.

"Eve did that," said Nick. "She gets smarter and more creative every day, just like her mom. Remember the other day when she explained the five love languages to us? I don't know where she learned that, but I looked it up later and she was spot on."

Kara double-checked that the door was locked. Nick put his arm around her and they retreated back to the couch. Nick hadn't noticed the ax that was missing from the multitude of tools and implements he left in the unfinished addition.

Chapter 39

Gordon Frost had worked late that night. When he arrived home, the house was relatively dark and it seemed that everyone had already gone to bed. He was a chief engineer over at Tinsel Inc. and had been freelance consulting for Yule Love It Christmas Corporation over the past week.

His wife Patience was aptly named. She had been a teacher in the Tinselvania school system for over forty years and was retiring after the current school year. She was beloved by her students and coworkers for her tolerance, fortitude, compassion, and ability to make everyone around her feel loved and supported.

Patience had left him a plate in the fridge from the dinner he missed. He decided to eat later, instead heading to the garage, where all of his electronic equipment and doodads were set up. He wanted to spend some time fiddling with his shortwave radio and working on his own pirate radio station, where he played his favorite obscure songs and shared his thoughts with tens of listeners. He used the anonymous handle "Cliff Garlicthroat" as his deejay moniker.

He had a special radio that was tuned into a numbers station, though he had no idea where the broadcast originated He was addicted to the rhythm and cadence of the numbers that were read over the ether, in an unidentified woman's voice, as he wondered what they meant and if he'd ever discover who sent them.

His house was full of company for the upcoming weekend. His birthday was on Saturday, so his sons Dodd, Bear, and Rye were visiting with their wives and children. They were all staying in their old rooms. He would see them in the morning for breakfast.

Once he listened to the measured reading of the numbers, he went back into the house and heated up his dinner. He sat at the dining room table with his plate in front of him, listening to the quiet and tranquility of the house. It was so silent that his ears rang. He was all alone at the empty table, smiling as he looked at the vacant seats surrounding him. He recalled watching his sons grow up, having dinner together as a family, the laughter and stories that were told around this very same table for decades.

Gordon did not see the reindeer as it rushed into the dining room from behind him, from the connecting area, the ax in its hands raised high in the air.

Thwack!

The reindeer brought the ax down on top of Gordon's head in one crushing blow. Gordon's head split open like a soft-boiled egg, his blood and brains exploding and oozing everywhere. The reindeer lifted the ax again and again, striking Gordon with it even as Gordon slumped forward onto his dinner plate. The ax blade made a sickening squishing, squelching sound every time it hit Gordon's head.

Once the reindeer had turned Gordon's skull into mush, it walked into an adjoining room. There were the bodies of Gordon's family, propped up as if they were alive. The room was decorated for the surprise party they had planned for Gordon that night: streamers, a "Happy Birthday" banner, confetti, balloons, noisemakers, party horns, wrapped birthday presents, a giant cake on the table with unlit candles.

The reindeer had arranged the corpses of Gordon's family– his wife Patience, his sons and their wives, and their teenage children– around the room. As if they were awaiting Gordon's arrival so they could yell, "Surprise!" It had placed colorful party hats on all of their heads and then sprinkled tinsel over them.

It had gotten to the Frosts' house earlier and crept around the house, attacking each of the family members when it had the opportunity. Had Gordon ventured farther into the house when he got home, he would have seen the blood and viscera that stained the floors and coated the walls.

The reindeer sat on the couch between the lifeless, vacant-eyed bodies of Patience and Bear. Its breathing was so steady and controlled that even with the mask, there was no sound. It stared at the crime scene around it, planning and plotting its next move.

Chapter 40

Mary and Bright weren't ready to call it a night yet. She offered to take him on a walk through town to see all of the houses lit up with Christmas lights and festive décor. Whole neighborhoods whose lights and colors could probably be seen from a satellite in space. Inflatable snowmen, plastic Santas, Nativity scenes, massive wreaths, and the like. Nobody did Christmas like Tinselvania did, day after day and year after year. It was their way of life. Most of the houses themselves were as old as the town, many having undergone restoration and refurbishing over the years.

"I never get tired of looking at these houses," Mary said. "I see these every day and I still love it."

"It's beautiful," said Bright. "It's like being in an alternate dimension. But instead of aliens, it's reindeer and angels and elves. What's it like here in the summertime?"

"Hot and muggy, but nowhere near what you probably get in the city. In the summer, I'm a sweaty, wet, gross mess and get chubrub. Then in the winter my skin dries out so badly that I can't shave my armpits or wear deodorant because of how bad my rash gets," Mary said, not sounding as seductive, intriguing, or enticing as she had hoped.

Shut up, Mary! she berated herself. *Is this your first time talking to an attractive, interesting man? Rashes are not sexy talk!*

"I hate when that happens," Bright chuckled. He enjoyed how awkward and goofy Mary could be. It made him want to embrace his awkward and goofy side too. "When I was young, I went to Boy Scout camp, and this older kid dared me to climb to the top of a really big tree. I made it all the way up, but when I looked down, I realized how high I was in the air. I instantly had explosive diarrhea that shot out of the legholes in my shorts and rained down on my Boy Scout troop. And that was how I learned I'm afraid of heights. My nickname was 'Thunderpoop' from that day on."

"What's wrong with us?" Mary asked. "We are in the middle of a Hallmark Christmas movie and we're blowing it."

"This is a really fucked-up Hallmark Christmas movie."

They laughed for a moment, stopping to admire more beautifully-adorned houses. After a quiet second of looking at each other in anticipation, Mary sucked in a breath and started walking again. Bright strode beside her.

"When I was younger, I'd put my *Christmas with The Jets* cassette in my Walkman and get all bundled up and walk around town and imagine that one of these houses would be mine someday. Remember The Jets? The band, not the football team. They sang 'You Got it All.'"

"No."

"Oh yeah, me neither," Mary said, pushing aside her inner dork and recovering. "What do you usually do for Christmas?"

"Get Chinese takeout and watch *Lethal Weapon* and do work. What's a Classen Christmas like?"

"Big dinner, the whole family together, opening gifts, Christmas movies, lots of drunk Aunt Elaine singing Christmas songs like she's a famous lounge singer. Read Christmas stories to the kids. I read R.L. Stine's *Fear Street: Silent Night* every year on Christmas Eve. It was a book I loved as a kid. We play a huge game of Win, Lose, or Draw. Tinsel everywhere. My mom makes ham, turkey, and ravioli every year. My dad loved ravioli so it's a Christmas tradition in our house."

"Do you miss him more this time of year?"

"Some days I miss him a lot. Others I feel like he's with me somehow. Everything reminds me of him. My office was his office. He's a part of me. I wish he were here. But I also don't believe in dwelling in the past. I have so much more I want to do with my life. My life is more than tinsel and Christmas."

"I always thought the legend of Santa was kind of creepy. Some fat guy with a big beard who watches you all year and breaks into your house at night while you're sleeping. Who employs elves in what's basically a sweatshop in the North Pole. Judging you for what you do, as if he is the final say that determines whether you're 'naughty' or 'nice.' Making his reindeer pull his fat ass all over the world once a year."

"Wow, that is cynical!" Mary laughed. "You're like a human lump of coal. Do you run through schoolyards shouting 'Santa is a lie!' to all the kids? Organizing anti-Christmas squads of angry malcontents who tear down decorations and burn them in a bonfire while yelling 'Damn the man'?"

"No, of course not," Bright said. "We're an anti-Christmas unit, not a squad. We're in the union. We only burn gross Christmas food like those layered Christmas dinners in a can and undercooked cranberry sauce. Sometimes we'll break up Ugly Christmas Sweater parties because they're just tacky and lame. The only thing worse is gender reveal parties. We have to come together as a society and say, 'Enough is enough.' Stop the madness. We have to draw the line somewhere."

They paused in front of a particularly well-decorated, beautiful home. It looked like something out of a Christmas special. As if dancers dressed like Santa, in red outfits and white trim, were going to burst into synchronized dance on the lawn, surrounded by the ornaments and lights.

Mary took another step and went sliding down a patch of black ice. Bright leaned forward to grab ahold of her. Instead, he slipped on the icy ground. They waved their hands wildly, attempting to balance themselves, as Mary spun around and crashed right into Bright. They held on to each other, their faces only inches apart, their breath visible in the cold of the night.

Bright looked into Mary's eyes. She stared back at him. He leaned down for their first kiss. Fireworks exploded within each of their bodies. Every synapse and nerve in their body turned electric. Mariah Carey's "All I Want for Christmas Is You" played over the speakers of their imaginations. The world around them disappeared. All that was left was the two of them and their unbridled passion as their lips locked and their spirits soared above the clouds.

Chapter 41

The desperate urge to pee woke Beef up from his slumber. He was still slightly inebriated from earlier but felt much more clear-headed. Wendy slept peacefully beside him inside the tent. Camilla and Devin were sound asleep in their own tent. Beef didn't bother to put any clothes on except for his boots, quietly exiting the tent stark naked. The fire had died out, only embers and ash remaining. He grabbed a flashlight and walked a few feet down a nearby trail to relieve himself. The woods were still, only the sounds of distant animals making any kind of noise.

He noticed the train tracks on the ground, enveloped in dirt, moss, and branches. There used to be a railway system that ran through this part of town eons ago, as well as a logging operation. That was all gone now, but the railroad tracks remained. He stared down at them, following along, when he heard the music.

The melodic notes of a Christmas tune wafted over the wind. Beef, puzzled, searched for the source, following the sound as it grew louder. Among the barren shrubs, in the melted snow, stood an eight-inch dancing robotic Santa. Burl Ives' "A Holly Jolly Christmas" emanated tinnily over a small speaker on Santa's base. Beef bent down to get a closer look at it. He felt a wave of distrust and suspicion wash over him, as he scanned his surroundings.

He took a step back. A twig cracked under his foot. He could feel something hard and metallic click beneath his boot. He didn't realize until it was too late for him. Beef had sprung a trap.

A dozen long, sharpened sticks shot up from the ground beneath him, impaling him vertically through his body. One of the spears sliced straight through his back and out of his gaping, bleeding mouth. He gagged on his own blood. His head was tilted back by the wooden stake jutting from his throat. He made a wet gargling sound, unable to form words, his body stuck in place.

The reindeer stepped out of the shadows, crushing the Santa underneath its hoof. Its black eyes stared at Beef, poking him as if he were a rag doll. Tears and blood streamed down Beef's face. He couldn't even scream as the light faded from his twitching, trapped body.

The reindeer turned its attention to Beef's campsite.

Wendy stirred inside her sleeping bag, pulling the extra blanket over her. She was cold. She heard Beef entering the tent, zipping it up, climbing underneath the covers next to her.

"I was having the weirdest dream," she said groggily, eyes half-open. "We were on a shire with a bunch of hobbits. They were having a huge rave with traveling minstrels and lute players. Everything they said had subtitles. Then the Burger King mascot guy showed up. You know, with that big, scary, grinning plastic mask. Everyone turned into replicas of the Burger King guy, all staring at me while they chanted limericks about pickles and thousand island dressing. And then the bats came."

Beef didn't move beside her. He remained silent and still. Wendy reached out for him, rubbing his side. She bristled, her eyes opening up instantly. She felt soft, cold fur.

"Beef?" she said. A wave of fear washed over her.

She sat up, staring at the unmoving figure outlined underneath the sleeping bag. She couldn't see Beef's face. She saw his breathing, the blanket moving up and down. She reached out to pull the covers away.

"Hey, this isn't funny," she said quietly.

Beef lurched forward from beneath the blanket. It wasn't Beef. It was the reindeer. Wendy was so shocked that she didn't react at first. It didn't matter. The reindeer thrust a hunting knife into her over and over, giving her no time to scream.

Devin and Camilla were asleep in their tent when they heard the scraping sound against the outside of their tent. As they slowly emerged from their respective slumbers, their eyes focused on the shadow that circled their canvas. The shadow was dragging a knife blade along the polyester and nylon, making a distinct, unsettling noise.

"Cut it out, Beef!" Devin said.

The shadow disappeared from view. Devin and Camilla could hear footsteps fading away in the distance. They relaxed, getting comfortable and attempting to go back to sleep.

They didn't hear the footsteps approaching, softer and quieter this time. The noise of the tent's zipper slowly opening shook them back to reality.

Camilla shined her flashlight on the tent flaps, scolding Beef for waking them. Beef poked his head inside the tent.

Devin and Camilla sighed in frustration. The realization sank in immediately. Beef's eyes were vacant, his mouth opened in an expressionless stare. It was Beef's head, dripping blood and gristle. An unknown, pawed hand grasped Beef's decapitated head by his hair. It let go of Beef's head, allowing it to spill forward onto Devin and Camilla's blankets. They recoiled and screamed.

Slash!

Their tent was being torn to shreds by a madman wielding a machete. Camilla grabbed Devin. They leapt to their feet and dashed out of the tent.

Camilla's first step landed her foot squarely in the center of a bear trap that snapped around her leg. She screamed out as Devin reached down to help her. When they looked at the area surrounding their tent, they saw that dozens upon dozens of bear traps had been laid out, as if waiting for them.

They saw the reindeer emerge from behind the tent and brandish the machete, making sure they saw it clearly, felt the threat and the implications. Devin struggled to free Camilla's leg. He felt the machete hit him in the side of his arm.

Devin spun around to face the reindeer, trying to watch where he put his feet. The reindeer swung the machete at him wildly. Camilla grabbed a rock and threw it at the reindeer. It responded swiftly, kicking her down. She fell on top of several other bear traps, which clamped down on her, cutting her open and maiming her as she screamed.

Devin held on to his wounded arm and made a run for it into the night. The reindeer wasn't far behind. Another slash to his side and he stumbled. He tried to fight the reindeer off, swinging his fists at it.

The reindeer picked Devin up in the air and impaled him on a low-hanging tree limb. Devin cried out, almost in disbelief, as he saw the branch that was sticking out of his body. His feet kicked against nothing as he was suspended in air by the skewer, the ground beneath him so far away.

The reindeer backed away to admire its handiwork. It listened to the gurgling, fruitless twitches and noises Camilla and Devin made as their lives drained from their bodies.

Chapter 42

Mary practically floated home. She and Bright had gone their separate ways for the night but she was already excited to see him at work the next morning. It had been so long since she'd felt like this toward someone.

She reached her front door. At the top of the frame hung mistletoe. It hadn't been there earlier. A note was attached to it. In pretty, dramatic calligraphy someone had written, *You better watch out.*

Mary shook her head, dismissing it as one of her mom's silly Christmas decorations. When she got inside, she went to the kitchen to get something to eat. The house was quiet and still. Mary sat on the couch in the living room and pulled a blanket over her. The wood in the fireplace crackled and popped as the warm fire blazed. Mary felt cozy and safe. It was late and she was tired, but she wanted this feeling of hope and joy to last a little longer.

Her phone buzzed. It was Robin calling. Mary picked up. Robin launched into her pitch right away.

"There's a foam party tonight at The Barco-Lounge in Portland. I'm with Angus and Chuck. Chuck keeps asking about you. You should come meet us after you get done being a good girl. Jenna Elfman is going to be there."

"I have to do some work," Mary said. "And the last time you made me go out with you, we ended up at Hot Lips and you told the manager I would audition. He thought you were serious. He literally greased up the pole for me."

"I was as serious as a zebra in a lion's den," said Robin. "I had singles. We made it rain!"

"I have to finish this paper on fiscal responsibility and tinsel."

"What happened to fun Mary? Where did she go? Can you please find the real Mary, my forever best friend, and tell her to get on the phone instead of this pod person I'm talking to?"

"This is reality-check Mary. She's much less delusional about our lives. You want to go to a club full of trashy guys who wear trucker hats and way too much cologne and drink like fishes and regret it in the morning? I will support you, but I will not go on this journey of self-loathing with you. Bring condoms, please. You do not want the STDs those guys are surely giving out like it's government cheese. Or worse, getting knocked up by one of them and having your baby come out with its hair already gelled."

"Your social life is a big black hole," said Robin. "Include that in your paper. You're on the couch watching *Under the Tuscan Sun* and pretending you're Diane Lane and eating pink Sno-Balls, aren't you?"

Mary looked down at the empty Sno-Balls package on her chest, then at Diane Lane in *Under the Tuscan Sun* playing on television.

"You don't know me."

"I can hear the wrapper crinkling!"

"Good night, Robin."

"Wait! You should watch *Blockers*. Gary Cole goes full-frontal, peen out! I'll DM you screenshots later. It's Must-See TV."

"Good night, Robin."

"Wait! Did you know, if we were in prison, we would be the 'new fish'? I learned that from watching Linda Blair prison movies."

Mary laughed as Robin disconnected. She watched the movie and let her mind wander. She was excited to get to know Bright. She liked how she felt around him. It didn't matter that it had only been two days. She could feel it in her heart. This was different this time.

She tried responding to work emails from Ethan, Liza, Kara, Josh, and Robin, but her thoughts remained elsewhere. She wrote notes down for her tinsel article. It was no use. She was distracted. She usually hated being distracted, but for once she allowed herself to be. She imagined Bright moving to Tinselvania and working at Tinsel Inc. with her. She envisioned him at family gatherings, becoming a part of this town she loved so much. It had been so long since she had met someone she felt butterflies for.

"What are you doing up so late?" Alvinia asked from the doorway. She was in her night clothes and poofy robe. "You're going to be a zombie tomorrow."

"I'm going to bed in a minute," Mary said. "What are you doing?"

"I couldn't sleep. I keep thinking about the party. I have to get the rest of the groceries and odds and ends for the *Family Stone* event," Alvinia said. "Elaine and I will go shopping tomorrow."

Alvinia sat next to Mary, getting underneath the blanket with her.

"We used to watch all the Christmas specials like this when you were kids," said Alvinia. "Every year, your father and I would scoop you up and get comfy so we could watch *Rudolph the Red-Nosed Reindeer* and *Frosty the Snowman* and *Santa Claus Is Comin' to Town* and *The Year Without a Santa Claus*. Do you remember?"

"Yes, of course," said Mary. "I think our favorite was *A Charlie Brown Christmas*."

"You were all such good girls growing up. I'm so lucky that you all stayed so close to me. Sometimes I'm sad for Elaine because all of her children moved away from her. That's why it's so important for us to take care of her. Sisterhood is an important bond. But remember what your grandma used to tell us. 'When life gives you lemons, don't cry over the molehills that you spilled your milk in because there's always a light at the end of the tunnel under that mountain where you get lemonade.'"

"Grandma used to tell me she had a trunk full of stuff for me when I got married. Every year she'd hang an empty stocking in honor of the husband I didn't have."

"She was from a different generation," Alvinia laughed. "I hope you know that even though I give you a hard time sometimes, I am so happy that you live your life the way you want to. You don't have to be just like me. In the end, all that matters is that you are happy. You are such a hard worker, Mary, and everyone looks up to you. It's a wonderful thing to see."

"Mom," Mary said, embarrassed. "Why are you being all maudlin?"

"Sometimes, late at night, when I'm all alone, I put on *Pirates of the Caribbean* and pretend the couch is a pirate ship," said Alvinia. "I put a picture of Jack Sparrow on an upside-down mop and make-believe that he's come to rescue me from rogues and scoundrels."

"Mom, that's so… pitiful," laughed Mary. "We all get lonely."

"I was the country bumpkin who married my high school sweetheart and popped out some kids. I never wanted to live anywhere else. Do you know that your father brought me flowers every week, the entire time we were married? There were so many women whose husbands were out cavorting with other women, but your dad was completely devoted to us. I didn't have any of the ambition that you and your father had, but I like my small little life. You are allowed to do things differently and to want more than domesticity. But don't be afraid to let yourself love someone. You can love someone and love your job too."

"Okay, Mom."

Chapter 43

Deputy Nash contacted Graham Cerne, the caretaker of The Morning Light Cemetery. He agreed to take Sylvia and the ladies through the gravestones although it was well after midnight. Nash did not join the women. He stayed home and ate the leftover pizza in his bunker.

Graham was a stocky older man, born and raised in Tinselvania. He was an amateur historian and archivist, knowledgeable about the family trees, events, politics, and happenings of the town he grew up in. He kept a collection of photos, papers, documents, and news articles at his home, where he worked on a historical record of the town's genealogy and accounts. He considered himself the unofficial town chronicler.

When Graham did the research on The Morning Light Cemetery, his online findings uncovered testimonials from people who had experienced petrifying, unexplained paranormal phenomena there. Online were dozens of videos featuring ghost hunters and amateur detectives who recorded themselves wandering around the graves and crypts. He had unearthed historical records and reports about some of the people who were buried there. Many were hardworking, decent folks, but there was a huge subsection where the criminally insane or "undesirable" were buried. Their crimes ranged from stealing and robbing to accusations of having ties with the supernatural to cold-blooded murder.

Pike waited in the car as Graham led Sylvia, Frances, Willa, and Belle into the cemetery. He stopped the vehicle outside of the squeaky iron front gates. The cemetery was two acres, located within the center of a larger plot of grassland. It was surrounded by a stone enclosure that wrapped around its entirety. At the edge of the field was a dense woodland.

Graham informed the women that it was a cemetery, not a graveyard. A graveyard denoted association with the church and holy grounds, whereas a cemetery was not necessarily indicative of any religious association.

"The ghosts of Tinselvania past," he said as he unlocked the chains on the front gates to the cemetery.

"Thank you for doing this, Mr. Cerne," Sylvia said.

"Oh, not a problem. I don't have much going on these days anyway," he said. "I usually just watch *ALF* and *Night Court* repeats and go to bed."

The gates didn't close properly. They hung crookedly from their hinges, swaying with the wind. Some of the cemetery's signs and plaques had been defaced or vandalized years before, making their inscriptions difficult to read.

The parts of the cemetery that hadn't been decayed or demolished through time, weather, or hooligans were lush and pristine. Even beneath the moonlight, it was obvious that Graham took great care tending to the headstones and statues. Headstones, grave markers, statues, monuments, and mausoleums were spread over the brown grass of the cemetery.

Frances ate a leftover chicken salad sandwich as they walked.

"Frances, why are you taking your sandwich with you, you big wackadoo?" said Willa.

"I'm still hungry," Frances said. "And there's no Cracker Barrel out here."

Frances took a big bite of her sandwich. She maintained direct eye contact with Willa as she chewed.

"Put a rocket under it, guys," Sylvia said, waving everyone over to her.

"The Persimmons mausoleum is over that way," Graham said, motioning to a general and nondescript area in the distance.

The sound of a bell ringing carried on the wind, faint and unhurried. Graham called the group over to one of the headstones.

"I've heard about these," Sylvia said. "People in the old days would sometimes accidentally be buried alive. So they invented these contraptions. If you woke up and you had been interred, you could pull on a string and the bell would alert everyone that you weren't really dead."

The bell was rusted and brown, attached to a crude and antiquated rigging system built into the earth next to the burial plot. It tinkled and dinged casually, unobtrusively. Any breeze made it ring.

Graham pulled a plastic bag filled with mustard seeds out of his pocket. He sprinkled the ground with them.

"See that grave?" he pointed, shining a light on a headstone with a strange symbol carved into it. "Supposedly that's the resting place of a vampire. I throw these on the ground as a precaution. Just in case vampires are real and can return from the dead. That way it will be too distracted by counting the mustard seeds to come after us."

"There could have been medical reasons for vampirism," said Sylvia. "Porphyria is a disease that causes sensitivity to sunlight and an urge to drink blood. Haematodipsia is a sexual thirst for blood. It's called Renfield's syndrome. Hemeralopia causes day blindness, an extreme sensitivity to light. The guy's psychotic tendencies aside, he probably suffered from those afflictions."

"How do you know that?" Graham asked.

"I used to Google a lot of vampire facts when I watched *Buffy the Vampire Slayer* and *Angel*."

"The Balkans believed that pumpkins and watermelons could become vampires," Willa added. She turned to Frances. "I watched *Buffy* and *Angel* too."

"Or maybe he was a vampire," Belle said. "Just because there's no definitive proof doesn't mean it doesn't exist. Like Bigfoot or aliens."

"Is all of this true or just fakelore?" Frances said. "Like how there's supposed to be a ghost in the background of *Three Men and a Baby* but it's just a cardboard cutout of Ted Danson?"

"Think about the misinformation that we have today," said Sylvia. "We have Christians Against Dinosaurs and people who don't believe in science or medicine. Back in those days, news and belief systems consisted of neighborhood gossip and conjecture, fear of angering imaginary deities, condemning anything different or subversive that goes against what people justified by their religions and moral superiority. Not much has changed with people, just nowadays we have ways to combat the ignorance. People just choose to ignore it."

"I read about an atheist who said that the idea of no afterlife wasn't disturbing for him, but it was disturbing that the bad people and hypocrites won't see any afterlife justice," said Frances. "That's always stuck with me."

"Maybe I'm just a superstitious old fool," Graham laughed at himself.

"Do you ever wonder about all of these people?" asked Belle. "What were their lives like? They were here once, just like us. They had whole lives filled with all kinds of dimensions and now it's over. We'll never know their stories or how they ended up here."

The headstones were scattered erratically, different sizes and configurations, with no discernable pattern as to where they were placed. Many of the tablets and monuments were severely damaged by weather, untended to for a nebulous amount of time. The writing and dates etched on the grave markers had faded away, making them difficult to read. Graham navigated the ladies through the cemetery.

"Over here," said Graham.

A large, locked mausoleum stood at the farthest end of the cemetery. Graham led the gang to its huge stone doors. It was covered in moss and other plants, as nature's elements began to swallow it up. There were ornate stained-glass windows on either side. Window-shaped small openings sat above them, as if to let air filter in and out.

"The Persimmons family," he said. He explained that it was a mausoleum with a crypt beneath it. The burial chamber was set up differently than others. There was an empty front room, then the sarcophagi of the Persimmons family in a second connecting room. Inside the walls of the mausoleum were more internment niches. He assured them that it was structurally sound.

"If we open that door, are we going to be attacked by a swarm of locusts? Or invoke some Pharaoh's curse and start dying mysterious deaths afterwards?" Belle asked. She had gone on many missions and faced danger hundreds of times in her life, but cemeteries and anything to do with rituals of the dead unnerved her.

"Let's find out," said Frances. "I hope they have those fancy seashell-shaped decorative soaps inside."

"Remember the Oregon Trail?" Belle said. "'You have died of dysentery.' This could actually happen to me here tonight."

A withered, dried-out wreath was hung on the doors of the mausoleum, adorned with a deep red-colored cloth ribbon. It looked old and weathered, but Graham pointed out he'd never noticed it there before.

"Enough standing around already," Sylvia said. "Let's rip off the Band-Aid."

"All right," Graham said. "Are we ready? As advertised. The final resting place of Chester Persimmons' family."

"If this turns out to be a giant escape room, I'm going to be really unhappy," said Frances.

Graham and Sylvia opened the large stone doors. They creaked and moaned in protest, as if they hadn't been moved in decades. The waning light from outside cast an orange glow in the doorway.

The inside smelled musty and old. The entry room was bare, aside from the cobwebs and dust. Air seeped in through the high windows. It was so dark inside that everyone had turned on flashlights in order to look around.

"The graves are in the next room," Graham said.

Frances took pictures on her camera phone. The flash went off, lighting up the hallway to the next row of burial chambers. As the burst of light came and went, she could have sworn that someone was standing in the doorway. A figure, a shadow, unmoving, watching them. She double-checked his pictures. There was nothing but the blackened entrance to the next room.

Graham slipped into the adjoining room, beckoning everyone to follow. Chester's parents' final resting place were two rectangular, above-ground stone enclosures. There were etchings, symbols, and words carved into the stone. Fresh flowers had been placed on top of both of the graves. The walls were lined with memorial plaques and dates for whoever in Chester's family was buried within.

Candles, melted and forgotten, were placed in holders intermittently spaced on the walls. Wax had congealed in streams beneath the sconces. Graham lit the remaining wicks, allowing dim light to aid in their ability to see the room.

Photos, frayed and yellowed from time, were pasted and stuck to the walls. The pictures showed people of all ages, smiling for the camera, unaware their happy moments would end up in a burial chamber.

The women inspected the photos, noting the different eras and generation of people in them. Their clothes and hairstyles varied from photo to photo, as if these were collected pictures from generations past. There were newer photos as well, from Polaroid pictures to the ones you would get developed at a one-hour photo shop There was no other major thread linking the people in the photographs.

There were pictures of happy times with family, friends, new babies, holidays, special events, birthdays, celebrations. The smiles on the faces of the people in the photos, full of joy and hope. Happy memories captured permanently, now relegated to this dank, cheerless wall, surrounded by tokens of death.

Some of the photos were taken as if the subject did not know they were being photographed. Private moments of families having dinner or a lone woman in her apartment, taken from a distance through windows. Random people walking down the street, at the playground, hiking through the woods, drinking coffee alone on a bench. Some of them were clearly pictures of Chester and his family through the years, but most of them featured unidentified and unknown persons.

Five red stockings hung on the adjoining wall. The names of their intended recipients were scrawled on the white trim– Chester, Noreen, Garland, Shepherd, John Patrick. The Persimmons family.

"Someone's been here recently," said Sylvia.

In the corner of the mausoleum was a rumpled red sleeping bag, empty canned foods and drink containers, a pile of clothes, a backpack, and a reindeer costume. The women leaned down to inspect it, not touching anything.

"Is it him?" asked Willa.

"It has to be," Sylvia said. "He's here."

Boom!

A loud bang emanated from beneath them. It came from within the crypt below their feet. Graham shined his flashlight on a trapdoor in the corner.

"Call Fuller," said Sylvia. Belle pulled out her cell phone and dialed.

The women heard more rustling and scraping noises from within the crypt, muffled by the trapdoor.

"Graham, get behind us," Sylvia instructed as she and the ladies each took out their handguns, flanking the trapdoor. Graham did as he was told.

Frances reached for the trapdoor's handle. Sylvia gave her a nod. Frances yanked the marbled panel open. The women shined their flashlights into the darkness below. There was a small, wide wooden staircase leading to the wet ground inside the crypt.

All noise and sound ceased. Fetid, moldy-smelling air poured out from the open trapdoor. Sylvia leaned down to get a closer look.

Before anyone could react, two large arms reached out from the blackness and pulled Sylvia into the crypt. The trapdoor slammed down hard. Frances, Willa, and Belle lunged forward to grab Sylvia and open the trapdoor but heard the sound of a deadbolt rapidly being locked. The door was now sealed shut.

Sylvia's eyes fluttered as she tried to adjust to the unlit chamber around her. The wind had been knocked out of her. She steadied herself and managed to get to her feet, gripping her flashlight. She banged on the trap door to no avail. She was trapped in this tomb. She shone the light around the tunnel, illuminating the cobwebs and the spiders that infested the corners. She was covered in dirt and grime from the fall, wet from the puddles from errant water that had accumulated in the soil over the years.

She heard the women above her banging and knocking, trying to break the door open to rescue her. She could hear movement and footsteps coming from within the crypt. The noise was faint and indistinct, Chester moving cautiously and purposely attempting to remain sly and evasive.

Her flashlight beam landed on three decomposing corpses propped against the wall. Sylvia couldn't tell if they were the bodies of the recently deceased in The Morning Light Cemetery that had been disinterred or if they were the latest victims of Chester Persimmons' latest murder spree. She lurched back, whacking her head on the exposed beams above her.

"I know you're in here, Chester," she said calmly, though her heart was racing. "It's Dr. Post. From The Calista Asylum. I'm here to help you."

"And who is going to help you?" a flat, low, gravelly voice intoned from the depths of the darkness.

"I'm going to take you with us so that we can talk. There doesn't need to be any more violence. You're safe now."

Unseen hands struck a match and lit a candle in the direction that the voice emanated from. It was so inky black that when the candle began moving, Sylvia couldn't see anything past the incandesce of the flame, which made the candle appear as if it were moving on its own, suspended in mid-air by ghostly, floating hands.

She raised her handgun. The phantom candle began to circle around her. As Chester drew closer, she saw that he was completely covered by a white sheet. He had dressed himself up as a twisted parody of a ghost. She couldn't see his eyes though he had cut eyeholes out of the sheet. He crept closer to her, then stepped back into shadows, toying with her.

Sylvia saw the quick gleam of the knife in his hand, its metal shining against the candlelight. The candle flame extinguished with one loud breath.

"Chester, you have to come with us," Sylvia said, maintaining her composure and gripping her handgun. "It's not too late. We can talk."

She felt Chester's hand brush the back of her neck. Sylvia spun around and kicked into the darkness. She felt her foot connect with his kneecap. He let out a pained groan and scurried back into the dark.

Darkness and silence. She heard her friends trying to dislodge the locked trapdoor. The crypt itself had gone eerily quiet, ominously tranquil.

"Aaaagh!" Chester yelled as he lunged for her, his face finally visible. He had taken off the ghost sheet. As soon as his face appeared in the beam of her flashlight, Sylvia reacted. She slammed her fist into him as hard as she could. He disappeared into the blackness.

It was definitely him, Sylvia confirmed. He was older and grayer, slightly heavier, but it was Chester Persimmons. She was sure of it.

Chester attacked. He pounced on her, throwing Sylvia to the ground. She lost the hold on her handgun and flashlight. Both tumbled to the floor while Chester launched into his ambush on Sylvia. They were like wild animals battling for the last scrap of food. It was a full-on, two-sided beatdown. As he hit and slashed at her, she struggled to see. She kneed him in the groin, throwing him off of her.

The beam of the flashlight illuminated where Chester fell. She picked up the flashlight and smashed it over his head. He still held the knife in his hand, wet with Sylvia's blood. Chester wasn't done. He kicked his leg out, tripping Sylvia. She regained her balance and pushed him onto the wooden staircase, where she repeatedly slammed his head into the slats of the steps.

"Sylvia!" she heard Frances yelling from above her. The marble of the trapdoor was cracking and giving way, allowing some of the light of the women's flashlights to shine into the crypt in slivers.

Sylvia backed away from Chester's motionless body. He was still breathing but unconscious. She found her handgun on the ground and aimed it at him. He began to stir, moaning and laughing, mocking her.

"This town needs to pay for what it did to me," he growled. As if making his last stand, he leapt to his feet and charged Sylvia.

She fired the handgun. Once, twice. Chester stopped in his tracks, almost shocked that he had been hit by the bullets. He felt his chest, soaked with his own blood, eyes wide in surprise. He made another rush toward Sylvia, his face contorted in a crazed, unhinged smile.

Bang!

Sylvia fired. Chester dropped to the ground. The bullet had him in the forehead. He lay crumpled on the ground, bleeding. He wasn't breathing anymore.

Chester Persimmons was dead. The nightmare was over.

Chapter 44

Nash, McCloskey, Jennings, Buchanan, and Cogan were all jolted from their sleep by their buzzing phones during the night with orders to come to The Morning Light Cemetery. They secured the crime scene, searched for any additional clues, collected evidence, and combed the expanse of graves for anything that could have been overlooked. Fuller had never been a part of a crime scene this large. Within hours, the area was overrun by police and CSI units. She had a mountain of paperwork to fill out, as well as meetings with law enforcement from other states and the FBI. She had to borrow the neighboring town's crime scene photographer since Tinselvania didn't have one of their own. She knew how the other police forces and law institutions looked at her town. She knew she was considered a small fish in a big pond.

Her investigation wouldn't be over yet. She still had to question witnesses, take statements, meet with detectives following the case, go through everything that was bagged and tagged, and keep the press from turning the crime scene into a circus. It was worth it to her. Tinselvania was safe. Her daughter was safe. Chester Persimmons wouldn't be coming back from the dead to avenge himself. She would have to notify his relatives and next of kin.

The story of Chester Persimmons' final moments was front-page news by sunlight. Media outlets, from newspapers to social media to online true crime blogs, recounted all of the grisly details for their readers. Television reporters, podcasters, and morbidly fascinated sightseers had already come and gone, with more on the way.

Pike drove Sylvia to the hospital to have her wounds cleaned and bandaged but they were able to return to The Happy Goose Inn by sunrise. Bertha and greeted them, asking questions that Sylvia wasn't ready to answer yet. She wanted a rest. Frances, Willa, and Belle met her at the inn and helped get her situated and packed their things. They would be leaving Tinselvania as soon as they could.

Chuck Brinkerhoff was in his room at the inn when the ladies arrived. He had already heard the news about Chester Persimmons on the local radio. He went downstairs to get some coffee and overheard Bertha's interrogation by Sylvia.

He returned to his room. A rage had built up inside of him. He was seething, his breaths ragged and angry. The fury and hate he felt boiled over. He smashed his desk chair against the wall.

Chester Persimmons was dead.

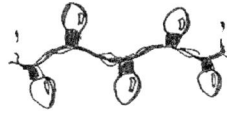

For the first time in as long as she could remember, Mary bounced out of bed with a fervor and energy that had nothing to do with work. She didn't turn on her self-help podcast. She didn't immediately check her phone or the stock market or the news. She ignored her computer altogether. Instead she played Jennifer Lopez's "Waiting for Tonight" and danced around her room as she got ready. It was Friday. She'd see Bright at work and then have the weekend free to spend quality time with him. He was going to be her date to the *Family Stone* party on Saturday.

Her mother and aunt were at the dining room table eating breakfast when Mary came downstairs. They filled her in on the Chester Persimmons story. Mary was shocked– Tinselvania was not a town used to crime-- but she was thankful that no one else was hurt and that he was stopped before it got too out of control.

Alvinia was lost in her own thoughts. Chester had been a family friend for many years, a partner in the tinsel business before he became the boogeyman people heard about on the news. She hadn't spoken to him in years. Yet she had a sadness inside of her because of it– the unnecessary loss of life of his victims, the senseless savagery, the decline of such a happy and hardworking man. His wife Noreen had been a friend of hers. She had babysat his children Garland and Shepherd. The Persimmons family had been a part of their lives, a part of Tinselvania.

She made up her mind that she would not dwell on it. She had never been someone who wallowed in sadness or pity. She wouldn't start today. She had a party to plan. She would include Chester's family and unfortunate victims in her prayers before bed that night.

"Oh, Mary," Alvinia said. "I need you to stop by your Uncle Cobden and Aunt Hepzibah's house and pick up a few things they borrowed over the years and never returned."

"I'll be at work, Mom," said Mary. "Why can't you and Aunt Elaine go?"

"Are you really going to make an old lady, your poor sweet mother who carried you for nine months and selflessly never asked for anything in return, schlep a whole bunch of heavy things in the cold?" Alvinia said. She didn't wait for Mary's answer. She handed Mary a list of items.

"Aren't they out of town?"

"There's a hide-a-key in the big rock next to their house. Let yourself in. See if they have any expensive wine we can borrow for the party."

"Borrow?"

"Fine, steal."

Mary grabbed herself a cup of coffee and finished getting ready for her day. When she finally looked at her phone, she saw she had dozens of missed texts and phone calls. When she read them and listened to her voice messages, she tried to control her increasing agitation and dismay.

She ran to her computer and typed the words "GleebGlob Tinsel Challenge" into the search bar. GleebGlob was the most famous social media video-sharing site in the nation. Thousands of results popped up instantly. Mary clicked on the first link and gasped as she watched.

Chapter 45

Ivy was in her car, parked in her driveway, rummaging through her backpack for her Advanced English Lit textbook. She had searched the house and couldn't find it anywhere. She reached underneath the passenger seat and pulled out a small, wrapped package. She sighed. She wasn't in the mood for another bloody, broken ornament.

She opened it anyway, despite her reservations. Inside the box was a gold-tinted translucent balloon filled with colorful bits of shiny confetti pieces shaped like tiny Santa Claus faces, icicles, and Christmas lights. The instructions included with the balloon directed Ivy to pop the balloon with the pin provided.

She did, as the glittery papers from inside exploded all over the inside of her car. She sighed, scolding herself for not thinking about the results of her actions, realizing now she'd need to clean out her car.

A note fell out of the inside of the balloon. It was wrapped up like a little scroll. Ivy unrolled it.

Dear Ivy, Will you go to the Christmas dance with me? Chip Wilson.

This was the gift Chip was talking about. Ivy stared at it for a moment. He didn't leave her the creepy ornament. This was the thoughtful and sweet gift he put in her car to find.

"Wait, Ivy!" Glory called as she dashed out of the house in her nightgown and robe, running to the car. She was holding Ivy's textbook in her hand.

"Where did you find this?" asked Ivy, rolling down the window and taking her book.

"Uh, your father and I needed it for something," Glory said.

"Did you guys use this to play 'bad teacher and naughty student?'" Ivy said. "You guys are disgusting! I'm going to throw up. I need to bleach my brain. Did you Clorox wipe this book down?"

"I don't know what you're talking about, sweetie!" smiled Glory, running off before Ivy asked any more questions. "I love you! Go be smart! I'm so proud of you!"

Ivy looked at the textbook in her hands, throwing it down and shuddering.

Chapter 46

Bright had made up his mind to tell Mary the truth. He was in town to convince the board of Tinsel Inc. to sell all of their shares to Yule Love It Christmas Corporation, thereby unseating her as CEO. He didn't want to lie to her. She didn't deserve it. Joseph tried to talk him out of telling her, pointing out the likelihood they'd both be fired. Bright didn't care. He could find another job. He'd take Joseph with him. He couldn't hurt Mary like that.

His good intentions were pushed to the wayside when he arrived at Tinsel Inc. and the staff and board members were abuzz with the public relations nightmare of the GleebGlob Tinsel Challenge. Thousands of videos from around the world showed tweens, teenagers, and college students (and some adults) who were taping tinsel to their butts and farting. The subsequent farts sent the tinsel fluttering and flying like ribbons tied to an air conditioner.

It was one of the most searched-for and popular memes and trending topics on the internet. The Tinsel Inc. hashtag was tacked on to all the ass-tinsel videos. Tinsel Inc. was in crisis lockdown and all of its employees were looking for a way to minimize the damage and gain control over the situation, as the association of tinsel and butts was not good for the company.

Mary held a staff meeting in the cafeteria. All of the board members, higher-ups, and employees were in attendance. Robin had already sent out press releases and statements that disavowed the use of tinsel for the purpose of dangerous, squicky entertainment and reaffirmed that tinsel was a beacon of hope, love, happiness, health, comfort, tradition, and Christmas. Liza and the legal team were crafted and sent cease-and-desist letters and emails. Tinsel Inc. made headline news for all the wrong reasons. The news of Chester Persimmons' capture and death had been eclipsed by the current calamity.

Mary reassured the staff that this was a fixable, temporary embarrassment for the company and to go about their workdays as usual. She asked that any links or videos the employees discovered be reported directly to her, Ethan, Josh, Liza, or Robin. Bright stood in awe of her; how she took command of the situation and heartened the employees that there was no need to panic or despair, even though she knew this was a publicity catastrophe that could seriously hurt their brand.

The meeting ended. Ethan, Josh, and Robin remained with Mary. Bright and Joseph made their way over to them.

"There's no such thing as bad publicity," Robin said. "Give me a couple of hours and I'll spin it so that even the most conservative, narrow-minded pinheads will be making their own ass-tinsel videos. It's all about presentation. We make tinsel-in-ass look cool. They'll do community theater plays about it."

"No, Robin," sighed Mary. "Shut it down."

"Remember, you are Janet Jackson and you're in control," Robin said to Mary as she headed off. She nodded at Bright and Joseph as she passed by.

"I know you have a crazy day ahead of you," said Bright to Ethan and Josh. "If you want to reschedule our meetings, we can."

"No, we're ready for you," Ethan said. "As long as a bunch of murder hornets don't show up and attack, we're still on like Donkey Kong."

"Yeah, no need to reschedule. We're all set," said Josh.

Ethan and Josh took off. Joseph made up an excuse to go do something, letting Mary and Bright have a minute together. He was going to go see Casper and make out with him in the janitor's closet.

"You handled yourself really well," he said.

"I don't know if my dad is laughing from up in Heaven or rolling over in his grave right now," said Mary. "'Ass-tinsel' is a word now. It's already on Urban Dictionary. How is taping tinsel to your butt fun or pleasurable?"

"Maybe we'll try it later and see. People eat Tide Pods, so you can't really look for deep meaning into why some people do the things they do. There's a reason there's a 1-800 number on shampoo bottles."

"'Ass-tinsel,'" laughed Mary, in spite of herself.

Bright laughed too. "It can't get worse, right?"

Chapter 47

Sylvia, Frances, Willa, and Belle had all given their statements and testimonies to Fuller and her crew. They were free to leave. They wished Fuller good luck and went to the inn.

They loaded their luggage and weaponry into the car. After saying goodbye to Bertha, they were on the road with Pike at the wheel.

Something nagged at the back of Sylvia's mind. She sat in silence on the drive, replaying the events of the previous night over and over in her head. The case was closed, as far as law enforcement stated. Yet for some reason, Sylvia was convinced they had overlooked something somehow.

She took a couple of Advil to deaden the pain of her wounds. The stabs and slashes Persimmons had inflicted on her were superficial, but they hurt like hell. Pike put on the SiriusXM Fleetwood Mac channel for the ladies. Sylvia leaned her head against the window and listened to "Landslide" as she tried to rest.

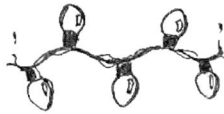

The police station had finally calmed down as the forensic teams and law enforcement from other states began to leave for their respective homes. Fuller was tired and sore, working on little sleep. She called Stacy to let her know everything was okay and she'd see her after school. She was at her desk, sorting through the paperwork and fielding phone calls when Deputy McCloskey interrupted her.

"Hey, Chief," McCloskey said. "I got a couple of phone calls that nobody has heard from any of the Frosts since yesterday."

Fuller sat up straight. "Okay, let's do a wellness check. Could you ask Buchanan and Cogan to come in here, please?"

Liza had spent the day exchanging emails and phone calls with the executives and legal team at GleebGlob, who issued orders for their users to remove their Tinsel Challenge videos. Liza herself had contacted users DumpsterDiver92, ButtGerbil, YourMama1234, KingDong, PimpDaddy, BoozeandCoozeCruise, BootlickerNJ, and KnittingGranny threatening legal action.

She stepped away from her computer for a moment to work out with her Shake Weight and listen to the soothing sounds of Enya's "Orinoco Flow (Sail Away)" to calm her mind and expend her anxiety-induced energy. She looked at the photo on her desk. Her favorite picture of her husband Fisher and ten-year-old son Paxton, smiling and laughing on the Tilt-A-Whirl at the town fair.

Liza's assistant forwarded a call to her. Liza braced herself, harnessing her inner stillness. She centered herself and picked up.

"Liza Wells," she said into the receiver.

The caller breathed heavily over the line. A dense, labored, leaden in-and-out wheezing.

"Hello?" Liza said.

"Tell them they got it wrong," the voice snarled.

"Who is this?"

"Tell them that I'm home."

The caller hung up. Liza, puzzled and unnerved, put her phone back on the receiver.

"Hey, Perry Mason," Robin said.

Liza jumped ten feet out of her chair. She clutched her chest and laughed, centering herself.

"Why so jumpy?" asked Robin. "Did I just catch you calling that 900 number where people just cry into the phone? Do you remember that commercial– $3.00 for the first minute, $1.95 for each additional minute?"

"You scared me," Liza said. "I just got a creepy phone call."

"College loan collectors?"

"Ah, just some pervy townie scrote, probably."

"I brought you some Fruity Pebbles cheesecake," Robin said, holding out a plate. "I figure we both deserve a break after what a shitshow today has been."

Robin sat down across from Liza's desk.

"So much for bowling tonight," said Liza. "We're not getting out of here til dinnertime. Fisher's going to have to make dinner, which isn't good for any of us since he can't even microwave Chef Boyardee. He made 'leftover surprise' once and the surprise part was that even the dog wouldn't eat it, so we ordered takeout. Remember that movie *Better Off Dead*, when the mom makes the green Jell-O mold and it starts to crawl away? I'd eat that over anything Fisher makes."

"And you guys always wonder why I don't want to get married. Reason number 575."

"Fisher and Paxton are my favorite things about Christmas. Aside from you guys, of course, and my family. But having your own little family during the holidays, it's really special."

"Gag me with a spoon. Okay, I'm going to go retch now," Robin said, getting up. "I have to get back to my regularly scheduled program. Public relations wait for no one. And I want to find Chuck. He didn't show up to work today. I hope I didn't scare him away after last night, when I put on *Gangbangs of New York* and brought Happy Gilmore out to play."

"Wait," said Liza. "Happy Gilmore, as in Adam Sandler?"

"No, Happy Gilmore is what I call my vibrator."

"Why do I ask?" Liza grumbled. "I only have myself to blame."

"He ran away before Happy got anywhere near him. He just asks lots of questions about Mary and Tinsel Inc. and the people who live here. Like an investigative journalist. Apparently, my heaving bosom doesn't seem to have much of an effect on him. Maybe I have cooties. I got my cooties shot in fourth grade. You guys gave it to me."

Robin got to the door and turned back to Liza. "Wouldn't 'Ass-Tinsel' be an awesome drag queen name?"

Liza laughed and went back to her emails as Robin went off to find Chuck.

Chapter 48

Officers Kenny Buchanan and Barnaby Cogan had been sent to check on the respective homes of the Frost family. They didn't get any answers when they knocked and announced themselves when they entered each home. All of the houses showed no signs of anything abnormal. No foul play, no cause for concern that anything was wrong.

Patience Frost had been one of their teachers growing up. When they arrived at her house, there were no red flags or bells to signal any reason to be worried.

It was odd that a birthday cake for Gordon sat uncovered in the center of their dining room table, even though no one was home. A few pieces had been eaten. The yellow cake inside looked like it had gone stale and dry.

They radioed Fuller, who called them back into the station. She was busy fielding phone calls and press conferences over the Chester Persimmons story. Their instructions were to call the Frosts' family members and then make another round to their houses in two hours. They were to file missing persons reports on all of them. At that point, Fuller didn't care if she was seen as an alarmist. She would rather be safe than sorry.

When Noelle went to pick Dashi and Acorn up from school, Acorn's teacher, Mr. Caldwell, pulled her aside to discuss Acorn's latest art project. Acorn and her class were tasked with drawing a picture of their friends. Acorn drew a reindeer named Rudy. Rudy was splattered in bright red blood, standing over the bodies of two victims whose eyes were X's and mouths were little screaming O's. All of this was drawn in cheerful crayon.

At home, Dashi went off to play with his Roblox and Avengers action figures while Noelle asked Acorn about her drawing.

"That's my friend Rudy," a guileless Acorn said.

"Why did he hurt the people in the picture?" asked Noelle.

"He said that they were bad people and he is going to bathe in the blood of his enemies."

"Who told you that?"

"Rudy!" insisted Acorn.

"Have you been watching cable when we told you not to?"

"No, Mom. We watched *While You Were Sleeping* together, 'member?"

"Rudy isn't real, Acorn."

"Yes, he is! He hates this family and everyone who lives here."

"Acorn, that's not a nice thing to say."

"I'm not lying! You can ask him yourself!"

Acorn dragged Noelle to her closet. She pulled the door open to prove to Noelle that Rudy had been there. Nothing was out of place. No sign or evidence to lend credence to Rudy's existence. Noelle looked at Acorn, trying not to seem angry or frustrated. She wanted to encourage Acorn's imagination, but not in the gory, graphic direction of the drawing.

"He must have gone back to the North Pole," Acorn said, shoulders slumped. Pleased by that answer, she trotted off to have some vegan cookies.

Noelle stood silently for a moment, staring into Acorn's closet, utterly befuddled.

"Okay then," she said, on the move to share some vegan cookies with her daughter.

Chapter 49

Robin had gone full investigative reporter in her quest to locate Chuck Brinkerhoff. She sent an email to Human Resources under the guise of innocuous business-related questions she claimed to need Chuck's paperwork for. The head of the HR department wrote back a half an hour later.

There was no one by the name of Chuck Brinkerhoff working at Tinsel Inc.

Robin called Bertha Havighurst over at The Happy Goose Inn and tried to play off her line of inquiry as innocent and breezy; she was just seeing if Chuck was around. Bertha would know; she was his aunt after all.

Except she wasn't.

Bertha didn't know him personally, let alone him being related to her. Bertha hadn't seen him that day and he hadn't checked out yet. When she called up to his room, there was no answer.

Who was Chuck Brinkerhoff? Robin texted Mary to reveal the information she'd uncovered.

Mary was so inundated with pushback and damage control over the Tinsel challenge videos that she hadn't spoken to Bright all day. The workday had ended for most people but she still had emails to answer, explanations to give, board members to reassure, and angles to spin from negative to positive. Casper left some ibuprofen and a Gatorade on her desk for her before he took off for his date with Joseph.

She had texted Kara, Liza, and Robin in their group chat to let them know she wouldn't be able to meet for bowling. They all responded the same; they had their own responsibilities to the company that would keep them occupied overtime and they'd see her tomorrow for the *Family Stone* party.

Then there was the whole Chuck debacle. Mary reasoned that he must have been a spy sent from a competing tinsel company to learn the inner workings of their company and capture their secrets. She made a note to hire extra security and have Liza prepare legal documents in case they had to charge Chuck with fraud. A security breach would not be good for the company. More emails she'd need to send before the day was through. She was concerned but couldn't get lost in that. There was too much else to do. This was her life. She was a high-powered executive and had to deal with everything that came along with that title, good and bad.

Ethan and Josh were at her door. She looked up and smiled at her cousins. They looked as battered and tired as she felt.

"What a day, huh?" Ethan said. "No fun being the boss sometimes."

"What are you guys still doing here?" Mary said. "Go home to your families. I don't want you to miss dinner."

"You don't have to stay either," said Ethan. "This'll all still be here Monday morning."

"Yeah, Mary," Josh said. "Let's call it a day. Susan's still at work so your mom is watching Hewney and Kyle. Last time she babysat, she told them if they didn't eat the crusts on their peanut butter and jelly, they'd never get hair on their chests. They're eleven and seven. They don't want hair on their chests yet. So now they scream bloody murder as soon as they see a bread loaf."

"Our tinsel brand now conjures up images of people's dirty bungholes. I need to be on top of this. You have kids and wives. This job is my version of that. You go. I'll take care of things here. There's no way to erase the internet, is there?"

"Years ago, I worked with a guy who had a nervous breakdown. He kept going up to random people on the street and on the subway and saying things like 'You got served!' and 'Maybe I'm born with it! Maybe it's Maybelline!' and he found a nice girl and got married and had kids. So, believe me, if he can find somebody, you can too," said Ethan.

"That's a really comforting story, Cousin Ethan."

"Dad would know what to do here," Josh said. "Your dad too, Mary."

"I don't know if either of them would be prepared for ass-tinsel videos," said Mary. "Really, please go. I have a conference call with investors from Ireland and Scotland in a bit."

Ethan and Josh nodded in understanding. As they left, they passed Bright in the hallway and exchanged pleasantries. Bright headed to Mary's office, knocking as he entered. He was carrying bags of burgers and fries.

"I thought you'd be hungry," he said. "And I thought you might like some company."

Mary dove into the bag, thrilled at the prospect of delicious burgers and fries. Bright held out a Diet Pepsi and a chocolate milkshake for her as well.

"You get me," she said.

Chapter 50

Sylvia was home again. Her husband was downstairs making dinner for them. Richard, her husband of over three decades, was a professional stuntman and daredevil like his idol Evel Knievel. He was an excellent sparring partner for Sylvia.

She was resting in bed. The Advil had worn off and she was sore from her bruises and slashes. That wasn't the only reason she couldn't relax. Something was eating at her, tickling the back of her mind and not allowing her to unwind.

Chester and Noreen Persimmons had two sons, Garland and Shepherd. Why were there five stockings in the mausoleum? There was one for someone named John Patrick. She had double-checked Chester's family tree and there was no John Patrick Persimmons.

She finally had time to check her emails. When she did, she saw that early that morning, she had a message from her contact at the asylum in New York that housed Persimmons. It was the visitor's log. She heard her husband calling for her to come have some food, but she was fixated on going through each and every name.

There it was. John Patrick, the name signed in and repeated over and over for ten years of visits. His name wasn't John Patrick Persimmons, though. It was John Patrick Colqhoun. Who was he? How was he associated with Chester Persimmons?

Sylvia texted Frances, Willa, and Belle and told them to meet her at her place as soon as they could. She was trying to put the puzzle pieces together. Chester Persimmons had help escaping. He had protection. His guardian was still out there. The danger wasn't over.

John Patrick Colqhoun was most likely somewhere in Tinselvania.

Chief Fuller was in the evidence room, searching through the items Sylvia and the ladies found in the Persimmons' mausoleum. Chester's backpack was full of paperwork, fake identifications, stolen clothing, copies of his patient files, and newspaper articles. One news clipping stood out to her. A fire that burned down a house and killed an entire family in the 1990s in Collinwood, leaving only one survivor. She couldn't figure out Chester's ties to the family or location. The fire had occurred before he had moved from Tinselvania to Nevada. What was the connection?

Nash interrupted her as she sorted through Chester's personal effects, many of which weren't even really his.

"Chief?" he said. "I just got off the phone with the folks over at the morgue in Spivey Point. Chester Persimmons' body is missing."

Chapter 51

Mary was finally on her way home from work when she remembered her mom's list. She went home, changed clothes, and hopped in the car. When she arrived at her Uncle Cobden and Aunt Hepzibah's mansion, there was only one outside light on and none from the inside. She wondered what part of the world they were in. It was accepted by the family that Uncle Cobden and Aunt Hepzibah kept everything. They were level-one hoarders and had so much impractical, unusable junk in storage at their place. They held on to everything.

She found the spare key and let herself in. The house was dark and almost sinisterly quiet. She wished she'd invited Bright to keep her company, not only because her uncle and aunt's house was somewhat frightening, but because she wanted to see him. She'd have to be patient until tomorrow.

She turned on lights as she went into each room, picking up the items her mother had requested. As she looked over the list, she realized her mom had sent her on a scavenger hunt to retrieve any and everything Uncle Cobden and Aunt Hepzibah had borrowed over the years, not just things she needed for the *Family Stone* party. Her mother was basically having her commit breaking-and-entering so she could get her ridiculous personal items back. She felt like she was invading Uncle Cobden and Aunt Hepzibah's privacy as she went from room to room. There were dozens of rooms to look through.

The mansion was so big and open that Mary's footsteps echoed as she walked. She checked off each item on the list as she found it. Her mother had written the word "my" before each individual item to emphasize her ownership claims. Mary sighed. She held her mom's list out.

Morgan Fairchild's Super Looks book. Pinwheels. Giant globe. Xylophone. 1998 "Sexy NYC Firefighters" calendar. Etch-A-Sketch. *Betty and Me* comics. Teddy Ruxpin doll. Easy-Bake Oven. Paintball gun set. Waffle maker. *Super Mario Brothers* Nintendo cartridge. Cracker Barrel gift card. Cadbury Crème Eggs. Antique clock. View-Master with *The A-Team* reels. ShamWow. Vintage curlers. *Rocky IV* soundtrack CD. Pogo stick. Folding chairs. Presidential commemorative plates. Pool floaties. Bagpipes. Kaleidoscope. Hula hoop. Rotary phone. Answering machine. Fuzzy seat cushion. Boogie board. *Jock Jams* CD. Velour painting of an angel looking down on Earth. *The Mentalist* throw blanket. Precious Moments figurines. Bedazzled corn-on-the-cob holders. Decoupage cookie jar projects. Neil Diamond's *Moods* vinyl. June 2001 *Good Housekeeping* magazine with Sally Field on the cover. *My Best Friend's Wedding* and *Bridget Jones's Diary* movie posters. Gingham tablecloth. Leg warmers. Dunkaroos. Afghans. Ecto-Cooler. Yurt. Ham.

Mary had so many questions. Why did she want some of these things in the first place? Why would Cobden and Hepzibah want them? Why did they never return them? What was her mom going to do with so many useless items? What was the meaning of life? Why did her mom ever buy a *Jock Jams* CD? What was the sudden rush to get these items back? And some of the objects were vague and nondescript, so how would she know which ones belonged to her mother?

She opened the door to Uncle Cobden's office. His desk was stacked with files and papers. Bills of sale, contracts, financial reports, personal histories, criminal reports, genealogy records, and thousands of photographs spanning decades; all pertaining to Tinsel Inc. and the townspeople of Tinselvania.

More papers and photos were pinned to a large corkboard hanging on the wall. Scribbled notes, dates, a timeline of events, sort of like something seen on a cop show. Uncle Cobden was researching and documenting something, but as far as Mary knew, he'd never mentioned it to the family. She'd ask her mom about it later.

Hanging high over the bookshelves were the mounted moose and deer heads from Cobden and her dad's hunting days.

Her Uncle Cobden, like her father, was fascinated by puzzles, contraptions, and engineering. A table in the corner was cluttered with tools, hardware, gadgets, and appliances. Cobden and her father used to make their own spring-activated mousetraps. Ethan and Josh had inherited the family aptitude for creating inventions and mechanisms, but it had passed by Mary completely.

Mary leaned in for closer inspection when she heard the noise.

Thunk.

Something on the floor above her. It sounded as if a large object was being moved. Footsteps followed. The ceiling above her creaked slightly. The noises were muffled but she could hear that someone else was in the house. On the floor directly above her. Mary paused and listened intently.

"Uncle Cobden? Aunt Hepzibah?" she called out hesitantly. They weren't supposed to be home. If it even was them. Had they come home from their trip early? Maybe Ethan or Josh had stopped by to pick something up.

She made her way quietly out into the hallway, listening for more sounds. She made it into the main hallway to the foyer. The house had gone silent.

There it was again. The creaking, its origin unobtainable. A shuffling sound, followed by footsteps. Mary tried to assuage her fears by reminding herself that it was an old house. Old houses make strange noises. Yet she couldn't shake the feeling of apprehension.

She gathered what she'd collected from the list. The rest of it could wait. She hesitated a moment before opening the door. Once she did, she nearly shrieked in terror when Ethan stepped into her path.

"Cousin Mary!" he said. "What are you doing here?"

"Having twenty years of my life being taken from me," she said. She held up her box of Alvinia's things. "I'm on a mission from Mom. What are you doing? Lurking in the dark and waiting to scare me?"

"Sorry about that," said Ethan, pointing at his house across the road. "I saw Mom and Dad's lights go on and came to see what was up. You go on home. I'll lock up here. I have some stuff I need to grab here anyway."

"I know this is going to sound cuckoo, but I heard noises inside. Like people walking around."

"This old house has lots of ghosts," Ethan said. Mary couldn't tell if he was kidding. He told her "good night" and went inside.

Mary surveyed the area outside. It was a star-filled, cool night. The street was empty and everything was quiet. She got in her car and headed home.

Chapter 52

Bertha wasn't in the habit of intruding into the guests' rooms, but she felt justified as she unlocked Chuck Brinkerhoff's door. She had placed several calls to his room to no avail. After she had spoken with Robin, her feeling of unease had increased, even knowing that Chester Persimmons was dead.

Chuck's room was tidy and well-kept except for a broken chair in the corner. Bertha looked under his bed and through his closet. His bags and clothes were still in the room. She went into the bathroom and pulled the shower curtain back. On his dresser was a police scanner that crackled and hissed as it picked up the calls and conversations between local law enforcement through the static and beeps.

In the tub was an artillery bag. It was full of weapons, from guns and knives to other sharp instruments of destruction that she didn't know the names for. Bertha closed the curtain and hurried out of Chuck's room.

When she got back down to the front desk, she placed a call to Chief Fuller.

Frances, Willa, and Belle met Sylvia at her house. She recounted the evidence and her theories that John Patrick Colqhoun was somehow involved with Chester Persimmons' escape and subsequent arrival in Tinselvania.

They pored over the visitor's log as Willa did an online search for John Patrick Colqhoun's identity. There were hundreds of John Patrick Colqhouns in the world.

"Bertha Havighurst," Sylvia said, as if struck by an epiphany. "She told us she lived in Tinselvania her entire life except for a year when she was in California. Right after her marriage to Chester Persimmons ended."

"What is her maiden name?" asked Willa, already typing Bertha's name into the government database Frances gave her access to.

Willa sat back and admired her handiwork as Bertha's information appeared on the screen. Sylvia, Frances, and Belle surrounded her.

Bertha Havighurst was born Bertha Colqhoun. She had given birth to a son, John Patrick, in California over forty years ago. He was given up for adoption. No father was listed on the birth certificate, but the timeline made sense.

"She had a child and never told Chester," said Frances, formulating a theory. "But the son found out who his parents were and reached out to Chester Persimmons. They formed a bond, based on their shared anger that they felt betrayed by Bertha. They created a plan to get Chester out of the asylum and punish Bertha."

"Nothing happened to Bertha, though," Belle said. "Do you think she knows that the son she gave away knows about her? Those records were supposed to be sealed. If she was Persimmons' intended target, he failed."

"Not if John Patrick Colqhoun is still in Tinselvania," said Sylvia. "We have to go back."

The ladies retreated back to their respective houses and assembled their belongings and gear. They had already informed Chief Fuller of their speculations and warned her that Bertha was at risk. Richard, who knew it was futile to try and convince her to stay home and rest, kissed Sylvia goodbye as she got into the car with Pike to pick up the rest of the women.

Chapter 53

Iola Fuller had never had to deal with this amount of crime in her entire tenure as chief. She assigned orders to her respective staff, letting them know they wouldn't be home for dinner. Deputy Nash was assigned guard duty for Bertha Havighurst at The Happy Goose Inn. Deputy McCloskey and Officer Cogan were tasked to locate Chuck Brinkerhoff and bring him in for questioning over his arsenal of deadly weapons and possible link to Chester Persimmons. Officer Buchanan was sent to keep watch at The Morning Light Cemetery in case any of Persimmons' suspected associates showed up. Officer Jennings was on patrol, making sure the neighborhood had a visible police presence.

The morgue at Spivey Point was locked down for the night. Nobody there had any new information to give anyway. Chester Persimmons' body was somehow stolen. The security cameras in the morgue captured the break-in. It was a lone individual, dressed in all black with a hood covering his face. The security detail at Spivey Point was minimal; like Tinselvania, it was a small town with little to no crime. The unlawful removal of a corpse was unheard of, something no one expected.

Fuller awaited Sylvia, Frances, Willa, and Belle's arrival. She sifted through Persimmons' belongings, searching for clues as to who his accomplice could be. If he even had an accomplice. There was no concrete proof that Persimmons had a co-conspirator, despite the fact someone had absconded with his body. It could be someone he had ties to, who was criminal in his own right; it didn't mean the unknown man was a murderer or violent degenerate.

She locked the front office and got in her police cruiser. While she waited for the women to get to town, she'd swing by and see if any of the Frost family had shown up at their houses.

Officer Kenny Buchanan walked the perimeter of The Morning Light Cemetery, trying to keep himself hidden amongst the shadows in case any suspicious-looking characters showed up. He'd parked his police cruiser by the edge of the trees, far away from the main roads that weaved through the cemetery.

He crept back to the car for the ziplocked sandwich and thermos of coffee he brought. The cemetery was empty, which was fine by him. He didn't want to see any bloodthirsty ghouls or shambling zombies or graverobbers.

He paused mid-bite of his sandwich. He swore someone was lurking by one of the trees in the distance. He turned his car headlights on, illuminating the area in front of him.

Nobody was there. He watched and waited. He flicked the headlights off.

Boom!

At the exact moment, someone bolted in front of his cruiser and into the woods. Buchanan watched the shadow run right in front of his windshield, opaque and fast. He sprung from his seat, gun drawn, and flashlight aimed into the forest.

Only the wind rustling against the branches of the trees greeted him.

Chapter 54

The *Family Stone* party day was here. Alvinia and Aunt Elaine spent the day decorating, setting up the movie room with red-cushioned theater seats and a large white screen, and organizing the table for the snacks, food, and drinks.

Mary worked all morning from home, still beleaguered by emails and phone calls from worried investors, vendors, and associates. Thankfully, most of the ass-tinsel videos had been shut down or removed from the internet. She knew she simply had to wait until another company had some sort of scandal, even better if it were a celebrity, and Tinsel Inc. would be old news and could go back to the business of spreading love and joy through tinsel.

Bright had sent her a video of a man dressed as The Grinch, dancing by himself on a disco dancefloor and really feeling the music. She laughed, not only because it was a cute video, but because she found it symbolic of Bright himself, though he didn't realize it.

Her mother insisted, as she did every year, that Mary wear a specific dress for the party. Alvinia had saved all of her own old clothes. This year, she'd hung a hunter green-colored dress made of thick, velvet-like material with a lace collar on Mary's closet hook. It was a shapeless, plain, old-fashioned frock that looked like it belonged to a prim schoolteacher in the 1800s, but Mary was not going to argue with her mother. Kara had promised to bring over a belt for it that would match. Mary wasn't exactly fashion-forward anyway; she wore nice clothes to work but didn't love to shop so it was one less wardrobe choice she had to make for the week.

"Mary!" her mother called up to her. "Where is the Sanka and the Five Alive?"

"Probably in the early 2000s, when they stopped being made, Mom!" Mary called back. "You ask me this every year! Sanka and Five Alive aren't fancy party drinks!"

"Where are the sacks for the potato sack races?" Alvinia shouted.

Mary stood up and made her way downstairs. She wasn't yelling down to her mom anymore. Alvinia and Aunt Elaine looked harried and unkempt, not dressed for the party yet but trying to put the finishing touches on all the last-minute details.

"Mom, it's like thirty degrees out today. Nobody is going to want to do potato sack races."

"I got a bouncy castle for the kids," Alvinia said. "The delivery driver is dropping it off at 2:00. Will you go put the big space heaters outside for me? And please put a nicer shirt on and brush your hair. You look like you just got back from one of those ayahuasca vision quests all the kids are doing."

"Yeah, like you two are ready for supermodel documentary hour. I'll alert the pageant circuit," mumbled Mary as she went to go change.

"What, honey?" her mom shouted.

"Love you!" said Mary.

Joseph and Bright were getting ready for the party. Bright tried on six different outfits, wanting to impress Mary but not have it be obvious that he was trying to impress her. It was a precarious balance. Joseph finally came to Bright's rescue and chose for him– a burnt orange-red button-down, pressed dark blue jeans, and a matching bow tie.

"What would I do without you?" Bright said.

"It's nice to see you happy," said Joseph.

"It's nice to be happy," Bright smiled. He kicked himself internally. He needed to refocus and remember his objective, what he was doing in Tinselvania in the first place. His blossoming romance with Mary couldn't be allowed to derail his ambition.

"You're allowed to be happy, Bright," Joseph said as he used a lint roller on Bright's clothes. "You are allowed to have hope for the future, to have a different life, to want things for yourself. Your dreams and goals can change. It's okay if they do, or if you're struggling with them."

Bright laughed internally. Joseph, his very own Dr. Phil. His cheerleader and supporter. He fixed his shirt collar in the mirror.

"What about you? Are you happy?"

"Yes. I really like it here. I really like Casper," Joseph said, his voice going soft for a moment. "I've even considered... I don't know, staying. Seeing how things go."

Bright knew that Joseph was waiting to see if he'd react poorly to the news. He wasn't going to stand in the way of Joseph's happiness.

"I think you should do whatever is best for you," said Bright.

"You'd be okay? You just said you don't know what you'd do without me."

"I'll manage. And who knows? Maybe I'll stay. You never know. Life is too short not to follow your dreams. You've been an amazing assistant. You deserve a chance to see what's out there."

"Okay," said Joseph. "This conversation is getting so cheesy we're going to need crackers to go with it. We should get going."

Bright and Joseph passed Bertha at the front desk as they left. They exchanged "good evenings" and were on their way.

Chapter 55

Bertha gave Deputy Nash a room at the inn to stay in while he was watching over her. She protested against the security detail but he refused to hear it, insisting she'd be safer with him on guard. She hadn't told Nash about the child she gave up for adoption, fearing his judgment, which never came. She wondered if their theories were correct. Why would John Patrick want to hurt her? She was his real mother, after all. He couldn't be so angry at her that his only solution was to team up with Chester and enact a violent plan against her, could he? She couldn't wrap her head around it.

The past always had a way of catching up with people. Bertha kept thinking that to herself as she went about her daily business, trying to pretend that everything was fine and she wasn't sad or scared. But she was. She wondered how Chuck Brinkerhoff fit into all of this. She had no connection to him. Not that she knew of, anyway.

She was going to bring Nash something to eat in a little while. For now, she was letting him get some rest. Nothing was going to happen to her.

She had no idea that Deputy Nash was dead in his temporary room. The reindeer had stopped by unnoticed and stabbed Nash repeatedly until he expired. It left Nash spread out on the bed, bloody and gored.

It had some other people to visit and then a party to go to.

The party was starting as most of the guests began to arrive. Christmas decorations covered every inch of the house, from the lights and tree to every wall and surface that could hold holiday spangles and trimmings. A mixture of white and rainbow lights blinked on and off along the walls, the windows, the hallway, the door frame, and the outside of the house.

Alvinia and Aunt Elaine were decked out in their most glittery and eye-catching eveningwear. Kara, Liza, Robin, Tyler, and Mike called up to Mary, who was in her room, staring at her reflection. The hunter-green monstrosity her mother chose for her was not making her feel confident and bold like she had hoped.

"Get your buns down here, Mary!" Robin called.

Mary sighed. This was the best it was going to get for now. When she rounded the hallway corner to the top of the stairs, she saw why her friends were so eager to get her downstairs. Bright stood with them, a beaming smile directed right at her.

Liza pressed "play" on her iPhone and "Kiss Me" by Sixpence None the Richer played while Mary descended the staircase. Just like Laney Boggs in *She's All That*. Her friends were recreating that moment for her. She shook her head at them, loving and hating them at the same time.

"Pretend you're walking in slow motion!" Kara instructed her.

"You look beautiful," said Bright as Mary reached the bottom of the stairs.

Bright got to meet the families of Mary's best friends in rapid succession. Kara introduced her husband Nick and daughters Eve and Astrid, Liza introduced her husband Fisher and son Paxton, and Robin introduced her "sort of" boyfriend Angus O'Connell, who looked like a young Bruce Willis.

Bing Crosby and Rosemary Clooney's "Silver Bells" played on the record player as Joseph and Casper drank wine and chatted on the couch. Ivy, Betsy, Ellie, Stacy, and Georgina were in the entertainment room. Ethan, Heloise, Josh, Susan, Noelle, Jed, Glory, and Cotter were mingling and laughing. The under-thirteen crowd– Dulcie, Maisie, Eugenie, Hewney, Kyle, Dashi, Acorn, Eve, Astrid, and Paxton– were outside jumping inside the bouncy castle and giggling. Kara kept checking on the kids until Nick finally pulled her away, reassuring her that they were fine and that Dulcie was watching over them.

"This is the first *Family Stone* party your parents have ever missed," Alvinia said to Ethan and Josh. "I hope they're having a good time, wherever they are this week. Tell them we'll miss their famous mincemeat pie."

"We talked to them earlier today," said Ethan. "They said to have a fun time and they'll be seeing you soon."

"Holidays aren't the same without family," said Alvinia. "I miss Bernard every day, but most of all around Christmas."

"We think about Uncle Bernard all the time too, Aunt Mary," Josh said.

"Oh, don't let me get all sentimental," Alvinia said. "We're making new memories tonight. We are blessed and grateful, right? Every day is a gift."

"That's why they call it the 'present,'" said Josh.

"That's some crazy shit about Chuck, huh?" Tyler asked.

"I knew there had to be a reason he wouldn't sleep with me," said Robin.

"Did you really want to make it with some weirdo whose name you don't even really know?" Kara said.

"Ah, it wouldn't be the first time," Robin shrugged.

"Hey, you ladies promised no business talk tonight," Fisher said.

"It's not business," Liza said. "It's like an episode of *Unsolved Mysteries*. I can hear Robert Stack's voiceover telling us the tale of the stranger called Chuck."

"How did no one notice he didn't actually work at Tinsel Inc.?" Mike said. "That seems like a huge lapse in security."

"Three hundred-plus employees, head of security out, small town mentality," Liza said. "Nobody would've thought that someone would use a fake name and identity to get a fake job here."

"I wonder what he wanted," Tyler said.

"Hey, guys, let's change the subject," said Bright. "It's a party! Let's celebrate Mary and her family and all the great, happy things in our lives."

The gang cheered to that.

Aunt Elaine tapped on her wine glass and directed everyone into the music room, over near the grand white piano. Noelle and Glory corralled all the kids. Alvinia sat in front of the keys as Aunt Elaine had the adults gather around her. She had a microphone in her hand. This was happening.

Alvinia began to play the notes Eartha Kitt's "Santa Baby" and Aunt Elaine belted it out like she was giving a concert at Madison Square Garden, vamping and serenading the audience. If Simon Cowell were there, it would be a "no" from him. That didn't stop Aunt Elaine. She may not have had rhythm, pitch, or talent, but she didn't care; in her mind, she was singing like Christina Aguilera. Mary could have sworn she heard dogs howling in the distance at Aunt Elaine's warbling and screeching.

"My ears hurt," Maisie said, looking up at her father. Ethan plugged her ears with his index fingers and stood in place behind her.

When Aunt Elaine was done, everyone applauded heartily, all in on the unspoken agreement to encourage and support her. They quickly realized their mistake when she launched into Bobby Helms' "It's Beginning to Look a Lot Like Christmas." They were trapped.

Once Aunt Elaine's performance was over and her captives were released to mingle, Noelle rearranged her mother's poinsettias around the table and repositioned the labels she'd created for each of the food dishes. The guests were eating, drinking, and mingling. The kids had retreated to the playroom and the teenagers went back to the entertainment room.

"If anyone needs any coasters for their drinks, they're right here!" announced Noelle, pointing at the spot on the table she'd placed them on.

"The table looks great, honey," Jed said, giving her a kiss.

Mary was with Kara, Liza, Robin, Tyler, and Mike in the living room as Nick, Fisher, and Angus went to get plates for their significant others. She looked up to see her mother sitting with Bright, flipping through an old photo album.

"Mom," Mary said. "What are you doing?"

"Just showing Bright some pictures of you!" Alvinia said cheerfully, pointing to a photograph. Bright was smiling and laughing at the old pictures. "That's from when Mary was little. She refused to go potty on the toilet and would hide behind the couch to make her doodies."

"Well, this should be good for my emotional well-being," said Mary.

"This was Mary and her father when they both went through their mullet phase," said Alvinia. "And this is her in eighth grade when she would dress like Debbie Gibson. She wore hats and vests to school every day and wore Electric Youth perfume. It didn't make her very popular with the other kids."

Alvinia flipped the page. Mary felt her face getting redder. Page after page of Mary in laughably cheesy outfits and out-of-date hairstyles.

All of her many awkward moments captured for posterity. Alvinia could barely contain her joy at getting to show them.

"And that's Mary and me at the square-dancing competition. She came in second place! And here's us at the Color Me Badd concert. That's her and the girls in the talent show. They sang and danced to Stacey Q's 'Two of Hearts.' Look at those side ponytails and jelly bracelets. And there she is at her Abstinence Club meeting. They gave all the kids promise rings and merkins to wear."

"I remember Abstinence Club," Robin said. "Mary, you were president, weren't you? I've heard Mormons tell Mary she's too frigid."

"I'm not in Abstinence Club anymore," mumbled Mary, mostly to Bright.

"Oh, and her on her horse Penelope!" Alvinia said. "Her uncle had a horse farm and she had a favorite horse. Unfortunately, Penelope had to be put down."

"You said Penelope went to live on a farm in Oklahoma!" Mary said.

"I know," said Alvinia. "You were so sensitive. Your father and I didn't want to hurt you and we didn't want to pay for a child psychologist. But think of the positive– Penelope lives on in all the glue you used for the collages you pasted together when you were a teenager."

"Mother, put that away or I'll tell everyone about that John Cena eight-by-ten autographed picture you keep in your room and kiss good night every night."

"Oh please," Alvinia said. "I'm not embarrassed. I have one of Garret Dillahunt too."

Mary suddenly realized why her mother used to watch *Raising Hope* with her.

"I hope that picture gives you lip herpes," Mary said.

"No, you don't, because then you'd catch it since I kiss you goodnight too!" Alvinia turned back to the photos. "Oh look! That's Mary and the girls in their grunge phase. I had to buy so much flannel. You wacky Generation X kids."

"And there's Mary before prom!" sighed Alvinia. "Mary had this huge crush on this guy on the wrestling team. What was his name? Walker Potard. He would always say hi to her in the hallway and told her he'd pick her up in his limo to take her to prom with his friends. Prom night comes and her sisters and the girls and I do this big movie montage thing with her where they got Mary all ready to ride with Walker, like crimping her hair and putting Clairol Glints hair color in for her, making her clean her face with Noxzema, putting Biore strips on her nose, all this stuff. She wanted to wear a dress like the one Molly Ringwald wore in *Pretty in Pink*."

"Mom," moaned Mary. "I hate this story."

"So, hours go by, and Mary is all ready, waiting by the door," Alvinia continued. "At this point, it's totally clear that Walker and his pals aren't showing up, and when she goes to look outside, there was a pamphlet for a Chunky Tots Fat Camp taped to the door. She locked herself in her room all night and listened to 'Everybody Hurts' by R.E.M. on repeat. Remember that, Mary?"

"Yes, of course I do. Why?"

"Oh, no reason. Just remember?"

"We got our revenge on Walker and his cronies," said Robin. "Kara, Liza, and I got all of the bags of manure from Mrs. Cheevely's reindeer farm and dumped them into Walker's brand-new convertible. Everyone called his car 'the shit-mobile' after that. Then I fucked all the guys on the wrestling squad. Except Walker."

"Yeah, you really showed them," said Kara.

"Why was prom such a big deal?" Liza said. "My prom night was horrible and my date was such a weirdo. When '(I've Had) the Time of My Life' from *Dirty Dancing* came on, he ran toward me so I would pick him up and lift him in the air. His boutonniere got caught in my scrunchie and ripped some of my hair out. I landed backwards into the fog machine. He was on *Cops* years later, getting arrested for stealing scratch-and-sniff Strawberry Shortcake stickers and a previously viewed *Community* Season One DVD from Cumberland Farms."

Mary took the photo album out of her mother's hands. "Okay, that's enough for the embarrassing CliffsNotes edition of my life. Maybe tomorrow we can show Bright pictures from my last pap smear. I'm sure there's more interesting things to talk about."

"Oh no, I was really enjoying myself," said Bright. "Alvinia, was Mary always this cool or is that something she grew into?"

"She was always super cool," Robin teased.

"You wore a wallet chain," said Mary. "That grunge picture is of the four of us, if you recall. And only one of us flashed their lady parts to the lead singer at the Candlebox concert, Robin."

Nick, Fisher, and Angus rejoined their respective dates, bringing gifts of food and drinks. Angus handed Mary a huge plate of Christmas cookies.

"Hey, Bright, how about you come ice fishing next weekend with us?" Fisher said. "We're going to watch *Time Cop* on the portable DVD player and catch some largemouth bass. It's a tradition."

"Yeah, let me check my schedule with Joseph and I'll let you know," said Bright.

Fisher, Liza's husband, and Nick, Kara's husband, were best friends who did everything together, which worked out well for Liza and Kara. There was no awkward ingratiating of spouses or boyfriends who felt forced to hang out together.

"Everybody eat up and get some drinks," said Alvinia, getting up. "We're going to start the movie in a little bit."

Chapter 56

The kids entertained themselves with Paw Patrol, The Octonauts, and Legos in the playroom. The reindeer stood outside in the cold, staring in through the window at the happy children.

Acorn gasped happily when she saw it in the window.

"Rudy!" she said, waving at it. The reindeer waved back, slowly and stiffly.

Noelle, Heloise, and Susan entered, checking on the kids.

"Mom!" Acorn said, grabbing Noelle's hand. "Rudy's here! He's outside! Can he come in?"

Acorn pointed to the window. There wasn't anybody there.

"Maybe he went back home, sweetheart," said Noelle. She made a mental note to fake a goodbye note from Rudy, telling Acorn that he had to go be with the other reindeer.

"This is my sister," Eugenie announced, patting Maisie's head. "She has two eyes."

"Yes, she does!" Heloise said. She wanted to be supportive of her kids, even when they were being Captain Obvious.

"Not a cyclops," said Susan. "Got it."

"Can we have some Hot Pockets?" Hewney said.

"Normally I'd say no, but now I have guilt that I'm a bad parent for subjecting you to Elaine's psychotic yodeling and caterwauling that she passes off as singing," said Susan.

Noelle, Heloise, and Susan went to grab some food and drinks for the kids. As soon as they left, the reindeer reappeared in the window, its black eyes peering into the bright and lively playroom.

Fuller had been trying to reach Buchanan at The Morning Light Cemetery. He wasn't responding to her calls on his cell phone or walkie-talkie. She was in the middle of collaborating with Sylvia, Frances,

Willa, and Belle; sorting through Chester Persimmons' belongings, and searching online for information on Chuck Brinkerhoff and John Patrick Colqhoun.

"Buchanan," Fuller said into the walkie. "Buchanan, come in."

Fuller put her walkie down. She texted Stacy to make sure she was okay. Stacy replied quickly, letting her mom know she loved her. Fuller smiled for a moment. She wished she were home with her daughter watching *The Facts of Life* reruns, but she had an obligation to protect the citizens of Tinselvania that she would not forsake.

Her smile faded away as she realized she still hadn't heard from the Frost family. She had asked some of the crime technicians to meet her tomorrow to go over to Gordon and Patience Frost's house to scan for evidence. Fuller wanted to believe that Chester Persimmons' arrival and the disappearance of the Frost family were coincidence, but the cop in her told her otherwise.

Where are you, Buchanan? Answer me now.

Chapter 57

Alvinia and Aunt Elaine gathered all of the adults for the movie. The teens and kids were excluded from having to watch the film if they didn't want to; the grown-ups were required. Ethan and Josh excused themselves, citing work they had to finish at the factory down the street. Other than that, seats were filled up. Bright sat next to Mary.

"Okay," Aunt Elaine said. "Before we start, a few things. Does everyone have their snacks and beverages? Good. Here's the rules. If you're one of those people who asks a million questions during movies, reconsider that right now. Don't talk at all while the film is playing. Silence your cell phones and yourselves. Talkers will be dealt with accordingly. Remember, I know where you all live. There's Kleenex underneath everyone's seats, because believe me, you'll need it for the emotional rollercoaster of *The Family Stone*. If anyone here does not love Sarah Jessica Parker or Diane Keaton, keep it to yourself and know there's a special place in Hell for you. Now enjoy the movie!"

Alvinia pressed "play" on the computer and the theater screen lit up. Bright took Mary's hand in his, squeezing it softly as the movie began.

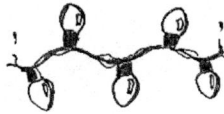

Ethan and Josh walked from Mary and Alvinia's house to the Tinsel Inc. factory. They had some business to discuss and weren't in the mood to watch *The Family Stone*. They had beers in their hands and some more in their pockets. They'd return later, either when they ran out of beer or when their wives texted and said it was time to go.

They didn't notice the reindeer following them down the street.

The reindeer made its way up the front porch. It opened the unlocked front door and slid into the house undetected. It could hear the kids playing and the sounds coming from the movie echoing from other rooms. It made its way through the house, checking out the space, taking in the decorations and layout.

It peeked into the movie room at the crowd watching the movie, oblivious to its presence. They had no idea what was coming for them.

It entered Bernard's office. Shelves of books, walls covered in photographs, desk stacked with papers, file cabinet with company memos. A posed, framed picture of Bernard and Alvinia with young Mary, Noelle, and Glory centered directly behind the desk. Another framed photo, from sometime in the 1970s, of Bernard and Cobden Classen with Emmett Branscombe and Chester Persimmons in front of Tinsel Inc.– a snapshot of the men who ran the company together once.

The reindeer pressed itself against the wall when it heard footfalls coming from the hallway.

Jed was on his way to the bathroom when he stopped to admire the impeccably decorated, ornate tree in the family room. Pristinely wrapped boxes and packages rested on top of the red-and-white tree skirt. He watched the changing colors that reflected off the string of lights onto the gift wrap.

He reached into his pocket and retrieved his Artemus Gordon action figure from the movie *Wild Wild West*. For the past few years, Jed kept an online account where he posted photographs of the tiny figurine in various locations, staged poses, and in front of a myriad of backdrops and arranged sets. The account had almost seven thousand followers at last count. The last photo he posted, depicting Artemus climbing a bowl of clementines, received almost three thousand "likes." It was a fun, harmless hobby that made Jed happy.

The gifts under the tree would make a perfect photo opportunity for the miniature Artemus. Jed leaned down and tried to balance Artemus amongst the present boxes. When he had Artemus in just the right position, he reached for his cell phone. He stopped and leaned back when he swore the presents moved slightly– a rise and a fall. Like the gifts themselves inhaled then exhaled.

Jed paused for a moment, laughing at himself. He must have been seeing things. He reached out to fix Artemus' stance under the tree.

He didn't have time to react as the arm reached out from beneath the gifts, sinking a hunting knife into the flesh beneath his chin. It pierced all the way through, the blade protruding out of his open mouth. Jed's blood doused the perfectly wrapped Christmas presents like a red geyser.

Chapter 58

The moviegoers were interrupted by the ringing of the landline in the kitchen. Mary volunteered to go answer it, excusing herself. She picked up the receiver.

The sounds of Darlene Love's "Christmas (Baby Please Come Home)" boomed over the line. It was a strained, slowed-down version; Darlene's voice and the music were stretched and warped, making it sound distorted and chilling, not festive and cheerful.

"Hello?" Mary said. She kicked herself, knowing if she was watching herself in a movie at that moment, she'd be yelling at the screen to hang up and run away from the freaky music.

"Mary…," an unknown voice seethed over the phone.

"Who's calling?" said Mary.

There was no answer, only the twisted notes of the music. She hung up and took a deep breath. Who was that? What was that about? There were some strange folks in Tinselvania.

"Mary!" Robin said, causing Mary to jump up in shock. Robin and Angus were in the kitchen doorway.

"Robin!" gasped Mary. "Don't sneak up on me like that."

"See? This is why you need to get out more and go to parties," Robin said. "That wasn't us 'sneaking around.' That was us being normal people who go into rooms normally and make normal amounts of noise. Why so jumpy?"

"I'm not jumpy, just hungry," Mary said, shaking it off and scanning the kitchen counter for more Candy Cane Marshmallow Peeps. "I get out."

"Last Friday night, you sat at home on your futon in zebra-striped Zubaz, eating cheese dip and watching *Must Love Dogs*."

"I had a Spin Doctors T-shirt on too," Mary said, as if that were a defense.

"We're going to circle back around to that a little later," Robin said, trying to choose her words carefully. "Listen. Your mom and aunt are currently occupied. On a scale of one to Anger from *Inside Out*, how mad at me would they be if I let Angus play Connect Four with my snorchdilly in one of the guest rooms?"

"You know people can't un-hear things, right?" Mary said. "Snorchdilly? Let's never speak of this again. You need to go sit on a dryer for a while."

"Hey, how's things going with Bright?" Robin said.

"Good, I think. I hope. I really like him. I'm not used to feeling like this."

"Later on tonight, do this," said Robin. "You reenact the ending scene from *Jerry Maguire*, except instead of saying, 'You had me at hello,' you say, 'You had me at let's bone.' And instead of 'You complete me,' you say, 'You can eat me.' It worked on Angus."

"It did," Angus nodded in approval.

"On the Likert scale, I'd rate that as a 'strongly disagree,'" Mary said. "You climbed to the top of Mount Filth and planted your flag yet again, Robin."

Robin and Angus started to leave. Robin turned back to Mary with a cheeky smile.

"Where's the dryer again?" asked Robin. "Downstairs, right?"

"May the odds be ever in your favor," Angus said.

"Calgon, take me away," said Mary, attempting to block the mental picture of Robin and Angus doing it in her house. Her mind went back to the spooky phone call. Other tinsel companies had pulled some weird and creepy things in the past, but this year, between putting a mole in her company and the bizarre notes and calls, she was genuinely disturbed and irritated.

"Relax," she said to herself. "It's a party."

Chapter 59

Kara went to check on the kids while Nick went to the walk-in pantry to get more libations. Once she made sure the little ones were happy and preoccupied, she went to meet up with her husband and offer him assistance.

She noted how many of the lights that were on earlier were now turned off. Maybe for ambiance, to show off the Christmas lights.

"Nick?" she called out.

She could see Nick through the partially open pantry door. She said his name again and pushed it open. She choked back a scream.

Nick was suspended off the ground, the noose of a rope tied tightly around his neck, his face blue and expressionless. His legs swung back and forth slightly, the rope creaking against the wooden slat it was rigged to.

The reindeer stepped out from behind Nick's swinging corpse. As if it had been waiting for her. Kara cried out and turned to run.

The other reindeer blocked her path, filling the doorway. It raised the ax in its hand, bringing it down and silencing the scream erupting from Kara's throat.

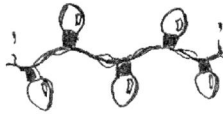

Deputy McCloskey and Officer Cogan radioed Chief Fuller from their police car. Chuck Brinkerhoff was in cuffs in the backseat. They found him skulking around town square, drunk and wandering. He was waving a gun around when they found him but they talked him down from whatever temporary intoxicated madness that drove him. He had no identification on him but gave his name as Chuck Brinkerhoff when questioned. Fuller radioed back to say she was headed to The Morning Light Cemetery to check on Buchanan and would be back to the police station as soon as she could.

Brinkerhoff mumbled and groaned incoherently in the back, kicking at the seats. McCloskey and Cogan threw him in a cell when they reached the station, hoping he'd sober up and provide some answers for them. Jennings was already at the station when they arrived.

Chuck banged against the bars of the jail cell. Cogan brought him a cup of water to help him sober up.

"The chief will be back soon," Cogan said. "You just relax and have a nap."

"He killed my brother," Chuck said, a sense of calm washing over him.

"Who did?" said McCloskey.

"Chester Persimmons," said Chuck. "He killed my brother. When I heard he escaped, I came here to find him and kill him. Someone beat me to it."

McCloskey, Cogan, and Jennings were dumbstruck. They didn't know what to say. If it were true, they almost felt bad for him.

Chuck sat, staring off into space, as if the officers weren't even there. "He has no idea what he took from us. He wasn't there to see all the damage he caused, the fallout he created. The impact his actions had on the lives around any of us. My brother was a good man. He had a family and friends and people who loved him. And Chester Persimmons came along and took him away from all of us."

"You know there are people who advocated for Persimmons to go free? They held protests and posted their opinions online. They said he deserved a 'second chance' and his actions weren't his fault. Who cares about the people he killed, who will never get a second chance? Who cares about the lives ruined because of what he did? 'He's a person too,' they would say. Instead of the death penalty, he got to go to a state asylum. He got to have free health care and three square meals a day. How does that make any sense? A depraved murderer."

"We had to listen to all of his supporters for years. They didn't see the holidays where the ghost of my brother haunted us. The empty seat at the dinner table every night. His absence cast a pall over everything. Nothing was the same. My mother had a nervous breakdown. His wife and children had to rebuild their entire lives. And there were people out there telling us that Chester Persimmons 'made a mistake' and 'deserved forgiveness' and was not a monster. Chester Persimmons wasn't the victim. My brother was. And our family. Victims of grief. Empty shells of who they used to be. It ate away everything in our lives."

"Did you take Chester Persimmons' body from the morgue?" McCloskey asked, even though she knew she should have waited for Chief Fuller.

"No, that wasn't me," Chuck said, laughing emptily. "I turned out to not be very good at surveillance or much of a spy. I have to rethink my career as a serial killer hunter. I just wanted to avenge my brother. I wanted to be able to tell my family that I took that piece of shit off of this horrible planet. I wanted to look Chester Persimmons in the eye as he died and tell him who I was and what he'd done and why I had come for him. I'm glad he's dead but I wish I had been the one to pull the trigger."

McCloskey, Jennings, and Cogan were speechless. Chuck looked like a lost little boy, sitting on the cell bench, lost in his sadness and helplessness.

Chapter 60

Mary made hot chocolate for the kids and handed out cups for them while they played. She could hear the teenagers laughing and chatting in the entertainment room and the film running in the movie room. Her dress was making her sweaty. She adjusted her undershirt in the quiet of the hallway, making a strained face. Her hands behind her back, struggling to situate herself, she looked up to see Bright, who was smiling at her misfortune.

"Ugh," she said, caught in yet another awkward moment. She decided to own it. "Will you please scratch my back? Right there?"

She spun around and Bright gave her back a good scratching. She sighed with relief.

"Thank you," she said, exhaling grandly.

"What kind of material is this?" he laughed.

"It's definitely not cotton," Mary said. "I think it's a combination of wool, polyester, and nylon. Fabrics meant for straight-jackets or Alaskan dog-sledding gear. You may have to cut me out of this dress at the end of the night. I need some air."

"Can I come with and keep you company?" asked Bright.

She brought him out to the sprawling back porch that overlooked their large backyard. The moon and stars shone down on them brightly. They could see the forest in the distance.

"Are you having a good time?" Mary said. "You're missing the movie."

"I've seen it before," he said. "I didn't want to tell your Aunt Elaine and let her down. Or have her hurt me. She's intense."

"You missed the year she made everyone dress up as characters from the movie. I tried my hardest, but I couldn't pull off my Claire Danes impersonation."

"I'm sure you did a better job than you think you did," Bright said. The way he looked at her made Mary feel weak in her knees. Foreigner's "Feels Like the First Time" played over both Mary and Bright's imaginations as they leaned in for a kiss.

"Does this count as a second date?" Bright said.

"With as much stuff as you learned about me tonight, I feel like you could call this the tenth date. You must be so tired of stories about me. Tell me stuff about you. What do you think about?"

"Hm," Bright thought out loud. "What is the meaning of life? What is our purpose here on earth? What would happen if Batman were bitten by a vampire? I wish I had my own woodland creatures like squirrels and birds to help me get dressed and ready every morning, like Amy Adams in *Enchanted*. Would I have to sing along with them while they make me pretty, though? If I had to choose 'start-the-day' songs, I would pick Bananarama's 'Venus' and Carly Rae Jepsen's 'Call Me Maybe.' I went to college for, like, eight years and the only thing I remember is the term for 'the fear of long words' is, ironically, 'hippopotomonstrosesquippedaliophobia.' I feel like Sisyphus most days."

Glory opened the sliding door to the back porch. Cotter was with her. She gave the "can-we-join-you?" look and Mary waved her out to the deck.

"I couldn't take Aunt Elaine's sobbing through the movie so we made a run for it," Glory said. She centered her attention on Bright. "So, young man, what are your intentions toward my big sister? You should know that if you plan to marry her for money, we're pretty certain our mom will outlive us all, so you won't be getting anything. That woman is like a black hole– she sucks you in and nobody's exactly sure what she does to you, but she's still the strongest presence in the galaxy."

"I plan for Mary and me to live on love," joked Bright. "Sunshine, glitter, unicorns, and double rainbows. When it rains, it will rain Skittles. We'll fly through the skies on a magical talking horse."

"Penelope," Mary sighed, remembering her horse friend.

"Oh, what I'd give for Ivy to bring a boy home," said Glory. "I'm thrilled my daughter is so smart and driven, but I swear she'd fit in perfectly at a convent. I used to tear it up when I was her age. I was always in trouble for sneaking out and going to parties and raves and hanging out with boys. Mary always told on me. I swear Ivy is more like her Aunt Mary than her own parents."

"I never told on you!" said Mary. "I just never lied for you. I wasn't going to be your alibi for your life of reckless debauchery. I was not going to aid and abet your crimes."

"I, for one, am completely okay that she has no boyfriends to speak of," said Cotter. "I personally love having a daughter who can do our taxes and explain *Inception* and *Interstellar* to me. I did not get those movies."

"Most parents would be thrilled to have a kid who loves books," Mary said to Glory.

"You would say that," said Glory. "I am totally, completely proud of my beautiful genius daughter. I just don't want her to miss out on life. I want her to feel fire and passion for things and have life experiences. She's friends with her teachers. She's the kind of girl I would've beat up in high school. I don't want her to spend her whole life learning about the world without seeing it and then someday settling for a dull marriage with a boring accountant who collects stamps in his spare time."

"Her fire and passion are for knowledge," Mary said. "And there's lots of really exciting accountants with hidden skills. Ben Affleck, *The Accountant*?"

"Hey, who's that?" Cotter said, pointing toward the tree line.

Llewellyn Barnes stepped out from the darkness. Mary recognized him from their previous encounter. He held a giant bouquet of flowers in his hands.

"Excuse me!" shouted Glory. "Are you lost? This is private property!"

"I'm sorry," Llewellyn said. "I didn't mean to frighten you. I... If I could just have a moment of your time."

Chapter 61

The movie had ended and the guests were congregated in the living room. The kids had been looked in on. Mary told Ivy, Betsy, Ellie, Stacy, and Georgina to come to the party for a minute. Everyone was happily drinking, eating, talking, and laughing. Mary, Bright, Glory, and Cotter joined the merriment with big smiles on their faces.

"Aunt Elaine," Mary said. "I think you should sit down. There's someone here who wants to say hello to you."

"Is it that heinous hog-bitch Valda Vickers from my couponing club?" Aunt Elaine said. "You tell her I do not forgive her for taking the last Stove Top stuffing coupon and she can ride on back home on her broom."

"No, it's not Valda Vickers," said Glory. Mary, Glory, Bright, and Cotter moved aside to make way for Llewellyn Barnes. He entered the room with a glimmering smile.

Aunt Elaine was so taken aback that she clutched her chest. She rose from her seat slowly, staring intently at Llewellyn with her mouth agape. Tears fell quietly down her cheeks. Llewellyn began to cry softly as well. He held the flowers out for her.

"Hayden Whitford?" she said gently. "Is that really you?"

"Hello, Elaine," Hayden (formerly Llewellyn, after he was formerly Hayden) said.

They embraced tightly as they cried tears of happiness and joy. Alvinia got choked up as well. Everyone looked on with a combination of delight and confusion.

"What's happening here?" Casper whispered to Mary.

Hayden let go of Elaine. They looked at each other lovingly and longingly. The guests held their breath, captivated by the odd but warm scene unfolding before them.

"You got old," Aunt Elaine said. A second later, her face got stern and serious. She hit his coat. "Where the fuck have you been for the last forty-five years?"

"I was on that *Gilligan's Island* tour," Hayden said. "One of the fans got overzealous and crashed the boat. A bunch of us made it to an uncharted island. No one ever came to rescue us. I've been there all this time. We made a whole colony there. A hundred of us, settlers living off of the land and hunting and foraging for food. I never stopped thinking about you, Elaine."

The crowd "aww"-ed.

"I finally made a makeshift boat and made it to an ocean liner. I stowed away on their vessel and made it to port. I came to find you," he continued.

The crowd "ahh"-ed.

"I had to assume a fake identity because I wasn't ready to come back to the real world. I've missed so many years. I didn't know if anyone remembered me. I didn't know if I could handle all of the changes. I didn't know if you were still here. I was afraid I'd be arrested or questioned because of the shipwreck."

The crowd "hmm"-ed.

"How did you survive all these years? Why didn't you try to come back before now?" Aunt Elaine asked.

"Well, we did try. We lost a lot of people along the way. In the end, I ate everyone on the island to survive. I was the last one standing! I had to kill and cook every single survivor to get back to you. But once the meat was all gone, I had no other option but to try my fate on the great ocean."

"You killed and cannibalized all of the other people to come back to me?" Aunt Elaine said, as if it were the most romantic thing she'd ever heard.

"I ate all of them," Hayden nodded. "I would eat them all again if it meant I got to see you one more time."

The crowd "huh"-ed.

"This story did not go the way I expected it to," Tyler said.

"I don't want to be away from you for another minute," said Hayden, producing a ring from his pocket. "Marry me, Elaine."

"Yes, of course I'll marry you, Hayden!" she exclaimed. They hugged and kissed. Hayden spun her around.

The crowd cheered.

"I'll take you anywhere you want to go, my love," Hayden said.

"Just no island trips," said Aunt Elaine.

The crowd laughed.

"Oh," said Betsy. "Old people are so cute. I'm going to get them some Activia and Metamucil for their wedding gift."

Alvinia blasted Cyndi Lauper's "Christmas Conga" on the stereo as everyone raised their drinks to Aunt Elaine and Hayden Whitford. People danced and hugged, celebrating the happy news.

"Who are we missing?" Alvinia said. "There were more people here earlier. They missed Aunt Elaine's big moment."

"Has anyone seen Kara or Nick?" asked Liza.

"I was just wondering where Jed went off to," Noelle said.

"I haven't heard from Ethan and Josh either," said Heloise. "They left a while ago and should've been back by now."

"Wait," said Tyler. "Where are Robin and Angus?"

"Try the laundry room," Mary said.

"I'm going to go check on the kids," said Susan.

Chapter 62

Casper and Joseph took a break from the party and breathed in the night air. Casper pointed out the constellations to Joseph, who wasn't used to seeing so many stars. New York City was too smog-filled for that. All Joseph knew was that he really liked Casper and hoped that Casper felt the same way. It had been a quick courtship, but something inside of Joseph knew he'd found someone he wanted to spend his time with.

Barbra Streisand's "What Are You Doing New Year's Eve?" played over the imaginary speakers of Joseph's mind. He didn't know that Casper had the same song running through his head, except it was the Ella Fitzgerald version. He wondered if it was too soon to pick out "His and His" bath towels.

"This has been a really amazing week," said Joseph.

Casper opened his mouth to speak but the only sound that emitted was a horrific gurgle. The blade of a hunting knife poked out from Casper's mouth as his eyes fluttered and he fell to the ground. The handle of the knife was jammed through the back of Casper's skull. The reindeer was standing where Casper once stood.

Joseph had no time to run. The second reindeer was behind him. It grabbed Joseph by the forehead and pulled him back onto the blade in its hand, tearing Joseph wide open.

Once Joseph had collapsed to the ground in a heap, each reindeer grabbed either of the dead men's legs and dragged them off of the porch, leaving huge, bloody swaths behind.

"I have to go call my children," Aunt Elaine said to Hayden. She let go of his hand for the first time since she saw him that night and went into the kitchen. Hayden smiled as he watched her walking away, feeling as if his life was starting again. He was going to have a new chapter in the book of his life.

"Did anyone see where the kids went?" Susan called from down the hallway. It was muffled under the music and chatter. She came bounding into the living room, her face streaked with worry, repeating the question louder and more frantically.

Alvinia turned the music off and everyone went silent.

"The kids aren't in the playroom," said Susan.

"Okay," Alvinia said. "They have to be around here somewhere."

"The phone isn't working," Aunt Elaine said as she returned. "I have no reception on my cell phone and the landline is dead."

Everyone began to pull out their own cell phones, checking them. No bars, no service, nothing, on all of the respective phones. A general sense of confusion, lined with an undercurrent of panic, settled into the group.

Tap! Tap! Tap!

The knocking sound at the picture window caused everyone to turn their heads. Nick was at the window, his face pressed against the glass. His expression was off– empty-eyed, emotionless, flaccid, poised at an unnatural angle.

The smears of blood stretched across the glass sent a hush over the crowd. The squeaking sound of Nick's skin pressed against the window pierced through the quiet as he rose. But it wasn't Nick.

It was his decapitated head.

The reindeer held Nick's head in its hand by his hair. It held the severed head in the air, as if showing off its gruesome handiwork to its screaming audience. The partygoers reacted in shock and revulsion, recoiling back in horror. The reindeer slammed Nick's head against the glass.

"What in creation?" Aunt Elaine whispered.

The second reindeer made its presence known, emerging from the shadows. Behind the first two reindeer stood two more. There were four figures in total—dressed in identical reindeer costumes, standing on the lawn, staring into the house. Enjoying the reactions of terror and heartbreak they caused. Weapons in their hands– an ax, a machete, a knife, a crossbow. Like Santa's vigilante gang of homicidal sadist reindeer, escaped from the North Pole on a mission of murder.

"There's four of them," Cotter said.

"Who are they?" Alvinia asked. "What do they want?"

"Lock up the house," Mary said, cutting off any more questions and speculation. Everyone stared at her for a moment. "Now! Every window and every door. Lock everything up! Find anyone who's missing. Go! Arm yourself with weapons– anything that can be used to defend yourself. Move! Now! We can't let them in the house."

"Where are the kids?" shouted Noelle as everyone separated to secure the three-story house. People were screaming their kids' names, running from room to room in an effort to locate them.

"Everyone meet back here as soon as this place is locked down!" Mary shouted.

"The landline is dead!" Alvinia shouted from the other room. "No dial tone!"

Mary grabbed a fireplace poker with one hand and Bright's arm with the other and pulled him to the mudroom overlooking the backyard. They frantically locked every window and door, wedging broomsticks and whatever else they could find against the tracks of the sliding glass. Mary peered out into the darkness beyond the motion light.

The reindeer were gone.

"Where did they go?" she whispered. Her mind wouldn't stop racing. Nick was dead. She had no idea where Kara was. Or Robin and Angus. Or the kids. Who were those people in reindeer costumes?

"Who would do this?" Bright said. He was beside her, his eyes scanning the dark for any sign of life.

Mary stared out into the night. She had no idea. She laughed to herself, thinking about the reindeer costumes. In the daylight, those would look so festive and playful. In the nighttime, those same silly costumes became something sinister and menacing.

"Where does your dad keep his guns?" asked Bright.

"There's no guns in this house," Mary said.

"Your dad was a rich, straight, old white man. He has guns!"

Smash! Smash!

They heard the sound of glass shattering as the lights outside the house began to die out one by one. The reindeer were obliterating all of the light sources around the perimeter, covering the surroundings in complete darkness.

Chapter 63

Georgina, Ivy, Betsy, Stacy, and Ellie went up the staircase leading to the attic. The fear running through them was like static electricity. Their chatter was filled with questions without any answers; none of them knew who donned the reindeer costumes or why.

The attic was stacked with boxes, cluttered with forgotten furniture and appliances, and racks of old clothing. Piles of old photographs and papers, toys, electronics, and long-disused remnants of the past. Dust hung in the air like a fog, illuminated against the light. Several clear plastic tarps hung against the walls to prevent rainwater from leaking into the house.

There were two sections of the attic, separated by a door. Ivy, Ellie, Stacy, and Betsy went to the window to secure it, while Georgina went into the spare room.

The spare room was dusty and silent. Moonlight shone in through the only window. Georgina tried the light switch to no avail. She took a few steps farther inside, the sound of her heartbeat pounding in her ears.

Her back was to the door. She slowly turned her head when she heard the pained, discordant creak behind her. The door was steadily, leisurely swinging closed.

The reindeer stood in the darkness behind the door. The eyeholes in its mask only gave way to two empty, dark orbs that Georgina saw were fixed directly on her. In its hand was a machete.

Georgina threw a dusty antique fleam at the reindeer, who sidestepped it and pushed her to the floor. As she tried to stand back up and move out of its way, she tripped over a stack of old magazines. The reindeer brought its machete down in one strong, swift motion, slashing into the paper pile beside her.

Georgina didn't hesitate. She scrambled to her feet and out the door, slamming it shut behind her. Ivy, Betsy, Ellie, and Stacy's panicked looks met hers. They pressed their weight against the door as the reindeer on the other side smashed against it.

The reindeer's force on the other side of the door came in steady bursts as the door itself slightly opened with each bang. The girls held steady, formulating a plan.

Ivy took her weight off the door and grabbed a nearby baseball bat hidden amongst her grandmother's piles of forgotten items. Stacy, Ellie, Betsy, and Georgina saw the look in her eyes.

Slice!

The machete blade slashed through the wood, narrowly missing stabbing Ellie and Stacy. They jumped back. Ivy brought the bat down on the blade, lodging it further into the wood as the reindeer struggled to remove it.

"Get back," whispered Ivy, as the other girls scoured the attic for weapons of their own.

There was only silence. The machete blade stopped moving. They couldn't hear the reindeer anymore. As if it had run away. The girls, wielding their weapons, stood silently as they waited for any sound.

"Stacy," Ellie said, nodding her head toward an old dresser near the door. Stacy inched over next to Ellie as they put their hands on top of the dresser.

Smack!

The reindeer's kick at the door broke the silence. Ellie and Stacy, their nerves and reflexes acting like lightning, pushed the heavy dresser down in front of the door. It crashed against the ground, right in front of the doorway, effectively blocking the reindeer from getting through.

Whack! Whack!

The reindeer wasn't giving up. It had extricated the machete blade and was bringing it down hard on the wooden door, pieces of cracked wood splintering and exploding everywhere. More and more of the door was decimated. The reindeer became visible through the open space in the door, its eyes boring holes of hate and anger into the terrified prey it was after.

Ivy swung at the door with the bat. The reindeer staggered back to avoid the blow. The plastic sheeting made crinkling, crackling noises as the cold air from the spare room began rushing in.

A high-pitched, animalistic sound echoed from outside the house. Like some kind of signal or call-and-response, as if to communicate to the reindeer. It backed away from the door and disappeared. The girls heard it rummaging around and scampering off.

"Let's go," said Betsy. Ivy, Georgina, Ellie, and Stacy followed her toward the stairs.

Ellie stepped on a piece of paneling that had been rotted out over time. It snapped as she put her foot on it, as that part of the floor gave way. Her leg went through the board, trapping her between the attic and the ceiling below her. She let out a cry of pain as she struggled to extricate herself. The other girls ran over to help dislodge her leg.

As the girls attempted to break Ellie free, her eyes widened. She saw the reindeer before anyone else did.

The reindeer had crept through the hole in the door and was almost upon them. The girls screamed in terror. Before they could stop it, the reindeer brought the machete blade down on Ellie, embedding it in her skull.

Ivy knocked the reindeer out with one swing of the bat. It sprawled on the ground. The girls turned back to Ellie, seeing the machete submerged in their friend's head. She wasn't moving. A pool of blood gathered around her, dripping down into the wooden slats where her leg was trapped.

There wasn't time to grieve. Georgina grabbed a rope from an old box and the girls tied the unconscious reindeer to a pole. Ivy leaned down to unmask the reindeer when they heard shouting from the floor below them. They bolted, leaving the reindeer incapacitated, not too far from where the body of their friend lay.

Chapter 64

Tyler and Mike were shouting out of the second-story window from a spare bedroom. Every year for the *Family Stone* party, Alvinia and Aunt Elaine hired the local Christmas carolers, led by Hester Branscombe, to sing outside for them around 11 p.m. Hester and a dozen other carolers, including members of Alvinia and Aunt Elaine's book club like Iris Pickleberry and Eudosia Dingle, had arrived. They were bundled in their warm winter coats and hats and singing "O Come, O Come, Emmanuel" as both Tyler and Mike screamed warnings for the carolers to run away and get help. Their cries were drowned out by the cacophony of music coming from the passionate singers on the front lawn.

Hester, Emmett Branscombe's ex-wife, stood in front of the pack. They were oblivious to Tyler and Mike's protests, thinking it was their cries of approval and encouragement.

"Behind you! Run! Get help!" Tyler and Mike yelled out the window. Hester waved at them cheerfully, pleased with herself that they were so moved by the carolers' harmony.

Three reindeer emerged from the shadows outside and crept toward the unsuspecting carolers. Hester put her arms around her grown daughters Hilda, Hortense, and Zinnia, hugging them to her as they sang. Hilda, Hortense, and Zinnia's husbands stood next to them.

Georgina, Ivy, Betsy, and Stacy joined Tyler and Mike at the window, adding their voices in protest to try and save the carolers. Once the realization spread over Hester's face that she recognized something was wrong, there was nothing they could do.

The three reindeer launched into a full-on assault of the carolers like a spring-loaded catapult. The attack happened with unbridled speed and fury, as the reindeer used their weapons to carve, defile, and obliterate the baker's dozen of people on the lawn. Some tried to escape the frenzied rush of violence, the night air filled with screams of terror. It was useless. The reindeer pounced upon them like wild animals. The blood spray in the air looked like a giant, low-hanging red cloud. In minutes, they had all been hacked and slashed as if their lives never mattered. The sounds of a singing chorus were replaced by eerie, deafening silence.

Tyler shut and locked the window furiously. They backed away, not wanting to see any more of the carnage and evil that waited outside.

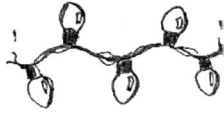

Mary sifted through the boxes in the garage, looking for any of her father's guns. She couldn't recall if her mother had donated them or if they ended up at Uncle Cobden's house. Bright dumped out plastic containers and toolboxes, hoping to find any kind of deadly weapons.

"Mary, in case something happens, there's something I should tell you," he said. "I didn't just come here to do an evaluation and assessment of Tinsel Inc. The board hired me to…"

"Not the time!" said Mary. "Tell me all about it once we get through this."

Bright went back to searching, silently scolding himself for adding awkwardness into a terrifying situation. When he looked back over at Mary, she jumped forward and kissed him passionately. He returned the affection, his entire body forgetting for a moment the danger they were in.

"Just in case," she said.

Glory, Cotter, and Noelle descended the steps into the basement. Noelle's mind hadn't stopped reeling. She couldn't calm herself. Her children were missing and she couldn't find Jed. She feared the worst but didn't want to let her thoughts drift there. She had to find them.

"Let's make this fast," said Glory. She knew Ivy would be okay with her friends. All she wanted was to get back upstairs with the others.

The basement held all types of tools and machinery. Her father used it as a workshop on all the gizmos he and Uncle Cobden would create together. Glory, Noelle, and Cotter armed themselves with what they could find; a hammer, a screwdriver, a wrench.

Cotter looked over at Glory. He had never seen his wife afraid of anything. For the first time, they felt real fear.

"We're going to find them," he said to Noelle.

A cold draft blew past them. The sole window in the basement was wide open. It was never open, especially in the wintertime. Cotter, Glory, and Noelle looked around them, wondering if someone was lurking in the darkness, waiting for the right time to strike.

The laundry room was off to the side. A faint light flickered from within. Cotter peered in, making out the forms of two people. They were motionless and balanced at an odd angle. He whispered for Glory and Noelle, who saw it too. Something wasn't right.

It was Robin and Angus. They were leaned up against the dryer, Angus resting on top of Robin. They had been impaled together, the rusty blade of a long scythe pinning them in a death embrace. The scythe had been left jutting out of Angus' back, its pointed blade protruding from Robin, sealing them as one. Judging from their stiff posture and the dried dark-red blood splattered around them, they had been killed much earlier. Glory, Cotter, and Noelle stifled their shock as Cotter lunged to close the basement window.

His foot caught on a wire that had been set up low to the ground and pulled taut. A groaning, mechanical noise emitted from each side of the trio. Cotter had sprung a trap.

A mechanism had been crudely built into the ceiling of the basement. Once Cotter inadvertently set it into motion, it popped out with rapid force. The wire was connected to a contraption; a long, thin metal sheet that had been rigged with several dozen blades, mirror shards, glass pieces, and other various serrated-edged weapons.

The metal sheet unfurled from its hiding place and swooped down, hitting Glory, Noelle, and Cotter in their midsections. The various deadly implements sliced and slashed their skin open, running through their bodies like skewers. It happened in a fraction of a second. There was no time to stop it.

Glory reached for Cotter's hand weakly as the light faded out of their eyes.

Chapter 65

Chief Fuller parked the SUV near Buchanan's police car. Its lights were off and the driver's side door was slightly ajar. There was no sign of him. She radioed him one more time, to no avail. She didn't want to assume the worst, telling herself there could be other explanations for his radio silence. Her police training wouldn't allow her to panic and worry or take over the rational parts of her psyche.

"Buchanan!" she shouted into the darkness of The Morning Light Cemetery.

Sylvia, Frances, Willa, and Belle were with her. They had set off into the cemetery itself to see if the Persimmons mausoleum had been further disturbed. The ladies saw the police tape still encompassing the mausoleum and decided to investigate the rest of the cemetery. They heard Fuller in the distance, calling for Buchanan.

"Something is still wrong here," Sylvia said. Her instincts had gotten her this far. Though Chester Persimmons was dead, she knew there was more to this story than they'd figured out.

"I have a call in to a friend of mine who works with sensitive documents, like sealed adoption records," said Frances. "Maybe she can help me find out what happened to John Patrick Colqhoun."

"My parents used to warn me about living in the city," Belle said. "I always told them, the real horrible stuff happens in the country. All that quiet and nothing else to do. You may get mugged in the city, but the small towns are where the real depraved crazies are."

"What is that?" Sylvia said, pointing.

There was a faint glint in the moonlight. Something shiny, a flash that would appear and then disappear off in the distance by a set of large headstones. The women made their way up the hill toward the intermittent gleam.

Bernard Classen's grave had been exhumed. Someone had dug it up. His resting place was beside a mammoth tombstone. A pile of freshly dug dirt sat next to the open hole in the earth.

Someone had placed cheap, glossy helium balloons, like the kind bought at the local drugstore, on top of Bernard's headstone. The balloons had expressions like *Congratulations!* and *Happy Graduation Day!* scrawled on them, whipping around in the wind, tied to a pastel-colored basket.

They looked inside the open mouth of the grave. Bernard Classen's coffin had been tampered with and left agape. Officer Buchanan's lifeless corpse had been dropped inside. Bernard's body was gone.

"That poor man," Sylvia said.

"Chief Fuller," Willa said into her walkie-talkie. "You need to see this."

Chapter 66

Alvinia's mind raced with the thought of who would do this to her family. Her husband had made enemies in the past through business, but nothing that would constitute this level of vengeance. She was friendly with almost everyone in town. It had to be strangers, drifters, vagrants, or even some kind of cult that had targeted them. There wasn't any other explanation that made any sense.

She had double-checked that her bedroom was sealed and fastened against any impending danger. Aunt Elaine and Hayden were securing the room next to hers. Alvinia wrung her hands and stared at the photos on the wall of her bedroom. Her family, her husband, Tinsel Inc. All of the things that mattered the most to her, represented on one wall. She didn't know what she would do if anything happened to them.

She tried the landline in her room with no success. She paced around the room, waiting for Hayden and Elaine. She stopped and looked at herself in the mirror.

Someone was standing directly behind her. Half-concealed by her own figure, but a partial view of the reindeer that towered at her back, standing stationary and glaring at her. She was frozen in fear, unable to move.

The reindeer clamped its paw on her mouth as she whimpered.

Aunt Elaine and Hayden had locked down the remaining rooms on the second floor. In the spare bedroom, Hayden surveyed the outside through the window. He swore he saw shadows and figures darting back and forth, choosing dark places to cloak themselves in.

"I can't believe this is happening," Aunt Elaine said. "I just got you back. It's not fair. After all these years, to lose you now. We just found each other again."

"Maybe this is the universe taking its revenge on me," said Hayden, his expression grim. "My karma. The ghosts of those I've consumed come back to make me pay for what I've done."

"You can't really believe that. These aren't ghosts. They're flesh-and-blood, like you and me."

"It's retribution."

Aunt Elaine looked at Hayden, putting her hand on his face. They did not notice the figure emerging behind them, crouched down beside the bed. First it revealed its paw on the mattress, then more of itself, keeping level to the bed to avoid detection.

"We have many years left to live and love," Aunt Elaine told Hayden.

The reindeer stood up straight behind Aunt Elaine, revealing itself. Hayden's eyes widened in shock as he saw it. He pushed Elaine out of the way as the reindeer advanced.

Heloise and Susan stood in the playroom with the lights off. They could see out of the windows better that way. They saw no sign of their children, though they saw child-sized footprints in the mud and melting snow covering the ground. They went from the ground outside the playroom window toward the tree line.

"Uncle Bernard built that big treehouse in the woods all those years ago," said Heloise. "I bet the kids all went there. There's a heating unit inside, so they'll be warm."

"We have to go get them," Susan said.

"We're no good to them if we're dead. I know they're all right. I know it."

Susan didn't know if Heloise was trying to convince her or herself. Their children were missing and they weren't sure whether their husbands had made it to the factory safely. Or worse, if Ethan and Josh had tried to come back to the house and met with the reindeer on their way.

"We can probably get a better view from this one," Susan said, going over to another window. She pulled back the curtains to peer outside but stepped back as soon as she did.

Written on the window in what seemed to be blood was the phrase "Look outside."

Susan and Heloise instantaneously spun around. No one was there. It was only them in the dark, quiet playroom. Alone.

Through the silence, they heard the vague sound of sleigh bells being shaken. It was coming from outside. From the trees. It started and stopped intermittently, barely audible enough to chime through the air.

"Do you see that?" Heloise said, pressing her face against the glass. Susan stood beside her, struggling to make out what Heloise was referring to.

Enveloped by the darkness, set against the tree line, were two scarecrows hoisted on wooden slats, like the one Rock Miller had previously left in Ethan and Heloise's yard.

As they stared harder and their eyes adjusted to the blackness, they realized that it wasn't two scarecrows raised on frames. It was Liza and Fisher. Heloise turned on the flashlight on her phone in a futile attempt to see them more clearly, aiming the beam out the window.

Liza and Fisher were strung up on the scarecrow stands, unmoving. Their wounds could not be determined from Heloise and Susan's distance. They didn't appear to be alive. They must have attempted to make a run for their car and try to find the kids, but clearly didn't make it.

"Should we go get them?" said Susan. "We can't leave them out there."

The silhouettes of two of the reindeer appeared next to Liza and Fisher's body. They were circling the bodies.

"Oh God, what are they doing?" Heloise whispered. The helpless feeling that washed over her was unbearable.

There was nothing they could do. The fires had begun. Both Liza and Fisher's dead bodies were lit up by gasoline and a match. The red and orange flames cast ominous, dancing shadows in the yard and along the trees, illuminating the reindeer that watched the blaze with fascination. The sound of the fire roaring replaced all of the silence. Susan and Heloise staggered back from the view. The reflection of the fire against the window's glass created a strange yellow glow in the playroom.

Chapter 67

Mary and Bright were exiting her father's office after securing it when they heard the sound of the projector start up in the movie room. As soon as they entered the hallway, they felt the cold breeze that billowed through the house.

They did not see the reindeer obscured in darkness in the corner behind them. It watched as they crept down the hallway. Both of them were oblivious to the presence waiting for the right time to strike. The presence that was having fun watching their fear and useless endeavor to survive.

Mary and Bright followed the cold draft to the foyer at the end of the hall. The front door was wide open. Mary rushed forward to close and lock it tightly.

"They might be in the house," she panted.

"We need to regroup," Bright said. "We don't know that anyone is in the house. Someone might have just tried to get to their car."

"I don't think everyone is alive," said Mary. The realization was hitting her. "I think some of the people I have loved my whole life may be gone."

"Don't think like that. Let's all meet back up and see who is missing."

Bang! Bang!

Knocks and thumps, slams and thuds, strikes against the walls of the house. They came from all sides, every direction. The reindeer were circling the house, banging on the outside, letting everyone inside know that they were next.

Ivy, Betsy, Stacy, Georgina, Tyler, and Mike appeared at the top of the stairs. Once they saw Mary and Bright, they breathed a collective sigh of relief and joined them. They listened intently as the banging noises against the sides of the house continued, harsher and more frenzied.

The banging stopped. Everything fell still. Stacy stepped forward to look out of the glass partitions on the side of the front door.

"Stacy, don't," said Betsy. Stacy put her hands up as if to say, "It's okay."

She stared out into the pitch black of the night. She almost let out a sigh when the reindeer's frame filled the glass, its eyes locked on hers. She lurched back with a small scream. As quickly as the reindeer had appeared, it disappeared back into the dark.

"Okay, everybody," Mary said. "We need to reconvene and create a distraction. There's safety in numbers. There's four of them and plenty of us. We have weapons. Now let's round everybody up."

"There aren't as many people to round up now, Aunt Mary," Ivy said. Her thoughts were on Ellie and how she'd never see her again. Betsy and Stacy took Ivy's hands in theirs.

"I know," said Mary, not knowing what else to say. "We're getting out of here."

They moved as a group to the movie room, where *The Family Stone* played against a shredded, torn screen. It looked like someone had burst through the movie screen to attack. The chairs had been moved and knocked around.

"They're inside," Mike said.

They found Susan and Heloise but couldn't find anyone else. The group shouted out the names of the missing, with no response. It was decided that they would remain in the living room for the time being.

"This was planned," said Heloise. "This whole night, this attack. This was premeditated."

"Where is my mother?" Mary said, trying not to become frantic.

"We have one of them tied upstairs in the attic!" Ivy said. All attention turned to her. "At least, I think he's still there."

"We have to go get him then," asserted Mary.

Chapter 68

Chief Fuller was in her SUV with the ladies, on her way back to the police station. They left Buchanan's body in Bernard Classen's grave for now. Once she got back to the station, she'd make some calls. For now, she was trying to keep a level head, as she'd tried to contact the other officers but wasn't receiving any response. She hadn't heard from Stacy in a while, and Nash hadn't checked in. The concern and worry she was trying to push aside began to creep in.

"McCloskey! Jennings! Cogan! Come in. Over," she repeated into the CB radio. "If you're all out getting a pizza, you better bring me back some. Come in. Over."

"I kept thinking about the article we found in Chester's things, about the family that was killed in that fire," said Sylvia. "What does he have to do with the Perkins family in Collinwood? I couldn't find a single tie, personal or business, between him and any member of that family. Then I realized. There was only one survivor of the fire, an unnamed foster son. It has to be John Patrick Colqhoun. The article even says the fire was 'suspicious' and it was likely arson, but none of the follow-up articles I read on it ever had an actual suspect in the crime."

"Because it was that little fucker John Patrick Colqhoun," finished Frances. "Kid got an early start on killing. He was a minor, so they didn't print his name in the paper."

"We need to find his other names and what other families he was shipped to stay with," Sylvia said. "I bet every one of the towns he lived in has had accidents or unsolved murders wherever he went."

"And now he's in my town," Fuller said.

Chapter 69

The plan was set. Weapons were in hand. Tyler and Mike would make a dash for their car while everyone else stood guard and fanned out on the front porch as lookouts. Georgina and Stacy would stay inside the house to listen for any unusual noises that indicated an unknown presence.

Tyler slowly opened the door into the darkness. The only sound they could hear was the wind blowing by. The house had been quiet and there was no evidence that the reindeer were nearby. Tyler and Mike held hands as they stepped onto the porch. Mary and Bright were right behind them. The rest followed, delicately choosing posts to keep watch from.

"Are you ready?" Tyler asked. Mike nodded.

Ivy and Betsy walked to the far end of the porch facing the road. They could see Tinsel Inc. from there. Ivy gave the signal that the coast was clear, as did Susan and Heloise from their position.

Tyler and Mike steadied themselves, feet dug into the wood, ready to run.

"Go," Bright said in a hush.

As they ran down the steps and to the parked vehicles, nobody noticed the razor-wire noose that descended from the roof of the porch. It tightened around Betsy's neck as she was lifted off of the ground, screaming and kicking her legs wildly. Her throat sliced open with ease and her blood rained down upon Ivy, who desperately attempted to free her from the taut garrote. Mary, Bright, Susan, and Heloise ran toward Betsy to help.

Tyler and Mike made it to their car. All of the tires had been slashed open, relieved of whatever air was inside.

Swoosh!

A carbon-aluminum composite arrow, launched from a bow and arrow, whizzed through the air and pierced through Tyler's chest and into Mike, who stood behind him. Then another. Then another. Three arrows protruded from Tyler's front and out of Mike's back. They coughed and choked on their own blood.

All everyone else could do from the porch was watch helplessly as their friends were taken down.

Susan and Heloise pulled Ivy with them back into the house. Mary and Bright were right behind them, slamming the door shut.

"What happened?" Georgina said, seeing Ivy covered in blood.

"We're trapped in this house!" said Susan.

Boom!

The explosion shook the entire house. The cars were on fire. One by one, each car lit up in a flaming ball like a chain reaction.

"If we can get out the back, we can make a run for the factory," said Bright.

"There's something we have to do first," Mary said, formulating an idea in her head. "The one that's tied up in the attic? He's our leverage. If we have him, they won't hurt us, right?"

"We don't know that," Heloise said.

"It's what we've got right now," said Mary. "They don't want us killing one of their own."

"Look!" Ivy shouted, her attention drawn outside.

The fire had lit up enough of the yard for everyone to see the large tree in the front lawn. Hayden had been tied to it. He was cut completely open, from sternum to groin. His innards were spilled at his feet, steaming in the cold.

Beside him was a large wooden stake sticking up from the ground. Aunt Elaine's head was skewered on its point.

Chapter 70

Fuller and the ladies arrived at the police station. All of the lights were off. It didn't look like anyone was inside. Fuller drew her gun, the feeling of dread and foreboding fully washing over her now. There was no reason the station would be empty and dark.

"Stay behind me," she ordered the women.

She was unprepared for the bloodbath that greeted her when she kicked the door open and flipped on the lights. The walls, the floor, and the furniture were all soaked in thick red blood. It had been the scene of a massacre.

Someone had mutilated Deputy McCloskey and Officers Jennings and Cogan. Chuck Brinkerhoff lay dead in his cell. It looked like an ambush, as the likelihood of someone being able to overcome three strong deputies was low. A full-on attack on police officers, her friends, who were unprepared for such violence and vengeance.

Fuller choked back any emotion, scanning the area for any signs of life. Officer Cogan was slumped over his desk, while McCloskey and Jennings were sprawled out on the floor. The women treaded carefully, their shoes and boots slipping in the pools of blood.

"Iola," Sylvia said. "I'm so sorry."

Fuller took a deep breath. She was not going to fall apart. She was going to find whoever was responsible for this. Her thoughts narrowed as only one person came to mind.

"Stacy," she said.

Mary and Bright elected to go to the attic to retrieve the incapacitated reindeer. Susan, Heloise, Ivy, Georgina, and Stacy were in charge of making sure nobody got inside the house. They huddled together in the living room, brandishing their weapons of choice. No one knew what to say. There were people unaccounted for. There were dead bodies only hundreds of feet away from them.

"We're going to be okay," Heloise tried to reassure everyone. She didn't know if she believed her own lies.

As Fuller and the ladies loaded themselves into her SUV, Sylvia's phone received a notification of a new email. She opened it immediately, recognizing the name of her friend from the federal adoption agency.

Fuller peeled out as the women listened to Sylvia read the email aloud.

"John Patrick Colqhoun, born December 25, 1976. Thirteen foster families until adopted in 1990, after which his name was legally changed," read Sylvia.

The women in the back leaned forward to see the pictures of the birth certificate and official court documents of the social security card and driver's license. Sylvia continued on, having found the information they needed.

"John Patrick Colqhoun is now officially known as Bright Harmon."

Chapter 71

Mary held back from screaming when she saw the carnage in the attic. She wondered who would do something this vicious and evil. All of these people, all of these decent people, whose lives were horribly snuffed out for no reason.

"Where is he?" she said, searching for the reindeer.

All that remained was a tangle of rope. The reindeer had broken free. Or someone had untied him.

"Mary," Bright said.

"We have to get everyone and get out of here," said Mary.

"Mary, there's something else I need to tell you."

"Can it wait?"

"No, I don't think it can."

"What is it?"

Mary noticed that Bright was now looking at her with a strange, almost disconnected stare. She thought maybe the night's blood-soaked events were finally crashing down on him. He wasn't as stoic as he wanted to seem.

"Mary," he said again.

"Yes, Bright?"

"I didn't just come to Tinselvania for work."

"Okay. We can discuss this later."

"There were other reasons for me to come."

"Let's go, Bright. Please. Let's just go. Everything else can wait."

"I can't wait anymore," he said, his mouth twisting into a smile that filled Mary with fear. He didn't even look the same. His eyes were empty, soulless.

She was too busy trying to figure out what was happening to notice as he lifted a table leg and hit her on the side of the head, knocking her unconscious.

Chapter 72

Heloise and Susan continued to stare out of the living room windows, searching the darkness for the reindeer or for any sign of their children. The room was silent except for their breathing.

"They're probably using a cell phone jammer," said Georgina. "That's why none of our phones are working."

A single note from the piano echoed through the house. Another. One by one, the sound of piano chords cut through the quiet. It was coming from the music room. Ivy, Stacy, and Georgina stood, looking out into the hallway. The sound stopped.

The plinking was replaced by loud, insistent static, as if coming from a television set. On top of the constant static, The Waitresses' "Christmas Wrapping" blared from another room down the hallway. The house was filled with discombobulating noise. It rang in everyone's ears, meant to drive them mad.

The reindeer stood at the very end of the hallway, its silhouette lined against the darkness. Like it was challenging them to a fight. Susan and Heloise rallied around the girls.

The electricity went out.

All sound and light ceased. Panic set in, causing the women to cry out. Ivy ushered the other women into the next room, locking the door behind them. At the same time, they heard the distinct sounds of footsteps thumping down the hall toward them.

The reindeer shook the door handle from the other side. When that didn't budge, it swung its ax against the door. The women backed away, running to the windows.

Susan and Heloise's hearts both leapt into their throats when they saw the children outside. They were walking toward the house from the woods.

The kids were alive. They looked confused and scared, trudging through the snowy yard. Some of the older kids were carrying the younger ones.

"Susan? Heloise?" Ivy said. They looked toward the other women, smiling in spite of their terror because they had found their children.

The reindeer had stopped trying to break down the door.

"Where did he go?" Stacy said.

Heloise threw the window open and leapt out. The others followed. They ran to the children, scooping up as many as they could, not wanting to look back at the house of horror behind them.

Stacy was the last at the window. The door burst open and the reindeer lunged to grab her. Instinctively, she remembered everything her mother had taught her. Her brain was blank and her body went into self-defense mode. She punched it in the stomach, slammed her foot down on its booted foot, smashed her fist into its nose, and then kicked it in its groin.

The reindeer fell to the ground in pain. Stacy vaulted out of the window onto the lawn and ran to the others.

Another reindeer stood at the corner of the house, watching them run into the forest.

The Classen house was on fire. Smoke swelled and rose to the sky, emanating from within the confines. As the fire grew and spread, taking over the different rooms and decimating everything inside, the women ran and didn't look back.

The fire raged and roared, as the sound of windows shattering, wood crackling, and objects exploding from within filled the night.

Chapter 73

It took Mary a few seconds to realize where she was. Her head hurt and she felt like there was a fuzz on her brain. Her vision steadied and she saw the familiar layout of the Tinsel Inc. factory line before her become clear. The spacious, sprawling room was filled with machinery and electronic equipment that was quiet now but roared during the day.

The lights buzzed above her and she heard voices chattering softly somewhere in the bowels of the building. Christmas music played softly over the loudspeakers.

Mary was tied up with rope and sparkly garland and placed in a plush office chair. She tried to break free of her restraints but they were tightly wrapped all around her. She was covered in tinsel, as if someone had taken a bucket of it and poured it all over her. The tape on her mouth was hanging off.

Flanking her on both sides were gigantic Christmas presents. Shiny red wrapping paper with a large green stripe running down the middle, capped with a mammoth gold bow. They were approximately five feet tall and three feet wide.

Bright. The memory came flooding back to her. Him smacking her upside her head after turning into some weird, crazed imitation of The Joker.

As if he was reading her mind, he appeared on the other side of the conveyor belt. He wasn't smiling. He looked peaceful but not happy. Like he had found some kind of contentment but it didn't necessarily bring him the joy he'd wished for.

"Bright," Mary said. The realization swept over her. She didn't know whether to laugh or cry. The guy she pictured starting a life with, someone she could see herself having the first dance at their wedding to Bon Jovi's "Bed of Roses" with, was a maniacal killer. There weren't any Hallmark cards for that.

"You know how they say killing isn't like it is in the movies?" said Bright. "They're wrong. Sometimes it is. I mean, if I'm being honest, not everything went according to plan. We had to improvise some stuff. But that's what makes it so exciting."

"Who's 'they'?"

"I don't hear voices in my head, Mary. That's for crazy people. I'm completely sober and sane. I see things clearly. I see you and the people of this town for what you really are."

"What have you done, Bright?"

"Don't you want to know if our love was real, Mary? Did I fake it all? Did I use you so my associates and I could kill everyone you love?"

"I don't care," Mary said, digging her heels into the ground. She didn't need to know now.

"Santa brought you some Christmas presents, Mary," Bright said. The way he said her name– with a harsh, pointed inflection– made her stomach flip.

He lifted each of the boxes, the one on the right first. Mary didn't look. She didn't want to know what Bright had chosen for her gruesome gifts.

"You can look now," said Bright. "I went to a lot of trouble to wrap those nicely."

She looked to her right and saw her mother. Alvinia was alive, but also tied up in a similar chair. On Mary's left was Bertha Havighurst, similarly incapacitated, with several bruises and cuts all over her. She was wide awake, her eyes like saucers. Her face was stained with tears. Her mouth, like Mary and Alvinia's, had been duct-taped shut.

Bertha shook her head at Mary as if to say, "There's no use fighting this. We're never getting out of here." Despite this, Mary still tried to wriggle out of the ropes. She wasn't going to give up this easily.

"This is where I give my great, big speech about why I did it," he said mirthlessly. "It's how all the scary movies end."

Bertha flinched as soon as Bright spoke. Alvinia began to stir. Mary stared at Bright, trying to fight the tightening fear in her chest. She had to get out of this situation. She had to think. She couldn't freak out now.

"Tonight was fun, wasn't it?" he continued. "I've had fun nights before, but nothing at this level. It was so easy to hide your dad's guns and unlock all the windows and doors while you were mooning over me like a smitten schoolgirl."

Alvinia's eyes were terror-stricken. She looked over at Mary pleadingly. Mary nodded to let her mom know that she was okay.

"How fucking stupid is tinsel? This whole ass-backwards town, obsessed with tinsel. It's literally everyone's entire life here. If the tinsel industry shut down, you'd have to close the entire area and turn it into a ghost town," said Bright. "It was me. I started the 'ass-tinsel' GleebGlob trend. I'm ShinyHappyButt37."

"You're a monster!" Mary screamed.

"Tinsel isn't stupid," said a voice from the dark corner. "We made our livelihoods from it."

The four reindeer entered the room, flanking Bright on either side. Bright sighed deeply, rubbing his temples. He laughed; not an amused laugh, but a humorless one. The reindeer had taken their masks off. They were still in their costumes but their faces were fully visible now.

"You may know my friends, Santa's reindeer," he said. Mary could see how impressed with himself he was.

Uncle Cobden, Aunt Hepzibah, Ethan, and Josh. Her own family. Alvinia breathed heavily, barely able to mask her disbelief.

Josh flipped a switch on the wall that started up the conveyor belt. A decomposed, rotted corpse, seemingly both wet and dried out at the same time, rolled into view. Josh turned off the machine, the body in full view.

"Look, your father wanted to join us!" said Bright.

It was her dad. She recognized the suit he had been buried in. It was tattered now, but it was definitely his. Mary almost threw up at the sight of her father's body. Alvinia was crying, struggling to get out of the chair she was in.

"Your dad," Uncle Cobden said. "He was supposed to be my best friend. My brother. My older brother, who was always supposed to look out for me and protect me. We're family. Instead, he pushed me out of the business our family made."

Alvinia screamed against the tape over her mouth. She shook her head side to side vehemently.

"Money and tinsel, that's all he cared about," continued Cobden. "He stole the company right out from underneath me, just like he did with Chester Persimmons all those years ago. He didn't care who he hurt or what the fallout was. The rumors and the gossip around town about us. He wanted the company all for himself."

Cobden ripped the tape off of Alvinia's mouth.

"You embezzled from the company!" she shouted. "He tried to save you. You were going to get caught. You were going to go to jail. The only way he could keep you out of prison was if you gave up your position at the company!"

Hepzibah, Ethan, and Josh looked at each other with shock. They had never heard that story before.

"You are a liar!" Cobden roared. "You're just like him. Anything to get me out of the way and have the company all to yourself. You loved being the wife of a successful businessman. Prancing around town like you were the First Lady of Tinselvania."

"He loved you, Cobden," Alvinia said. "We all did. He was trying to protect you."

"What about my dad?" interjected Bright. "It seems like there's a pattern here and the variable is good, dead old Bernard here, right?" He patted Bernard's corpse.

"Your dad?" Alvinia said.

"My dad. Chester Persimmons."

"You're not one of Chester and Noreen's sons," said Alvinia. "I knew those boys. Garland and Shepherd. You're not either one of them."

"The fact remains, I am still Chester Persimmons' son," Bright said, turning his attention to Bertha. "Isn't that right, Mom?"

Alvinia looked to Bertha, whose eyes confirmed everything. Her shame, her fear, her regrets, her sadness. Mary and Alvinia couldn't believe what they were hearing.

"Mom took a vacation to hide me from the judging eyes of the townspeople, then dumped me off at the nearest fire station once I popped out of her," Bright said. "Then she ran back here and never looked back. I grew up in foster homes, being beaten and starved and pissed on and wearing dirty hand-me-downs. Mom here ran a cozy bed-and-breakfast while I slept on a mattress so filthy and disease-ridden, you wouldn't give it to a dog. Do you know the things that my foster parents used to make me do, Mom? Do you? You don't want to know."

Bertha attempted to speak. Bright took the tape off her mouth for her.

"I was young and afraid, John," she said, tears streaming down her face. "I'm so sorry. I wish I could go back and fight for you. I would do anything to make it up to you. I had no one. I had no support and no money. My family threatened to disown me."

"You had me!" Bright screamed.

"John," said Bertha. "I thought about you every day of my life. I gave you up so you could have a better life than I could've given you. I would take it all back if I could. I swear. I'm so sorry, John. Please forgive me."

"My own father didn't even know about me until I stole my files and found out who my birth parents were. You lied to him and you lied to everyone in this town. I am the sin that you hid from the world, here in the flesh!"

"John, your father knew I was pregnant with you."

"You are lying! Shut your lying mouth!"

"I'm sorry, John, but he knew. I don't know what he told you, but he knew. He paid for me to go away and take care of it."

"My father would never have done that. I visited him in the asylum. Did you? No, you never did. You were glad to be rid of him. Just like you were glad to be rid of me. He told me how you lie and how you never wanted me. My only regret is that I didn't kill your children while I was here. But there's still time."

"John," Bertha implored him.

"Stop calling me 'John!'" Bright shouted. "That's not my name. That boy died a long time ago. Because of you."

Bright ripped the tape off of Mary's mouth, enraged. He just wanted to cause pain. He grabbed his head and mumbled something to himself.

"Imagine how lucky I felt when I met Ethan and Josh at a Christmas convention," said Bright, composing himself. "We got to talking about the town they were from and how their uncle duped their father out of the business. Just like he did mine. How Bernard Classen, upstanding citizen and noble businessman, was really just a snake oil salesman who only looked out for himself. And then, when my father moved to a new state to start his own Christmas business, your father made sure to slander him and bury him with lies so nobody would do business with him. All those years ago, a chance encounter with people who understood me brought us to this night."

"Chester wanted out," Alvinia said. "He wanted to start his own business. He told Bernard that he could buy out his shares. Your dad was having some sort of midlife crisis at the time. We never knew the extent of it or what was really going on, but he needed to get away from Tinselvania. When he started his own business, it was just bad luck and faulty investments that took it down. Not my husband."

"You're just like him. You refuse to take any blame for what he's done."

"There's so much more to these things that you don't know, Bright," Alvinia said calmly. "It's not all black-and-white. He wasn't well when you knew him. He did horrible things and couldn't face it."

"That's the wrong way to talk about my father," Bright said, without any emotion. His tonelessness was a threat.

"Bright," Mary said. "Weren't you happy here? Even for a moment?"

"Cousin Mary," said Ethan. "You think you're so much smarter than everybody else. It must be nice to have everything handed to you. The company just waiting for you to be CEO while the rest of us bust our asses in school and at work and will never be rewarded because they're not the boss' daughter. No matter how good we are, how smart, how successful, it's always you, Mary. Perfect Mary with her perfect life. Nobody else gets any praise or attention because we all have to live in your shadow."

"Yeah!" Josh said.

"How could you all do this?" Alvinia said.

"Because, dear Alvinia," said Cobden, getting uncomfortably close to her. "You deserve this. You reap what you sow."

"Those people at the party had nothing to do with this!" said Mary.

"Collateral damage," said Bright. "Wrong place, wrong time. They were in the way. And it was fun."

"Aunt Hepzibah," Mary said pleadingly. "Why?"

Hepzibah drew closer to Mary. Their eyes met. Hepzibah almost seemed repentant and sorrowful, like she was trying to apologize to Mary through her eyes. Until she slammed the knife down into Mary's thigh. Mary squealed and jolted up.

"We were never that close," Hepzibah hissed.

"How do you think you'll get away with this?" said Alvinia.

"What do you mean?" asked Cobden. "Hepzibah and I aren't even here. We're on a cruise somewhere in the Atlantic. Ethan and Josh were in the factory all night. Bright was just an innocent victim who survived the massacre. There's no other witnesses who can say otherwise."

"You're all fucking stupid," Mary said.

"What did you say?" sneered Bright.

"You heard me. All of this. How pathetic," said Mary. She looked between Ethan, Josh, Cobden, Hepzibah, and Bright. "You're a bunch of weak crybabies, sobbing into your oatmeal because I got to be CEO. Well, you can have that job if you want it so bad. And you blame my dad because you're a thieving cretin who wasn't smart enough not to get caught. Josh, do you even take a dump unless Ethan goes first? And you're all too dense to see how insane and ridiculous this whole situation is. You murdered people because you can't take responsibility for yourselves or you're too busy blaming everyone else because you're a bunch of psychopathic assholes."

"It's not a smart idea to mock the very same people you're trying to convince not to kill you," said Ethan.

"You're going to kill us anyway," Mary said. "Might as well go out with the truth."

"People have killed for less," said Bright.

"Yeah, they're a bunch of assholes too."

"We're going to play a Christmas game," Bright said, unfazed. "Look up."

Mary, Alvinia, and Bertha did as they were instructed. Above them was a mechanism attached to the ceiling that looked like an upside-down swing set; an apparatus constructed of various gadgets, wheels, and ropes. Fastened to the various components were three axes in front of the women, three cinder blocks directly overhead, and three shotguns pointed diagonally toward them from behind. One of each kind for each of the captive women. Taut strings affixed to the weapons kept them rigid and still, high above their heads but close enough that the damage to them would be lethal.

"It's my own invention," said Ethan. "Maybe I should've been an engineer and not a CFO. I could've gotten more credit."

"I helped," said Josh.

Bright, Cobden, and Hepzibah rushed toward Mary, Bertha, and Alvinia with deranged, gleeful expressions painted on their faces. The people Mary once knew, who she thought that she knew, had taken their masks of sanity off. All she could see now was their madness, their raving and demented ideas that had consumed them for years.

They spun Mary, Alvinia, and Bertha's chairs around, facing them toward the far back wall. A vast, wide, maroon-colored curtain spread from ceiling to floor, clearly obscuring whatever surprise they had in store for their victims.

Bright stood before the curtain. Ethan held a long, thick rope that was attached to the top of the curtain. Bright produced one of those slender, pencil-thin microphones that game show hosts used in the '70s.

"Are you ready to play?" he asked. Josh shone a giant spotlight on Bright, maneuvering it as he walked.

Ethan yanked the curtain. It crashed to the ground to reveal a crudely made, colossal replica of the *Hollywood Squares* set. A behemoth-sized tic-tac-toe set, taking up the entirety of the wall. Cobden, Hepzibah, Ethan, and Josh could barely contain their exhilaration at the sight of it.

In each of the set's squares was a corpse with a handwritten name tag placed before them. The center square was the newly deceased, newly stolen body of Chester Persimmons. The empty, blank eyes and bloated carcasses of Emmett Branscombe, Estelle McGarrigle, Gordon and Patience Frost, Jed Kubiak, Kara and Nick Halloran, and Aunt Elaine stared back at Mary, Alvinia, and Bertha from their seats. Some of them were headless.

"We can't call it *Hollywood Squares* or we'll get sued," said Bright. "So welcome to today's edition of *Tic-Tac-Toe-selvania.*"

Mary started to laugh. In all her horror and disbelief, her instinct was to burst out into uncontrollable, disbelieving laughter. She shook her head from side to side, unable to even hide her incredulity.

"What's so funny, Mary?" Bright said.

"None of you even realize how fucking crazy this is," chuckled Mary. "This is the dumbest, most ridiculous thing I've ever seen. I mean, you fruit-loop, cheese-headed maniacs actually took the time to build this insane thing and you don't even see how completely bonkers you are."

"There's no crazy people here," said Bright. "Only passionate ones with truth on their side."

"You sad, pathetic jackholes," Mary said.

Bright stepped up to Mary and thrust a knife into her other leg, the one that Hepzibah hadn't stabbed before. She screamed and grimaced at the pain.

"Don't speak unless spoken to or the next cut is your throat," Bright said.

"Mary," Alvinia said quietly, wishing she could help and comfort her daughter. She knew they were trapped.

"Okay, if everyone is done back-talking, we can start the game," said Bright, motioning toward the collection of cadavers behind him.

"First question to you, Mom," he continued, standing in front of Bertha, speaking into the microphone in his hand like a demented Wink Martindale. "It's a warm-up question, a really easy one. Don't be nervous. Let's see what our celebrity guests say. Aunt Elaine is going to answer and you see if you agree with what she says."

Bright leaned closer to Bertha. "Name the 2007 romantic comedy starring Hugh Grant as a washed-up pop star and Drew Barrymore as his writing partner."

Cobden stood behind Aunt Elaine's lifeless body. He treated her like a life-sized puppet, manipulating her head with his hands and lifting her limp arm to make it appear as if she were thinking of the answer.

"*We Bought a Zoo*, my favorite movie," Cobden said in a high-pitched, overdone imitation of Aunt Elaine's voice. He shook her head up and down.

Bertha choked back her sobs. She didn't know what to say. Bright's intense gaze penetrated through her, wracking her with fear and shock.

"Come on, Mom! You know this one. I bet you watched it all cozied up under some blankets on the couch with the kids you kept."

"I'm sorry you weren't given the love you deserved, son," Bertha said.

"Final answer?" announced Bright.

Bertha kept sobbing. Cobden maneuvered Aunt Elaine's head and arms in a "I don't know" motion.

"Judges?" bellowed Bright, looking toward his co-conspirators. They shook their heads "no" in unison.

"I'm sorry, Mom, wrong answer. We were looking for *Music and Lyrics*. That's *Music and Lyrics*. You don't get any points but you get an 'A' for the effort in your fake sincerity and make-believe contrition."

Bright turned his attention toward Alvinia. "Mary's mom, you're up. Another easy one. Name the group whose song 'Doctor! Doctor!' went to number eleven on the *Billboard* Hot 100 in July 1984."

Alvinia was silent. Her mind was blank. Her thoughts were only of Mary and her family. Of all of the things she still wanted to do. Of how she'd ever recover from this.

"Time's ticking, Mary's mom. You're going to need a 'Doctor! Doctor!' if you don't come up with an answer. I'll give you a hint. It's not A Flock of Seagulls." Bright paced before the women, his relish at what he perceived as his diabolical genius clearly written on his face.

"It's Thompson Twins," Alvinia said, her voice flat and defeated.

"You are correct! For your prize, I'll bury you in the same unmarked grave in the woods as I do your husband's corpse," Bright announced. She glared down at Mary. "Now, Mary. If you could have a do-over on any moment of your life, what would you choose?"

"I think today as a whole would be a solid pick," said Mary.

"I'm sorry, Mary. We were looking for, 'When I stole the CEO position from my cousins,'" Bright said. "But your humor is noted and appreciated. It won't win you any points for the game, though. And I know you want to make it to the bonus round."

"Now, Mom," he resumed. "What do you think will be your last thoughts on this earth as you die?"

"They'll be of my family," Bertha said. "That includes you, son. It's not too late to stop this. You can put an end to this madness. You can have a good life. I'll help you. I'll be there for you. Things can be different. It's never too late, son."

"Ah, Mom, the dozens of dead bodies we've left around Tinselvania would disagree with you. You're not sorry for what you did. You're sorry because you're being punished for it. There's no winning for people who are disingenuous. It's unbecoming of a competitor."

Bright pulled a remote control out of his pocket. Bertha opened her mouth to say something to him. He ignored her and pressed a red button.

Blast!

The shotgun aimed above Bertha fired. The bullet launched directly into her head, causing it to burst and spray blood and brain matter on Mary, Alvinia, and the floor. Bright wiped away the gore splatter that splashed his clothes. Mary and Alvinia screamed, struggling harder than ever to break free of their restrictive binds.

"It's a cutthroat game, folks. We had to send my mom off with some parting gifts. There will be no consolation prizes for you ladies, though. This is the lightning round."

"Enough," said Cobden. "These two are ours. You had your turn."

"Wait, just one more thing," said Bright, pressing another button on the remote. The cinder block above Bertha came crashing down upon her body, splitting her open and smashing her bones. Bright stood like a statue, staring at Bertha's demolished corpse.

"Was it the fairy tale you had in mind?" Cobden said, as he, Hepzibah, Ethan, and Josh made strides toward Mary and Alvinia.

"I have one question for you," Mary said, as serenely as she could muster. "If Bright was sent here to help take over the company, then you would've gotten what you wanted anyway. I'd be out of the way. So, what is the point of all of this for you?"

Bright's smirk at Mary said it all. He had no idea that she knew that he had been hired to manifest a takeover. He thought she was clueless about the whole situation. She was even smarter than he thought. It made her even more attractive to him. He hadn't meant to find Mary so interesting and charming; it happened despite his ulterior motives for coming to town.

"Bright was never going to get control of the company," Ethan said. "But with you and your family dead, that leaves me next in line for CEO, wherein I bring my father back into the fold."

"What about me?" said Josh, as if this just occurred to him. "Why can't I be CEO? Why does it automatically get to be you?"

"It doesn't matter, Josh," said Hepzibah. "You'd both have the controlling share in the factory. The business would be ours again. We'd be out from under the militant, watchful judgment of queen bees Mary and Alvinia Classen. For once. Finally."

"You guys are all real dicks," Mary said, her jaw set defiantly.

"Family should always stick together. And support each other. And have each other's backs. And look out for each other," raved Ethan. "Your dad only looked out for himself. He abandoned us. He renounced his loyalty and disregarded the people who were there for him and made him all of the money he loved so much."

"You've covered this already, Cousin Ethan," Mary said. She wanted to sound strong and brave, but she was shaking inside. She didn't want her life to end this way. "You're risking losing your audience."

Clank!

The sound of doors opening in the distance echoed through the factory. People were there. Bright, Cobden, Hepzibah, Ethan, and Josh instantly swiveled in the direction of the noises. Footsteps and voices reverberated from the depths of the building.

"I thought everyone else was dead," said Bright.

"Well, almost everyone," Cobden said. None of Cobden and his family's immediate relations, or any of the children, were meant to be harmed. Susan, Heloise, and Georgina had no clue who were underneath the reindeer costumes anyway. The only people they hadn't taken care of who were on the original hit list were Ivy and Stacy, and there'd be time to find them later.

"Help us!" screamed Alvinia. She hoped whoever was there could hear her. "Help! Help us!"

Bright put the duct tape back over her mouth. Alvinia fought against it but wasn't strong enough. Cobden directed his sons to check out the sound. Ethan and Josh went into the hallway.

"It's over, Bright," Mary said.

"Our relationship or the fun we're all having here?"

"Both. You won't get away with any of this."

"Such big threats for someone all tied up. We'll still have time to kill you and your mother and get away, after we take care of whoever stupidly decided to make a late-night visit to the factory. All of the security cameras are off. No one even knows we were here. And the fire we're going to start will take care of any incidental evidence. Think of it. You're all dead, we get the insurance money and the company, and we rebuild it in our images while we stomp all over the ashes of where you burned. Now, no more talking."

Chapter 74

Ethan and Josh went from room to room, searching for the interlopers. Ethan tapped Josh's shoulder and pointed in the direction of the office. They saw motion coming from inside.

They cautiously entered, their eyes adjusting to the dark room. Josh flicked on the overhead lights.

As soon as they did, they saw Willa and Belle waiting for them, their guns pointed directly at them.

"Have a seat, boys," said Willa.

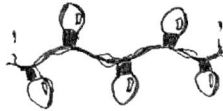

"Ethan? Josh?" Hepzibah called down the dark hallway. Bright and Cobden were by her side, struggling to see in the blackened distance.

They did not see Sylvia and Frances crouched down next to the factory line. They stayed low to the ground, making their way over to Mary and Alvinia. The women hid behind Mary and Alvinia's chairs and began to untie all of their restraints.

Bright turned and saw what Sylvia and Frances were up to. He clicked a button on the remote in his hand.

The axes all swung down with brute force. Sylvia and Frances yanked Mary and Alvinia's chairs out of the way, the ax blades swooshing by them. Bright clicked another button and sent the remaining cinder blocks crashing down.

Mary and Alvinia were freed from their binds. They reached down to undo the tethers at their feet as Bright, Cobden, and Hepzibah rushed them.

"Freeze!" shouted Fuller. The chief appeared from a side door, gun drawn. "Hands up!"

Bright, Cobden, and Hepzibah had their backs to Fuller. They all stopped in place, barely raising their hands in the air. Sylvia and Frances had guns aimed at them as well. Fuller strode toward the murderous trio as Mary and Alvinia got behind Sylvia and Frances.

"Drop your weapons!" Fuller commanded. Cobden and Hepzibah obeyed. Bright turned toward Fuller, his eyes filled with defiance and ego. He pressed a button on the remote.

Bang! Boom! Boom!

Bombs and explosives set off throughout the building. Homemade incendiary devices placed strategically around the factory were now activated. The walls and ground vibrated and convulsed, the edifice rocked to its foundation.

A barrage of nails flew from one of the combustible devices, showering the factory line. Everyone hit the floor. Flames erupted all throughout the building. Some of the walls cracked and the ceiling rumbled, spraying mineral wool and fiberglass.

In the office, where Willa and Belle held Ethan and Josh at bay, the explosion knocked the women down and allowed the criminals to dash out of the room. Belle got back to her feet, helping Willa up. Willa had a bloody gash on her head.

Ethan and Josh took off down the hallway toward their parents and Bright. In the factory line room, Bright used the distraction to make an escape, as Hepzibah pulled Cobden out of the way off debris that collapsed and blew past them. His body had become dead weight. Hepzibah screamed as she realized his whole face and torso had been punctured and destroyed by hundreds of the sharp nails.

"No! Cobden, no!" she sat beside him, her moans of sadness and loss louder than the fire that burned around her.

Ethan and Josh saw their father's dead body and helped their mother to her feet. Their faces were full of rage. When they scanned the room, they couldn't find Mary or Alvinia.

Fuller was hit by a shard of shrapnel that cut her side, even through the Kevlar vest she wore. She held her hand over the wound as Sylvia and Frances assisted her in getting out of the room.

They met up with Belle and the wounded Willa. Mary pushed her mother toward Frances, who was helping Fuller out of the building. She knew her mother wouldn't leave without her, but Mary had unfinished business to attend to.

"Mary, come on!" Alvinia said.

"Get them out of here!" Sylvia said. They heard Ethan and Josh clattering through the halls and rooms looking for them.

Frances took Fuller and Alvinia, while Belle held on to Willa. The building shuddered again, sending rubble everywhere. Mary realized that Bright must have disabled the alarm and sprinkler systems. The bombs had destroyed certain areas of the factory, but the fires seemed to be contained directly in the areas where the explosions were, not spreading or giving off too much black smoke.

The ladies made it to the main exit door. Mary and Sylvia waited inside as the others got Fuller and Willa to safety. Mary's legs throbbed and ached from the knife wounds. Sylvia put her hand on Mary's shoulder as they attempted to exit.

Slam!

The outside security gates crashed down over the doors and windows, leaving Mary and Sylvia trapped inside the factory. Frances spun around and pulled on the barrier, to no avail. It was locked in place. Bright had initiated the lockdown sequence for the factory, something Mary had never needed to use, as it was in case of extreme emergency.

"I know another way out," said Mary.

"Get Fuller and Willa to a doctor!" Sylvia shouted to Belle, Frances, and Alvinia.

"Mary!" Alvinia said.

"I'm all right, Mom," Mary said. "We'll be out with you as soon as we can."

Sylvia unholstered her gun. Bright, Hepzibah, Ethan, and Josh were likely still in the building. Mary concentrated on getting them out of there, trying to ignore her fear and the blood that ran down her legs.

There was an access tunnel to the outside in the basement. Mary and Sylvia fumbled their way over the rubble and the furniture and shelves that had been knocked to the ground. The lights flashed and blinked on and off, covering them in darkness and then bright light, making it hard to see. Mary knew the factory. She could get them out.

She stopped when she noticed the flickering light in the conference room. She wanted to see what it was. On the large table were dozens of candles. The room was decorated with wreaths, tinsel, garland, and Christmas lights. Torn photos of Mary and her family and friends, the factory workers, the associates, and product advertisements littered the room. Shadows danced and distorted over the walls.

Chester Persimmons' unmoving, swollen body was at the head of the table, propped up at a slant on a handmade wooden stand using wires and gadgets. A decrepit stench floated off of his corpse. A shrine to him, the man who started this nightmare.

Sylvia put her finger to her lips to shush Mary and guided her behind the door. As they did, Ethan and Josh entered, their eyes focused on Chester.

"We're gonna have to get this guy out of here," said Josh.

"Let Bright deal with it," Ethan said. "It's his dad. Tomorrow, the company is ours and we'll never see either of them again. There's something we have to take care of right now."

With that, Ethan whipped around and swung the ax in his hand at the door Mary and Sylvia hid behind. Both women jumped back and leapt from their hiding spot. Sylvia aimed her gun at the men.

"Don't move," she said.

"You're not going to shoot me," said Ethan, filled with confidence and bravado.

"You're right," said Sylvia.

Bam!

She kicked the door forward. It connected directly with Ethan's head, knocking him on the ground. Mary kicked the ax away from him and picked it up. Josh charged, screaming at Sylvia.

Mary didn't think. She buried the ax in Josh's torso. He looked at her in shock, as if he couldn't actually believe his cousin was capable of doing so. As if he were surprised by his own demise.

Mary wished at that moment that she had some kind of witty one-liner, like they did in the movies. Her brain was on autopilot, her fight-or-flight kicking in. Later she'd think about it and wish she'd said, "Consider this your resignation," or some similar wisecrack.

Ethan ambled to his feet. Before he did, Sylvia gave him a swift kick in the side, sending him back down. His head lay between the doorframe and the door. Mary slammed the door shut on his head. Once. Twice. Again. Again. Her insides were bursting with rage and anger at what these degenerates had done to her and her family and friends.

"Okay, Mary, okay, he's definitely dead," said Sylvia, trying not to step in the mush and gore on the floor that used to be Ethan's face and head.

Splash!

A bucket of tinsel waste– the disused, toxic, noxious odds and ends and rejected product that couldn't be used for the public– burst onto Sylvia from the darkness of the hallway. Sylvia tripped backward, surprised, rubbing her eyes and trying to get the fumes and harmful fragments off of her. Her eyes burned as her vision blurred. Her skin tingled.

Hepzibah's banshee-like scream tore through the air. She shrieked at the sight of her dead sons and launched on top of Mary, wildly clawing and kicking at her. Mary tripped backwards, trying to fight Hepzibah off. Hepzibah knocked Mary on top of the conference table, the bowie knife in her hand poised to strike.

Mary avoided the oncoming knife stabs that made dents and holes in the table beneath her. She managed to toss Hepzibah off of her, sending her into Chester's standing corpse. The force of Hepzibah's tumble caused Chester to crash down on top of both of them. His purple veins, open eyes, and wet skin bore down on Mary, who slipped out from beneath him.

Hepzibah, her hair wild and her screaming incessant, charged. She looked like a crazed woman who was raised in the woods by animals. Mary dodged her advance.

"You killed my sons!" she screeched.

Bang! Bang! Bang!

Sylvia fired three shots. Hepzibah crumpled to the ground like a rag doll.

"Helicopter moms," she said to Mary.

Why couldn't I have thought to say that? Mary chastised herself.

Mary brought Sylvia down through the stairwell and tunnels to the basement, over to the metal double doors to the outside. It was built like a storm shelter, an extra exit in case of emergency. Frances was waiting like a guard dog, helping Sylvia on to the snowy ground and to a waiting car. Pike, in the driver's seat, nodded at them.

Mary took a final look at the destruction around her. Her family's factory. It would take some time but this could all be rebuilt. She wasn't ready to face the things that couldn't be. Her friends and family, taken away from her.

The moment she put her foot on the first step to freedom, she felt the unseen hands thrust her backwards. Bright leapt out from the darkness, pulling the storm doors shut and latching them. Frances banged on the other side, unable to make them budge.

Pain shot through Mary's wounded legs, along with the new pain in her skull. She had hit her head on something in the dark. She backed away, still on the ground, as Bright approached. His game show host demeanor was gone, replaced by hate and seething anger.

"I did wonder if we could make a life here together, Mary," he said. "I really do like you. You're a weirdo, but the good kind of weird. For a moment, I pictured us having friends over for canasta and taking your mom shopping at T.J. Maxx. We'd watch *Hope Floats* together and I'd pretend I hated it but I would secretly love it because I was with you. But then I remembered your bloodline. You're a Classen. All the Classen family does is destroy everything it touches."

"You should look up the definition of 'irony' sometime," said Mary. *Ah, good one! Finally!* she thought.

Bright raised the ax over her. "Let's see that Classen blood."

"You first," Mary said, grabbing a rusty shard of metal on the floor and sinking it into Bright's leg. He loosened his grip on the ax and reached down to pull it out. Mary ran up the stairs and through the tunnel. She heard Bright in pursuit, screaming out her name.

Frankenstein's Laboratory. Chemicals, spare parts, scientific equipment that could be used as weaponry. A small fire amongst the rubble flickered in the corner. Mary didn't hear Bright anymore. He either ran down a different hallway or was hiding in wait. She went to work.

Mary moved the large spool of plastic and unraveled it, stretching it from one side of the open doorway to the other. She listened for Bright's approach.

"Come and get me, motherfucker," she said as she crouched down next to the door frame.

She didn't have to wait long. She heard Bright calling her name in a mocking sing-song, his footsteps getting closer. She saw his silhouette pass by the doorway, not noticing her in the darkness.

She took a deep breath. She could make it to the back exit if he were far enough away.

"Mary," Bright's voice said from the black.

He hovered for a brief moment, having spotted her. She pulled the plastic taut. He lunged for her, knife in his hand, losing his balance as the plastic caught on his legs. He fell forward. He tried to catch himself and regain his balance but sprawled face-first on the ground. He swung the knife at the air around him, trying to slash Mary.

Mary stood, grabbing a microscope off of one of the tables. She smashed him over the head. Then again. And again. Bright was unconscious, his head bleeding and cracked.

She dragged his limp body to the giant high-heel chair and wrapped him in plastic, sealing him in. He moaned, stirring back to reality.

"I'll kill you!" he screamed at her, trying to break free of his prison of plastic wrap. He struggled and shook like a shark caught in a fisherman's net.

Mary doused him with the various chemicals that they used to make tinsel. Bright was fighting, yelling, roaring to release himself. The chair teetered and wobbled, but he was trapped. Mary grabbed a handful of papers, putting them into the flaming rubble until they lit up.

"Nobody talks about how dangerous the tinsel industry is," she said, glaring directly into his evil, angry eyes.

"You'll never be free of me, Mary," he said, his murderous thoughts written all over his face. "I've already won."

"Let's see if winners are flammable," Mary said, dropping the flaming pages on him. The plastic and chemicals ignited instantly. Bright and the high-heel chair were engulfed in flames in moments. She backed away as he screamed, watching for only a moment in the doorway, then taking off down the hall.

She reached the factory line, strewn with bodies and game show sets. She heard the sirens outside the building. The police and firefighters were there, trying to gain entry and rescue her.

The smell of charred flesh hit her before anything else. Bright, his entire body aflame, came barreling into the room. His skin was blackened and smoke billowed off of him, but his eyes were unmistakable. The rage, the anger. He ran full-speed at Mary.

She looked at the rotted husk of her father's corpse, still flat on its back on the assembly line.

"Sorry, Dad," she said. She grabbed his leg bone and broke it off of his body with a sickening snap. She held her father's jagged, decaying femur in her hands. The end of the break was sharp and pointed. Bright launched his attack.

As he did, Mary held the femur out in front of her. Bright knocked into her as they both crashed atop the metallic assembly line. The fire on his body burned her skin and clothes. She was laid out on the line, Bright on top of her.

Her father's femur bone had impaled Bright through his torso. Dark red blood, steaming and thick, leaked out of his mouth onto Mary. She flipped a switch on the line. The machine started up, the rolls and wheels grinding.

Mary pushed her father's corpse off of the line. Bright wasn't giving up. His body was weakened but he still tried to claw at Mary. She got out from underneath him and watched his final moments as his body disappeared up the moving line and into a giant machine used for pressing tinsel. The machine groaned and squealed as it smashed and thrashed Bright's corpse.

When he came out on the other side, his body was shredded and gored. Pieces of tinsel jutted out from various parts of his corpse.

Mary didn't stay to say goodbye. She made her way to the back exit, where EMTs rushed toward her and police officers and firefighters made their way into the building. Mary pushed past everyone as she saw Sylvia, who hugged her tightly.

"You're okay," she whispered to Mary.

EMTs loaded Mary into the back of a waiting ambulance, putting ointment and bandages on her. She watched her childhood home and Tinsel Inc. through the window as they drove away. The buildings grew smaller and smaller in the distance. She fought back tears as the reality of her night caught up to her. Sylvia held Mary's hand all the way to the hospital.

Chapter 75

Two men stood at the tree line behind the wreckage that once was the Classen home. They hid in the night, staring over the distance to the police and fire teams who pulled bodies from both the house and the factory. No one had noticed them.

Garland Persimmons looked over at his brother Shepherd. They had dumped their reindeer costumes in the house fire to be burned up. Their father was dead. Tinselvania had been punished for what they'd done to him. They had more things to discuss, but they had to go. They had to get back to their respective homes and practice their surprised reactions when the news of the night's tragedies broke. Without any words exchanged, they disappeared into the forest.

There would be time to decide what to do next.

THE END

Acknowledgments:

A very special thank you to Grandma, for always encouraging me. You are the best.

Lisa Stout, my writing guru, for all of your guidance, patience, time, and invaluable advice. "Thank you" doesn't even cover it.

Dr. Shannon White, for your endless enthusiasm, math homework help, and dedication to reading (and editing) every single thing I've written. You are incredible.

Katie, Gavin, Owen, and Simon Allen, for investing in me in more ways than one. I am beyond grateful to you guys for always believing in me.

James Sanguinetti, for your technical support, feedback, perfectly-timed Alice Johnson motivational video, and push to keep writing.

Meghan Buckley, the red-pen queen, corn maze champion, character guide Excel warrior, and pop-culture litmus test subject, for all of your heartfelt thought and genuine care.

Our goddaughter Frankie, who is as smart, strong, resilient, brave, capable, and resourceful as the most iconic final girls.

Dad, for letting me watch *Friday the 13th Part 3* on Fox Channel 5 when I was a kid and starting my lifelong love of horror.

For your constant love and support: Anna Maria Skiotis, Steve Galuna, Sofia Maria and Diana; Colin and Olivia Capelle; Danielle, Harry, and A.J. Providakes; Diane Treacy; Drew, Kassie, Carver, and Sailer McConville; Dylan Campbell; Erica and Brian Sheldon; Grandpa; Holly and Sharon Lemanski; Jessica Raymond; Jessica, Andy, and Leah Simon; Jim Paul; Julie and Jake Forgit; Kay Forgit; Kerri Allard; Kristin O'Brien; Maribel Palin; Mary Motley; Mia Turner; Paul Buckley; Roberta Townsend; Ryan, Sara, and Emerson Hastings; Shannon, Ryan, and Ryder Vogt; Stephanie Iscovitz and Frank Valdez; Tami, Travis, Mirren, and Porter Harless; Toni and Steve Weymer; the rest of the Forgit family; and every wonderful person who I haven't mentioned here.

A gigantic thanks and eternal appreciation to everyone who spends their hard-earned money to buy this book.

About the Author:

Matt Forgit lives and writes in New England. Other than his love of Christmas movies and everything scary, his interests include spending time with friends and family, trying to be a cool uncle, movies, television, music, reading, travel, eating, board games, folklore, being near the ocean, and the hope that someday *Chopping Mall: The Musical* will become a reality. He is terrible with social media, dreams of owning a haunted bed and breakfast atop a cliffside overlooking the sea, and doesn't usually talk about himself in the third person.

WHO'S WHO IN TINSELVANIA

The Classen Family

- Bernard Classen (deceased), former CEO Tinsel Inc. + Alvinia Classen

    - Mary Classen, CEO Tinsel Inc.

    - Glory Classen Ellis, Packing/Shipping Tinsel Inc. + Cotter Ellis
        - Ivy Ellis

    - Noelle Classen Kubiak, Art Dept Tinsel Inc. + Jed Kubiak
        - Dashi Kubiak
        - Acorn Kubiak

- Cobden Classen + Hepzibah Classen

    - Ethan Classen, CFO Tinsel Inc. + Heloise Classen
        - Georgina Classen
        - Dulcie Classen
        - Maisie Classen
        - Eugenie Classen

    - Josh Classen, COO Tinsel Inc. + Susan Classen
        - Hewney Classen
        - Kyle Classen

Mary's Friends
- Kara Halloran + Nick Halloran
    - Eve Halloran
    - Astrid Halloran

- Liza Wells + Fisher Wells
    - Paxton Wells

- Tyler Dawkins + Mike Hudson

- Robin Landes

Ivy's Girl Gang
- Betsy Scofield
- Ellie Branscombe: Emmett Branscombe's granddaughter
- Stacy Fuller: Chief Fuller's daughter

The Persimmons Family
- Chester Persimmons   + Noreen Persimmons (deceased)
  - Garland Persimmons
  - Shepherd Persimmons

Tinselvania Residents
- Aunt Elaine: Alvinia Classen's sister
- Bertha Havighurst: Runs The Happy Goose Inn
- Chief Iola Fuller: Chief of Tinselvania police
- Casper Capwell: Mary's assistant at Tinsel Inc.
- Emmett Branscombe: Retired former employee of Tinsel Inc.

Tinselvania Visitors
- Bright Harmon: Executive from Yule Love It Christmas Corporation
- Joseph Lowery: Bright's assistant
- Dr. Sylvia Post: Chester Persimmons' former psychiatrist
- Frances Boggs: Associate of Sylvia
- Willa Pataki: Associate of Sylvia
- Belle Mulvaney: Associate of Sylvia
- Llewellyn Barnes: Former Tinselvania resident

Printed in Dunstable, United Kingdom